In the Shadow of the Apocalypse

Dinu Pillat

EGRETTA PRESS

The current translation is based on the Editura Humanitas edition of Aşteptând ceasul de apoi, published in 2010.

Library of Congress Cataloguing-in-Publication Data
Names:
Pillat, Dinu (1921-1975), author
Brown, James Christian (1962-), translator
Sipos, George T. (1975-), Introduction
Pillat, Monica (1947-), Afterword.
Title: In the Shadow of the Apocalypse/ Dinu Pillat. Translated from Romanian by James Christian Brown
Description: Saint Louis, Missouri: Egretta Press, [2022]
Identifiers: LCCN: 2022937913 | ISBN: 9798985744705 (pbk) | ISBN: 9798985744712 (ebook)

Cover design: Eliza Claudia Filimon
Book Editor: Jessica Busch Sipos
Layout: Rodica Teişi

Egretta Press is an independent publisher located in Saint Louis, Missouri. For more information visit: www.egretta-press.com

Dinu Pillat

In the Shadow of the Apocalypse

Translated from Romanian
by James Christian Brown

With an introduction by George T. Sipos,
and an Afterword by Monica Pillat

EGRETTA
PRESS

CONTENTS

A Novel of Its Time. And Ours
George T. Sipos

The English translation and publication of Dinu Pillat's novel *Aşteptând ceasul de apoi* (In the Shadow of the Apocalypse, 1948—literally, "Waiting for the Final Hour") comes twelve years after the original publication of this long-lost novel by the Romanian publisher Humanitas in 2010. As evidenced in this edition's *Afterword* signed by the author's daughter, Monica Pillat, herself a celebrated Romanian writer, translator, and literary critic, the manuscript of *In the Shadow of the Apocalypse* represented the main evidence of the prosecution in the trial staged in 1960 to a number of prominent Romanian intellectuals and artists who were perceived as uncomfortably popular by the communist regime installed in the country by the Soviet occupation after War World II. The trial, triggered mostly by the fear of the regime of a revolution such as that of October-November 1956 in Hungary, is remembered in postwar Romanian history as the Noica-Pillat trial, after the names of philosopher Constantin Noica (1909-1987) and the author of the novel translated here, Dinu Pillat. A total of 25 people were arrested and sentenced to combinations of hard labor and deprivation of civil rights for many years, Pillat receiving, together with others, the maximum sentence: 25 years of hard labor and 10 years of deprivation of civil rights.

Pillat was released from prison in 1964, as a sign of political relaxation, and was able to re-join the ranks of the researchers at the Institute for Literary Theory and History. Although he rarely spoke himself of the prison years, the few personal testimonials, accompanied by those of other political prisoners of the time, reveal the physical and psychological trauma that the frequent and brutal beatings, the torture and the isolation left behind. At the end of 1974 Pillat was yet again politically purged and forced to accept a position way beneath his background and abilities. Sick with cancer, most probably contracted as a result of the prison torture, Pillat died at the end of 1975.

Perhaps more than the subject matter of the novel brilliantly translated here by James Christian Brown, Pillat's major power was his artistic and intellectual pedigree and stature within the Romanian intelligentsia, his name carrying the aura (and the burden) of one of the leading artistic and political families of modern Romania, with roots in the country's medieval history. Dinu Pillat's personality seems to have left an indelible impression on all those who knew him in whatever capacity, so much so that when his works started to be republished in the 2000s, decades after his death, thanks to Monica Pillat's arduous efforts, Romanian cultural magazines were flooded with recollections of Pillat the individual and not just with readings and assessments of his literary work. What stands out from these recollections is the profound humanity and care for others that the writer was capable of imparting to those around, a characteristic due perhaps, at least in part, to the nobility of spirit that had been inculcated in him from his upbringing and also to the tragic existence that he had the misfortune to lead.

Born in 1921, in Bucharest, Dinu (Constantin) Pillat had roots in the medieval Romanian nobility (the boyar class), the name of his paternal ancestors being mentioned in the *Descriptio Moldaviae* (1716), written by Moldavian prince and Renaissance scholar Dimitrie Cantemir (1674-1723).[1] And while on the maternal side, he belonged to the Brătianu family, one of the most respected and influential political dynasties of modern Romania, on the paternal side he was part of the Pillat family, prominent members of the artistic intelligentsia of the country. As such, Pillat was not only ancient nobility, connected with powerful political figures of the prewar period, but his very name commanded the respect of the literary and artistic establishment. His father, Ion Pillat (1891-1945), was a well-known poet, editor, publisher, and politician of the interwar period, who, after an initial interest in symbolism, decided that traditionalism represented him best and built a respectable literary career. His mother, Maria Pillat-Brateş (1892-1975), was a painter, whose artistic career was brutally interrupted by Romania's placement within the Soviet sphere of influence in the wake of World War II and the subsequent dismantling of the country's economy, democracy, government system, and elites by governments imposed by force from Moscow after 1946. Labeled a dangerous element by the authorities due to her family connections with the political top echelon of the interwar period and

---

[1] Mircea Anghelescu, "Ex Libris: Dinu Pillat," *România literară*, 17, 2014. p. 2.

found guilty of having belonged to the "moşierime" (landowner) class, Maria Pillat-Brateş was arrested in 1949 and sentenced to exile and house arrest in the Transylvanian town of Miercurea Ciuc, far from her Bucharest home.

Young Dinu grew up surrounded by an effervescent artistic environment in which his main struggle was not so much how to choose his own path but how to ensure that he was not perceived solely as an epigone or, even worse, as having built a literary career on the coattails of his father's renown. Early on he determined to commit to writing prose and literary criticism rather than poetry, and he made his debut during high school in the publication *Vlăstarul* (The Sapling)[2], which, albeit only a high school magazine, is famous for having gathered in its pages some of the most important names of interwar Romanian literature and culture, such as Mircea Eliade (1907-1986), Constantin Noica (1909-1987), Alexandru Paleologu (1919-2005), and Eugène Ionesco (1909-1994), among many others. In *The Sapling*, Pillat published essays and book reviews.

As a University of Bucharest student, the young writer wrote for and published in yet another important cultural magazine of the time, *Albatros* (Albatross), where his first serialized novel, *Jurnalul unui adolescent* (Diary of an Adolescent) appeared in 1941. His first novel written as a complete literary work, *Tinereţe ciudată* (Strange Youth, 1942) was followed in

---

[2] Significantly for the case of Pillat and others who made their debut in the pages of this high school journal, the Romanian word "vlăstar" also means "offspring", as in the offspring of well-known, famous people.

1946, right after the end of World War II, by *Moartea cotidiană* (Everyday Death, 1946), partly triggered by his emotional response to his father's death in 1945. Together with the novel translated in this volume, these three novels remained the only novelistic legacy Pillat was able to leave behind, as history finally caught up with him and his family soon after the regime change in Bucharest and callously forced him to forego other such literary endeavors. He did, however, continue to write works of literary history and criticism.

Often read as a *roman à clef*, *In the Shadow of the Apocalypse* is first and foremost a fictional work about a generational clash. One that, unfortunately, would ultimately lead the entire world straight in the throes of a deadly war. For what Pillat is attempting to capture, analyze, and come to terms with in the novel, is in fact the disappointment and disenchantment of the 1930s generation with their parents' generation, one that benefited from sufficient stability and ability to accumulate wealth in the wake of World War I in order to create for themselves and their progeny a life without much material worry. Granted, that was only the case of those who fell into the category of the budding urban upper middle class or of those who already possessed inter-generational wealth, such as the Holbans in the novel. As such, tempting as it may be, reading Pillat's book exclusively as an analysis of interwar Romania's extremely violent and fascist organization, The Iron Guard (also known as the Legion of the Archangel

Michael), and seeking to identify the characters—in good *roman à clef* fashion—with prominent politicians of the time or with leaders of the extremist movement, is not necessarily the most productive way to understand its ultimate political message.

On one hand, the similarities with some of the political figures of prewar Romania seem so evident that it makes you wonder why Pillat would have chosen to direct his readership toward them in such an un-subtle fashion. On the other, having completed the novel in 1947 and re-edited it in 1955, it is doubtful that he could have been unaware of the fact that some of his characters might be mis-interpreted by the communist regime and used against him (as indeed happened in the end). Final proof that Pillat had no intention to write a *roman à clef* and only a *roman à clef* is the fact that many of the members of the Legion who read the novel complained that the text was not an accurate representation of the actual movement. No, in *In the Shadow of the Apocalypse* Pillat uses the Iron Guard and Romania's fascism and incorporates certain episodes from their despicable history, such as the antisemitic outbursts and violence against Jewish students—which would subsequently open the door for the Romanian Holocaust, during the military dictatorship installed in 1940 under the leadership of Marshal Ion Antonescu (1882-1946)—as a pretext for a broader meditation on the meaning of history and the inevitability of certain moments.

And it is in that meditation on history exemplified through the clash of the generations in interwar Romania that Pillat's novel is so acutely (and sadly) relevant today, as Europe is yet again shaken by a war of a magnitude that we have not seen since the end of World War II. For Russia's attack on Ukraine is also a clash between generations, one, the older generation, (represented by Putin, as well as his supporters in Russia and worldwide) indoctrinated with ideas that everything liberal, that freedom and democracy themselves, are dangerous, that people having a voice is un-necessary and that people need to be led with an iron fist, and the other, the younger, (unwillingly represented by the Ukrainian president Volodymyr Zelenskyy and his supporters in Ukraine and all over the world) that embraces the principles of humanity, human rights, inclusion and freedom. The generation clash in Pillat's novel ends up in violence as well. Isolated as they are, the acts of violence in the novel are perpetrated by the young generation. Its members are deeply dissatisfied with the world order, and entertain images of sacrifice and purification through blood, believing that bringing about the Apocalypse itself is a justifiable end goal, as long as that will cleanse and transform the world in the image that they consider right and just. An ordered world, a sterile world, a dead world.

That is not to say that the historical background that generated the novel, the religious mysticism, the nationalism, the anti-bourgeois, anti-capitalist attitudes need not be understood within their proper political, social, and economic contexts. But they matter only in so far as we might believe that there is true historical relevance to the events described in the novel. While, when it comes to fiction, be that even anchored in historical events, what ultimately matters is the narrative and its politics. And Pillat's politics in 1947 were more concerned with his own legacy as a writer, with what he was to leave behind that would be different than his father, the celebrated poet. He cared about the ways in which he could leave his own mark. And in that way, the fascist youth of interwar Romania with its wish for violent change, for carnage, its religious extremism was the perfect metaphor for how a generational clash can go horribly wrong. Pillat does not advocate violence and does not endorse the actions of his characters, but they certainly help him—a deeply humanistic member of the literary establishment—to ponder on the efficacy (or lack thereof) of such methods. And for their violence, for their murders, for their limited understanding of the world and how history progresses, the young fascists are punished not only by their fellow humans, but by history as well. In the end, their way, the writer seems to indicate, is not *the* way to fix history.

Their parents' generation does not come across much better either. Isolated, lost in futile endeavors, locked in illusory ivory towers and meditations about the past, trapped in nightmares, but lacking the will to change their way of being, and ultimately disconnected from reality and themselves, their world is equally dissipating, and they are equally engulfed by and left behind by history. For lack of action, complacency, and escapism are not *the* way either. In *In the Shadow of the Apocalypse*, Pillat does not try to offer a solution to the ongoing, irreparable, always-advancing bulldozer of history—as a *roman à clef* reading would indicate—, but to articulate the problem. At the end of the novel, the

Apocalypse is still around the corner, and unfortunately, the characters find themselves equally stuck, just as much as in the beginning. Neither complacency nor violence have stopped anything, prevented anything.

The overall impression one gathers from Pillat's novel is that, although he did think initially about writing a novel about the clash between the young fascists and their parents in interwar Romania as soon as he had finished his first novel, in 1942, by the time he completed it in 1947, and certainly by the time he was done with the edits, in 1955, *In the Shadow of the Apocalypse* had become more a warning to the newly-installed communist authorities, brought to Bucharest on the tanks of the Soviet Red Army. Violence may shake history, some major actors may die in the process, but it does not necessarily change the overall course of humanity: this seems to be the ultimate message hidden in the pages of the novel. Clad in the stories of Dinu Pillat's fictional extremists was an invitation to reason, to moderation, to calculated (rather than unreasonable) political action for the communists and the foreign occupying army supporting them. And in that way, Pillat's novel was indeed subversive, and it contained indeed a dangerous message from the perspective of the still-shaky order imposed by the communist authorities. In putting him on trial for it, they simply did not possess the artistic subtlety and refinement to discern its intended political message.

Read today, almost seven decades after its completion, in the midst of another war—perhaps yet another continuation of that same war that was started back when the plot of Pillat's novel takes place—*In the Shadow of the Apocalypse* is strikingly relevant. The same sentiments that animated the characters in Pillat's pages and triggered their violence are now present again all around the world. From the rooms of the White House to the Parliaments of Europe, to the bunkers of the Kremlin and the halls of the Beijing communist leadership, the world is once again bracing itself for what's to come. Intolerance, xenophobia, racism, prejudice, nationalism, and religious fanaticism have made their way back into our lives. And reading literary works such as Pillat's is now all the more important, as we ourselves try hopefully to avoid the mistakes that those who inspired the characters in this novel made.

Translator's Note

Dinu Pillat began writing *In the Shadow of the Apocalypse* in 1943, when he was a student at the University of Bucharest. He completed a first draft in 1948 and the final draft in 1955. In writing it, he drew on the reminiscences of participants in the tumultuous events of the preceding decades in Romania. The result, however, is not a historical novel as such, but rather a fictional distillation out of events in the recent past, through which Pillat explores the psychology of radicalization and the breakdown of understanding between generations

It is easy to find connections between the background against which the destinies of the novel's characters unfold and real events and personalities in the history of Romania between the World Wars. In reality as in the novel, liberal democracy in Romania was challenged in period by a political movement with a charismatic leader and a revolutionary nationalist and anti-Semitic ideology combined with an element of Orthodox mysticism—Corneliu Zelea Codreanu's Legion of the Archangel Michael, commonly known by the name of its paramilitary wing, the Iron Guard. Two Romanian prime ministers were assassinated by the Iron Guard, Ion G. Duca in 1933 and Armand Călinescu in 1939. On a number of occasions in the interwar years, Jewish students were violently ejected from university classes by their colleagues.

A philosophy professor with anti-Semitic views, Nae Ionescu, influenced a rising generation of Romanian intellectuals and writers, some of whom followed him towards politics of the Legion (while others, notably Eugène Ionesco and Mihail Sebastian, did not). All these have their fictional parallels in Dinu Pillat's novel. However, it is a matter of similarity, not identity: the process by which these personalities and events are distilled into a fictional construction involves more than just changes of name, and in the symbolic chronology of the book, events whose real-life counterparts took place over more than a decade are condensed into the space of twelve months, as we follow the characters from one fateful summer to the next.

If the historical background is reshaped for the author's purposes, the geographical setting remains recognizable as the Romania of the interwar period, and in particular the city of Bucharest. Despite the demolitions and new building programs of the communist period, much of the cityscape of the novel can still be seen today. Except in the case of two squares whose names simply express their location, I have kept the Romanian forms of street names unchanged. The curious reader will easily find those named in the novel on a map of the city. If English equivalents are sought, *Strada* may be understood as "Street", *Calea* as "Avenue", *Bulevardul* as "Boulevard", and *Piața* as "Square".

When the original Romanian edition of the novel was first published in 2010, the manuscript had only recently been rediscovered by a researcher working in the archives left by the Securitate, the secret police of the communist regime that ruled Romania from

1947 to 1989. Not surprisingly, much interest at the time was attracted by the tortuous history of the book itself, an account of which, by the author's daughter Monica Pillat, is appended to this English edition: how it was confiscated from the author in 1959 and was willfully misread in order to serve as prosecution evidence in a trial which led to his imprisonment for allegedly "conspiring against the social order", and how it subsequently remained "lost" for half a century in the Securitate archives, only to re-appear twenty years after the fall of the communist regime. In the years since 2010, however, events in more than one country around the world seem to have given Dinu Pillat's novel a new topicality. His fictional exploration of the radicalization of idealistic youth, the pull of extremism, and the temptation of apocalyptic solutions seems as relevant today as when he wrote it, and it is as a novel for our own time that it is now offered to new readers in this English translation.

As might be expected in a work that in its final form was twelve years in the making, Dinu Pillat's text is one in which it is clear that the words have been chosen and deployed with care, often with a concision in expression that is hard to reproduce in translation. Though nuances of style may elude transfer to another language, I have tried as far as possible in this English version to preserve as much as possible of the stylistic character and expressive effect of the original.

For the Biblical quotations and allusions, I have used the King James (Authorized) Version, except in the case of the quotation from Isaiah in Part Five chapter III, where the Romanian version of the text, based on the Greek Septuagint, is significantly different from the

King James and other English Bibles, in which the Old Testament is translated from the Hebrew. For the poem by Lucian Blaga recited in Part Three chapter II, rather than quoting any of the existing English translation, I have taken the liberty of offering my own fairly literal version.

Finally, I should mention that the original title of the novel, *Așteptând ceasul de apoi*, would, in a literal English translation, be something like "Waiting for the Final Hour". While working on the translation, however, I came to the conclusion, with which Monica Pillat and George T. Sipos of Egretta Press agreed, that "In the Shadow of the Apocalypse" would more effectively render in English the real meaning of the Romanian title. (*James Christian Brown, February 2022*)

In the Shadow of the Apocalypse

PART ONE

Chapter I

To the weary clip-clop of the two old horses' hooves, the cart rolled on through the darkness, across the emptiness of the endless plains. After all that had happened at the market, it was only under duress that the peasant had agreed to take the three students with him. He had kept silent since they set out, rigid as a scarecrow behind the horses, which ambled on as though no one were driving them.

Rotaru, a final-year student of Medicine, bent once more over the wounded man who lay on the floor of the cart under a bundle of hay. He took his pulse and leaned back.

"He has a high fever! But it's a good thing that otherwise he's settled down. That delirium of his with quotations from the Book of Revelation was dramatic...."

"I never imagined that someone could retain the memory of texts in the unconscious to such an extent," observed the third student, who, like the wounded man, was studying theology.

Rotaru said no more, his attention distracted by a falling star on its long descent through the depths of the July night. The silence had thickened again over the clip-clop of the hooves, leaving their thoughts in a state of numbness, like their bodies squeezed together in the narrow space of the cart.

"Ah! Do you see him? Do you see him? The angel…. He comes out of the temple and cries with a loud voice to him that sits on the cloud: Thrust in thy sickle, and reap: for the time is come for thee to reap; for the harvest of the earth is ripe…. Behold! Behold how the vine of the earth is cast into the great wine-press of the wrath of God! Blood…blood came out of the wine-press, even unto the horse bridles!"[1] The wounded man had begun to writhe again.

Rotaru grasped the carter's arm to get him to stop the horses. "I fear he may have a hemorrhage. How much further can it be to the clinic?"

The other theologian shrugged: it was the first time he had been in these parts, so he had no way of knowing the road to the village clinic, where Rotaru was on a placement.

In fact the question had been addressed to the peasant, whose answer came only slowly, after he had looked up at the arc of the sky. "We should be there about midnight, if God so grant…."

Rotaru placed his hand back on the wounded man's chest; his heartbeat was getting fainter. There was no time to be lost. As he crouched again, with his knees almost in his mouth, by the side of the fever-ridden man, he found himself cursing the moment he had taken up medicine. Otherwise he might not have felt so responsible for the life of his comrade. He would not have seen the gravity of the man's situation with such professional lucidity, coupled with the awareness that he was unable to do anything for him. At the first jolt of the cart, which had started moving again, he turned involuntarily toward the other theologian. He

---

[1] Cf. Revelation 14.15–20

could hardly believe his eyes when he realized that the man was on his knees, his head bowed and his hands clasped. Of course, he was praying. Why, in that same moment, could he himself not do likewise? Definitely Luther was right to believe in predestination: there were people endowed from the beginning with the grace of God, while others could never partake of it; they were denied from birth the right to salvation. If that was how things stood, what value could one still attribute to the metaphysical justice of Christianity? For a moment, he wanted to ask his comrade, but then he decided that the other's prayer ought to be respected. In the swaying of the cart, his uncertainties gradually disintegrated until, in the end, he was left only with his powerful impressions of the day's events.

In order to thwart their rally, which had begun in the marketplace at the end of the little Jewish town, what mind sick with fear had spread out of the blue the rumor that they had come to set fire to the grimy little booths? Rotaru had never before seen such a manifestation of collective psychosis. He recalled the sensation they had caused when they arrived in a marching column, as disciplined as a military unit. The bustle of the market, with all the haggling and dealing, had slowly died down. The motley crowd of peasants, among whom it was easy to distinguish the presence of the Jewish merchants with their caps and boots, had closed in around the group, as though gathering to watch some sort of fairground entertainment. Andrițoiu, the student who now lay wounded in the bottom of the cart, had taken the floor, speaking to the people as if from the Book of Revelation. Then, from somewhere down at the end of a lane, a woman's anguished voice had rung out, quickly followed by a tumult of hysterical shrieks. Rotaru had not caught the exact dialect words. However, the meaning was clear: a cry of alarm, warning that the town was going to be set on fire. Could it have been an organized maneuver? In any case, at that very moment, a number of gendarmes had appeared from different directions, ready to force their way through the crowd with the butts of their rifles. The fighting had started without further ado and had rapidly engulfed the whole area of the marketplace. An uproar, like the sound of a hailstorm, with screams and oaths mingled indiscriminately, had risen deafeningly along the edge of the town, where the shutters of the booths were immediately closed. Who had fired the first shots? It was hard to tell. At one point, as he was struggling to break free from the clutches of a group of people, Rotaru had seen Andriţoiu close by, slumped on the ground, with the other comrade from theology trying desperately to help him. He had been shot in the stomach. With great difficulty, the two of them had then carried the wounded man between the carts, steering clear of scuffles, till they reached the edge of the marketplace. There, it had taken the threat of Rotaru's revolver to persuade a peasant to take them with him.

"Excuse me, doesn't Dr. Weissman work here anymore?"

Rotaru started up from his chair. He had dozed off with his head slumped forward in the consultation room of the clinic. After their arrival in the middle of the night, he had hurried to give the first effective medical care to poor Andriţoiu, who was badly weakened by all that the journey by cart had inevitably meant for a man in his condition. Then he had telephoned a colleague in the city hospital to ask for an ambulance. Andriţoiu had to be operated on without delay. The vehicle had finally turned up in the course of the morning, and it was not long since it had left. The other theologian had accompanied the wounded man, determined to stay with him to the very end. With his hair greasy and his cheeks unshaven for the last two days, Rotaru could not but make the worst possible impression at that moment. Rising to his feet, he made a slightly uncomfortable bow. "Allow me to introduce myself: Rotaru! I am temporarily posted here, in Weissman's place. You know, as part of the summer work experience that the Ministry obliges us to do in villages…. Mrs. Răutu, if I'm not mistaken?"

Rotaru had been warned by Ghiţă, the orderly, that Adina Răutu had arrived with her husband on the estate, and that he could expect a visit any time, as it was well known that the clinic constituted one of her humanitarian works.

The wife of the minister Sebastian Răutu, a woman of around fifty, showed her age under the broad brim of her straw hat. Her thin summer dress, cut to a pattern that would have been more appropriate for a young girl, did not suit her in the slightest, but rather drew attention to the fatty bulk of her body. Feeling every bit as awkward as Rotaru, Adina Răutu let her eyes wander around the room, as though she were seeing its contents for the first time: the leather couch; the glass cabinet containing syringes for injections, instruments for minor surgery, and vials of medicine; the portrait of the Queen, which appeared to be spotted with fly excrement; and on the table, an ashtray full of cigarette ends, a glass of water, and the book *L'Homme, cet inconnu* by Dr. Alexis Carrel…. After a while she said with a forced smile, "I believe you're doing great work in our clinic."

Rotaru grimaced, revealing his bad teeth, "What great work? The clinic is miserably equipped. As far as I can see, the stock of medicines was shamelessly squandered by Weissman. Latterly he had ended up giving injections of distilled water. I have no neosalvarsan, no nicotinic acid, no quinine—in other words, nothing of what's essential here. And how then am I to meet the needs of a medical district that includes no less than five villages? Judge for yourself!"

Adina Răutu lowered her eyes. She had been spoken to in a tone to which she was not accustomed. Her susceptibilities as the founder of the clinic were hurt. She spoke with difficulty, "Never mind, all that can be put right!"

Rotaru made a gesture with his hand that said more than any words.

Overcoming her antipathy toward this young trainee doctor so lacking in manners, Adina Răutu tried to be friendly. "Doctor, won't you join us for an aperitif up at the manor? It will give us a chance to debate matters at greater length."

Rotaru was so little expecting a proposal of this nature that he did not know how to answer on the spur of the moment. As luck would have it, the whole village happened to be out weeding the maize fields, so there was no patient in the waiting room who might have given him a pretext to escape the invitation. In the end, having no alternative, he found himself forced to accept. He took off his consultation coat, remaining in his slightly worn black suit. Only his tennis shoes and the open collar of his less-than-clean shirt made any concession to the summer day.

Outside, as they started walking through the thick dust of the lane, with the burning midday sun beating down on them, Adina Răutu opened the conversation again, "And what exactly do you want to specialize in, Doctor?"

"Endocrinology."

"Interesting."

Interesting.… Rotaru could picture himself in his tiny room in the evening, reading from Simonnet and Brouha's treatise by the faint light of the oil lamp, while next door, he could hear his landlord and landlady snorting in their sleep now and then in the heavy air. It was only at such times that he managed to integrate himself to some extent in the destiny of his future specialty, which had almost begun to seem a chimera after this month cut off from civilization. He felt that he was made for laboratory experiments, destined, perhaps, to become a new Columbus for the continent of human physiology, a continent as yet not fully explored along the latitude of the glands. But instead of having time to work in the direction of his chosen field, he found himself forced to waste his energy in the desert, fighting syphilis without neosalvarsan and pellagra without nicotinic acid. Interesting...."

Adina Răutu said no more. She realized instinctively that all her good intentions were becoming distorted in the other's mind, as if refracted through a cracked prism. She maintained a resigned silence, with that consciousness of being alone that she experienced every time she tried to build a bridge between herself and other people and found herself forced to acknowledge that it was in vain.

By now they had arrived in the park, on the alleyway shaded by the bushy crowns of chestnut trees. To their right, the shiny surface of the lawn could be seen, freshly watered with a hose.

How was Andrițoiu doing at that moment? Would the operation be over? Had he come through after all? Rotaru's thoughts kept revolving around his wounded comrade, if only to take him out of the ambiance of the Răutu family estate.

"Sebasto, let me introduce the new doctor at the clinic. I've invited him for an aperitif, so we can get to know each other better. I'll leave him with you till I finish some things in the kitchen."

Once they were seated in the basketwork chairs that lay to hand on the veranda, Sebastian Răutu asked carelessly, for the sake of something to say, "Well, how do you find things around here?"

"I find that they are what they reduce to: squalor."

"What do you expect? Squalor is inherent in social life!"

"Very well, but...."

"Forgive me for interrupting you. Are you involved in politics?"

"Yes. Well, not exactly...."

"What do you mean? I don't understand."

"You see, I'm a member of the Herald movement."

A frown came over Sebastian Răutu's forehead, while the hand in which he held his cigarette stopped in the air. So, as was the way of things, he found himself once again faced with the problem that only a few moments before he had been trying to forget.

"And so? What do you mean? Why do you imagine you're not involved in politics, when you are militant in the ranks of the Heralds?"

"You see, I believe that politics in our country is represented by Caragiale's *A Lost Letter*.[2] Even today, although appearances might give a different impression, due to the formal evolution of things. The Herald movement doesn't regard itself as just one more political party among the others, fitting in with our parliamentary regime's mentality of continuity in opportunism and compromise, in which the reality is expressed by the citizen Mitică[3], 'Out go our lot, in

[2] The play *A Lost Letter* (*O scrisoare pierdută*, 1884) by Ion Luca Caragiale (1852–1917), a comedy satirizing the superficiality and corruption of provincial politics, is one of the most well-known and frequently quoted classics of Romanian literature. Its characters include the opposition politician Cațavencu, the county prefect Tipătescu, and the policeman Pristanda. (Tr.)

[3] Another of Caragiale's characters, introduced in his collection of short prose *Moments* (*Momente*, 1901), a witty and opportunistic man about town whose name has become a byword for cynical superficiality and lack of seriousness in social and political life. (Tr.)

come our lot….' We are trying to prefigure a new man."

Sebastian Răutu had listened with pursed lips, not looking at his interlocutor, delaying lighting another cigarette until Rotaru had finished what he had to say. The sharpening of his face made his nose stand out all the more prominently.

"I agree with you in just one respect. Indeed, *A Lost Letter* defines our political habits of yesterday and of today. And I would go further and argue that Caragiale's comic work will represent us equally well tomorrow too. But why are you so scandalized at that? Caţavencu, Tipătescu, and Pristanda are endemic among us. What do you expect? We are in the land of the Romanians, on the margins of the Orient… And as for opportunism and compromise, these forms in which our genius for irremediable servility manifests itself, let us not forget that they have repeatedly saved us as a state. What makes you suddenly revolted out of the blue that it has been given us to have Mitică as a citizen and not Jesus? Don't you realize how ridiculous it is?" Sebastian Răutu, who had been gradually warming up, broke off when the maid came out with the aperitifs.

"Please, have a drink."

Without any pleasure, Rotaru took with one hand the glass that was offered to him, and with the other picked up an olive on the point of a cocktail stick.

Just at that moment, however, the sound of carriage wheels could be heard coming from the entrance of the park.

"Ah, the guests must have arrived!"

With a feeling of relief, Rotaru put his glass down on the tray and said hurriedly, "Then I'll be going."

"All right. It's late, so I won't keep you. We'll meet again, though, while I'm staying here. Do you know your way out of the park?"

"Yes, I bid you goodbye."

Rotaru walked away, but he did not go out the way he had come, for fear of bumping into the newly arrived guests. Knowing that the wall around the park had a little back gate, which opened onto one side of the village, he turned into a series of short paths lined with maples and found the exit without too much difficulty. He tried to think only of Andrițoiu, as he had been picked up by the ambulance, with a lost look in his eyes, all the blood drained from his cheeks and his lips gone purple, but instead he was followed on his way by the face of Sebastian Răutu. Like a gramophone needle stuck in the groove of a damaged record, his mind stopped at a sentence whose words he was unable to pass over: "Cațavencu, Tipătescu, and Pristanda are endemic among us. What do you expect? We are in the land of the Romanians, on the margins of the Orient...."

Rotaru found the little gate locked and had to jump over it. The village lane was empty, just as he had left it earlier. Only a hen crossed his path, seeking something to peck at in the dust.

In the dining room of the manor, the sultry heat outside could scarcely be felt. Once the flies were driven out, the windows had been closed and the blinds lowered.

As the guests entered, Adina Răutu showed each to their place. The hosts sat at the ends of the table, Grigore and Raluca Holban on the right, and Colonel Ioanid on the left.

While the maid was bringing in the first course, Sebastian Răutu stifled a yawn of boredom. From force of tradition, every time they came to the country, they invited the neighboring landowners to dinner. Then they did not see them again until the summer of the following year, when the same meal would be repeated. Although in his fifties, and thus around the same age as Sebastian Răutu, Grigore Holban looked more as though he belonged to the generation of his host's father. Bald, pallid-looking, with a high collar in the old style, he was never seen in anything but a black jacket and striped trousers. He had pursued his university studies in Paris, where he had specialized in the ancient history of the Orient. After the First World War, his father, a member of the Academy and a respected figure in the leadership of the old Conservative party, had managed to persuade those with a say in the matter to set up a lectureship in the History section of the Faculty of Letters in Bucharest. But Grigore Holban's career as a university teacher did not last long, due to the fact that no one could be found who was desirous of attending classes in a field lacking any contingent interest. After the termination of his lectures under the pretext of budget cuts, he had retired permanently to his estate, taking with him his entire library. Since then, he had lived an owl-like existence, taking an interest only in his studies. Now and then, Sebastian Răutu and the other professors would receive the odd slim brochure, the extract of an article published by Grigore Holban in some specialized journal abroad. His wife, with their three children, came to join him for the duration of the summer vacation, otherwise staying in their house in Bucharest. To Sebastian Răutu, Raluca Holban was of much less interest. A model of domestic virtue who retained something of the romantic melancholy of the early years of the century.

Colonel Ioanid had none of the typical characteristics of a career officer. In fact, he had been retired for a decade and lived almost all year round on his estate. A bachelor, full of witty misogynistic theories. A pipe smoker. He was accustomed to drinking dozens of cups of tea per day, which he prepared himself in a samovar. He only ever read travel books. A great chess enthusiast, he could often be found sitting alone, engrossed in a game begun who knows when, reconstructing from specialized treatises the moves that had been set down as memorable. As he was something of a "personality" in the county, Sebastian Răutu had been eager to get him involved in politics as a member of the local branch of his party. The colonel had ended up accepting, just to keep the leader happy, not considering that this need entail any sacrifice of his relaxed lifestyle. Only at the height of election campaigning did he find himself obliged to accompany Sebastian Răutu around the county in his car. At meetings, he remained placid, somewhere in the vicinity of the leader, and always managed to decline with a joke if ever anyone proposed that he should take the floor.

Sebastian Răutu began by addressing Grigore Holban, who was eating without looking up from his plate, "Well, Grigore old chap, what are you working on now?"

"Something extremely interesting. Unfortunately I don't have all the necessary bibliography to hand. I've ordered the items that I lack from London, but nothing has come yet. My study is entitled *The Influence of the Reformed Philosophical School of Mo-Tzu on the Imperial Jurisdiction in the Period of the Han Dynasty*."

On the chair next to him, Raluca Holban blushed to the roots of her hair, as she noticed that both Sebastian Răutu and Colonel Ioanid could barely refrain from laughing.

Adina Răutu, whose thoughts had until then been elsewhere, suddenly had the presence of mind to break the impasse. She quickly changed the subject, asking her friend, "My dear, what has happened this year that the children aren't here with you?"

Raluca Holban hesitated before replying. How could she confess the truth and share with them openly the fact that the boys had refused to accompany her, as they usually did every year, on the grounds that they considered themselves mobilized in the service of the Herald movement for the duration of the election campaign? Sebastian Răutu would, of course, have made his usual ironic comments. And if she had learned to bear reluctantly the remarks that he made at the expense of poor Grigore, she did not know how she would be able to suffer in silence any that he might make about Ștefănucă and Lucian.

"Liliana is with us, but she has stayed at home because she thought there was no point in her coming alone, without her brothers. As for the boys, they're hanging on a bit longer in Bucharest. One's children do slip away from one as they grow up."

"Wasn't Ștefănucă due to sit his baccalaureate?" Adina Răutu asked for the sake of conversation.

"No, he still has another year."

Sebastian Răutu thought it was time that he said something too.

"I don't know Ștefănucă all that well. About Lucian, however, I am in a position to speak with some authority. He is the best of all the students I have had lately. A clear head. Thorough. Organized. Perhaps still not personal enough in his opinions, too much swayed by the influence of some of his reading, but that is only normal at his age. In seminars he always speaks up. Sure of himself, almost presumptuous. I like him!"

While the plates were being changed, Colonel Ioanid broached a subject which he had been eager to raise ever since he arrived. As he waited impatiently for the round of social questions and answers to finish, he had been fidgeting on his chair to such an extent that the maid serving at the table had felt fully entitled to conclude that he was suffering from cramp.

"You must have heard about how the Heralds see fit to spread electoral propaganda! Demagogy based on Christian premises… It's utterly scandalous! And when the gendarmes, alarmed at the anarchic character of their rallies, try to scatter the crowd, the propagandists respond by firing revolvers. Only yesterday I heard that in—"

Sebastian Răutu did not allow him to finish. "To all appearances, we are dealing with a case of mystical psychosis. Disoriented young people have fallen victim to Toma Vesper's pseudo-messianism. The individual is well known to me; we were at the Residential High School in Iaşi together. He's an idiot…I have to tell you a story that shows the comic side of his mysticism, which is surely syphilitic in origin. Back then, the incident was the talk of the school. Vesper was in fifth or sixth grade. Religious Instruction. The priest is up at the front talking about 'Miracles in the Christian Religion.' On the benches, total lack of interest: one step away from sleep. The priest hasn't even managed to finish properly when up stands Vesper, 'You know, Father, it's happened to me too, experiencing a miracle….' The priest looks at him askance, while the class breaks out in fits of laughter. But Vesper doesn't lose his cool, 'On the night of the Resurrection, when I was coming home from church, Saint George appeared to me at the end of the village. His stallion was prancing on the spot, frightened by the dragon that was waiting to pounce on it from the side. Saint George raised his spear and ran it through the body of the beast in an instant….' You can imagine the look on the priest's face! Saint George shows himself to a kid in the fifth grade who isn't even a prize-winner… The result: Vesper got a grade of three out of ten, and Saint George ended up as the emblem of the Heralds."

Sebastian Răutu fell silent. Caught up in the story, he had let his steak go dry. As he hurried to finish what was left on his plate, he observed to his displeasure that the effect was not what he had expected. The women seemed lost in thought, apparently in no doubt about the reality of the miracle. Grigore Holban was still looking down at his plate, so that it was impossible to tell if he was surprised, or at least amused, while the colonel limited himself to exclaiming stupidly, "Well, I say!"

As dessert was brought in, Sebastian Răutu felt the need to return to the subject. "The so-called Herald movement poses a greater threat than might appear at first glance. In public, they seek to mystify people with demagogy based on Christian premises, as the colonel was saying. Within restricted circles, however, it's a completely different matter. They are organized in shock groups. They have weapons. They are preparing to overthrow the political order of our form of state, with no regard for the consequences. We keep getting reports at the Siguranță[4] from agents infiltrated among them. It's no joking matter. Measures must be taken."

Raluca Holban started anxiously. There was a slight tremor in her hands as she took a slice of melon. "What measures?"

"The dissolution of the movement on the eve of the elections. Its lists of candidates annulled. Its headquarters sealed. The instigating leaders arrested. Almost all the members of the government have come around to my conclusion. It only remains to convince the prime minister. In his senile indolence, he still clings to the belief that the Herald movement is no more than an inoffensive children's game...."

---

[4] Literally "Safety:" the secret police of Romania in the first half of the twentieth-century. (Tr.)

Colonel Ioanid intervened in the discussion, "Very well, but how can we take such a measure before we are empowered by a vote of Parliament? The situation seems to me unprecedented."

"The form is the easiest thing to find. The dissolution can be carried out on the basis of the dispositions of a minuted decision of the Council of Ministers. Nothing could be simpler."

Before starting his melon, Sebastian Răutu continued a moment later, in a different tone, "Actually, what I find most appalling is the structure of social life desired by the young people of the Heralds. The world of the 'new man.' Absolute uniformity is the goal. You no longer have any right to see and judge except through a single prism, which is imposed on you automatically. The plurality of points of view, the weighing up of problems, the dialectic of intelligence are condemned as generators of chaos. After several millennia of evolution in thinking, is the ideal form of society suddenly to be revealed to us in the beehive or the anthill?"

Adina Răutu watched her husband with growing puzzlement. She was surprised at his vehemence on the issue of the Heralds, now, at dinner, among people without political preoccupations. She had always considered him to be eminently skeptical, if not downright cynical. He judged everything with a humor of his own. He never dramatized. So what was the matter now?

Chapter II

or several nights now, the great winds of autumn had been blowing. In her long hours of insomnia, Raluca Holban heard the darkness filled by the continuous rustling of the trees in the park, something like the sound of chaotic organ chords.

During the day, a cloudy sky closed in the atmosphere. It was in the autumn, more than at any other time, that the castle, with its air of a historic mausoleum, managed to be in tune with the landscape. Having no connection to the native architecture of the region, the Holban family's country residence might have suggested to their contemporaries the eccentric action of some American billionaire who had insisted on buying, dismantling, and then rebuilding, in his own land across the ocean, a genuine medieval French castle. In fact, the massive, gloomy walls, with their gothic arches, had been clumsily erected by an ancestor on Raluca Holban's side, an ancestor with some Polish blood in his veins, who, back in the reign of Stephen the Great, had seen fit to conform to the grand feudal style. Situated in the steppe-country of Northern Moldavia, close to the meeting of the borders, the simulacrum of a castle had had to suffer over the years all that the history of the region could throw at it, looking down in majestic decay on depredations and desecrations. Of all the repairs it had undergone, the latest and most substantial had been necessitated by the decision taken by Grigore Holban to withdraw to the estate. The heavy ceilings now no longer threatened to collapse into the unusually accommodating rooms.

In the grey of that autumn morning, in which the yellow of the leaves in the park had taken on the reverberation of lamps lit in broad daylight, Raluca Holban had suddenly felt a disturbing identity of atmosphere with a period of great rending in her childhood. How could she still retain in her possession memories from the age of five? And what unexpected intuition made her, after so many years, find herself a little girl again and Papa Andu in the last days of his leukemia, made her relive the events of back then through both of them? Finding herself prey to an oppressive unease, she had left the household in the care of the servants and had locked herself alone in her room, where now, much later, she found herself pouring out the suffering of her soul in writing:

1892. It was his last autumn. Andu knew that well. He suffered from a cancer of the blood in one of the forms that gives no respite. He sat as usual on the chaise-longue, with his beret on his head and his coat on, wrapped in a large striped rug so that he could not feel the viscous cold of the morning. A chestnut leaf had fallen by chance on his feet, where it had remained like the strange hand of some prehistoric being. Overhead, the crows kept scraping at the silence. In the frayed mist among the trees, the castle before him took on the shape of a ghostly ship.

"Papa Andu!"

The child's voice came along the pathway, rolling like a chestnut. And a moment later, the tiny figure of

Raluca appeared beside the chaise-longue. "Papa Andu, when are we leaving with the wild geese?"

With the flick of a finger, the question threw aside the days of a whole year. It was another autumn, and Andu, with the little girl holding his hand, had set out into the field. The frost had long lost its marine fluidity and spread with the opacity of lead across the wide steppes with their gathered harvests. A broad wind filled one's lungs. The hunting dogs raced ahead, tracking a scent across the deserted stubble. Andu had felt the need to walk at a stride, so for some time, he had carried Raluca on his back, with her legs wound around his neck. And suddenly the voice from above burst out and a finger pointed.

"Papa Andu, what's that over there?"

A flock of wild geese was passing under the low sky, rowing away from the reeds of the ponds. A flash of white, unreal in the ash grey of the season. And then the wings were out of sight on the horizon.

"Some wild geese, on their way to hot countries. They come from up in the north, where the darkness and cold have driven them away...."

As they returned in the early twilight, Andu found himself telling Raluca Selma Lagerlöf's story of the amazing journey of Nils Holgersson with the wild geese.

"Papa Andu, let's go away with the wild geese, us too, like the little boy."

"It's too late now. They've all gone. Never mind, next year...."

"Is next year a lot?"

"A year..."

"A year? How big is a year? As big as the castle, as big as the sky, as big as the church? How big?"

Beside the chaise-longue, Raluca was still waiting. Andu's silence led her to believe that he had not heard the question. "Papa Andu, when are we going away with the wild geese? When?"

"How can we go, Raluca? Can't you see your father is ill?"

"Yes, but aren't there any doctors in the hot countries?"

Over Andu's glassy face, a smile passed like an apparition. The fog thickened around them, ever more oppressive. Was death not perhaps a dissolution, like the fog itself?

Beside him, he could hear Raluca's plangent voice.

"Papa Andu, when are we going? Tell me! Why don't you tell me?"

The void of the fog was unexpectedly filled with the clang of bells from the church. A long, drawn-out clang, as each repeated stroke came before the echo of the last had had time to die away fully.

"Papa Andu, why are the bells ringing?" asked Raluca with a start.

"Who knows? Maybe someone has died in the village," replied Andu, feeling the same shiver.

"Why do the bells ring when someone has died?"

"I don't know. That's the custom. To announce a departure. The same as the engine whistle when the train leaves the station or the ship's horn when it leaves the harbor."

"When you die, do you go away?"

"Yes, in a way."

"How?"

Andu turned his head toward Raluca. Through the fog, he saw her image broken as if in a slightly misted glass: tiny and poignantly comical, with her rain hood like an elf's cap, she held in one hand a chestnut that she could barely get her fingers all around.

"Come on, Papa, tell me, how?"

"How what?" asked Andu, whose thoughts were immediately lost.

"How do you go away when you die?"

"I don't know, little girl. How shall I put it? You go out of yourself, you leave your body like a dry leaf.... You become something without containment...."

For Raluca, Andu's words came together strangely. It was like when she heard Gran'mama speaking French.

"Papa Andu, what's 'without containment?'" Raluca took the word as it came, like a butterfly on the tips of her fingers.

"Without containment? Something that doesn't start anywhere, for example, the air — "

Andu did not manage to finish his sentence, as Gran'mama's voice could now be heard calling from the castle, "Raluca...Raluca...Raluca...."

Andu's hand, ivory-colored for lack of blood, made a movement toward Raluca. A gesture of caress? To stop her?

"Here's the chestnut, Papa, until I come back! So you have something to play with!"

Around the chaise-longue, solitude formed itself into rings.

Ϙ

A new day had begun. Andu was sitting with his beret on his head and his coat on, wrapped in the same striped rug. Raluca had left him alone, to go and bury a swallow that she had found dead on the path. She had shown it to him. When he took the bird in his palm, it had seemed to him as heavy as a stone within the corset of its bark-like wings.

Since morning tea, Andu had been unable to eat anything. Lack of appetite? His pharynxes blocked any attempt to swallow, with boiling barriers that rose to the roof of his mouth. His thoughts, ever more slender in their precarious articulation, now wore him out like his frequent nosebleeds. As for his eyelids, they had acquired a heavy materiality that made it an effort even to open his eyes and look.

Fog? No. The evening was falling. And yet it did not seem to be that either. A rinsing in transparent water. In front of him, the phantom ship solemnly sank. The trees themselves began to lose their forms. The rug, his hands, himself? He wanted to raise his head, to move his arms over the water. Choked in his dry throat, his voice only managed to call out once, before drowning, "Raluca!"

Then nothing. Only silence, playing the organ over spaces without dimensions.

"Papa Andu, what is it?"

Raluca, who had run from the end of the path, looked at her father, puzzled. She tugged his arm. His hand slipped softly to one side. He was sleeping. The way his head had fallen forward showed that too. But how could he be sleeping with his eyes open like that? Even her doll closed her eyes when she laid her on her back. Who knows? Perhaps grown-ups slept with their eyes open, just as only they snored in the night.

Raluca slipped quietly away on tiptoe, so as not to disturb Papa Andu's sleep.

ଔ

In the great double bed, Raluca could lose herself completely. Until a short time ago, before she had started snoring, Gran'mama's hand had come searching for her at intervals, to check that she had not slipped too close to the edge or got smothered under the huge, old-style quilt.

Raluca turned over again, from one side to the other, but she still could not fall asleep. Through the tall windows, she kept hearing the same rustle of wings. The wind? Raluca's thoughts jumped like grasshoppers through the darkness. Everything had been so strange these last few days. They had taken her by the hand hurriedly, when she had still not properly finished the tomb of leaves for the dead swallow, laid out beside Mommy's grave. They had taken her to the castle and locked her in her room, where she had been given her food too. Why had they punished her, when even now she could not see that she was guilty of anything? In vain, she had wept and struggled. No one had given any answer to her questions, not even Gran'mama, when she had come in the evening to go to bed, with eyes red from weeping and trembling all over. The next day, she had still been shut in. She had tried to play with her doll, to look at her book with all the animals in it. But she had got bored quickly. She had called out, she had pounded the door with her fists, she had wept again. Then, finally, she had sat down on her stool, determined to keep the fish in the bowl company. But the fish was sleeping in the water and treated her like a complete stranger. It was then that she had observed to her surprise that he too was sleeping with open, staring eyes, like Papa Andu. Around midday, the church bells had kept ringing. For the dead swallow? Only toward evening had they let her out. She had run through all the rooms, calling for Papa Andu, wanting to cry in front of him. No answer came from anywhere. She had sat down at the table in the dining room; it was just her and Gran'mama. She had asked again about Papa Andu. And for the first time, Gran'mama had acknowledged, with downturned eyes, "Papa Andu has gone away with the wild geese...."

Suddenly it had all gone cloudy. In Raluca's eyes, everything had started to swim all over the place: the macaroni in her plate, the glass of water, the empty chair across the table, the sideboard and the dishes. She had burst into a fit of sobbing with hiccups. She could not swallow anything. That Papa Andu should go away with the wild geese, without her! Leaving her alone, with the darkness of the rooms, with the bare trees and the cawing of the crows! After dinner, as soon as she felt that the eyes of the others were not on her, she had rushed outside and headed toward the gate of the park. There she had stopped, out of breath. Beyond was the beginning of the fields and of the sky. In vain, she had strained to catch a glimpse of something moving up there, in the ever more complete darkness. All the wild geese had gone. Papa Andu had joined the very last ones. And there was not one left for her, not one!

With her head on the pillow, Raluca wept without restraint. Then, little by little, her breathing stilled. Only now and then, at long intervals, did a little hiccup of a sob jump to the surface, like a delayed echo.

Was she weeping? Why? Couldn't she hear from outside the sound of honking like a trumpet? And the fluttering of wings, very close, touching the window? Raluca jumped out of bed, her tears all of a sudden dried. She hurried across the room to the window. Joy filled her completely. She kept blinking. A wild goose, halted in its flight, was waiting for her there. No angel could have been more beautiful! It was beating its wings and honking its summons. What should she take with her? She put on what she had to hand: her rain hood on her head and her cape over her nightdress. She wanted to kiss her doll, to say goodbye to the fish in the bowl, to Gran'mama, to the coffee-colored dress, to the animals in the book (at least the Hippopotamus). But, lo and behold, she was already on the welcoming back of the goose, with her arms clasped tight around its neck! She shut her eyes so as not to get dizzy. She felt herself going up and up, while her ears were filled more and more with a growing sound of wing-beats on all sides. At last, she dared to open her eyelids. She was not flying alone. Around her, lined up in ranks, countless other geese were flying through the vast expanse of air. As far as the eyes could see, there were only white wings, taking the sky along with them.

Raluca Holban's hand let go of the pencil to cover and support her heated brow. When Liliana burst into the room, with the telegram in her hand, she found her mother motionless, in a posture that gave no clue as to what was the matter with her.

"Great news, Mom! A telegram from the boys. Listen: 'Coming tomorrow slow train. Send coach station. Hugs. Ștefănucă.'"

Rising to her feet, with her consciousness turned as if by magic back to the present moment, Raluca Holban took the telegram from the girl's hand. On her lips a curious, almost distant smile took shape.

"I have to leave you. I'm going to wash my hair. Pachița's heated the rain water for me."

Raluca Holban's eyes remained on the telegram. Only she knew what anxieties she had gone through until she received it. A month before, the Bucharest papers had mentioned ever more alarming incidents caused by the Heralds all over the country. The government's decision to dissolve the movement had been made public right on the eve of the elections, just as Sebastian Răutu had foretold. Then rumors had gone around about searches and arrests. And from Bucharest not a single sign of life, until today's news, which had come at last to scatter all fears.

Raluca Holban left the room, feeling the need to share the contents of the telegram with her husband. She went into his study without bothering to knock.

"Grigore, I've received a telegram from the boys. They're coming tomorrow, by the slow train!"

Grigore Holban, who was working at his writing desk, with his head buried behind a stack of books, raised his eyes in confusion, evidently surprised that there had been no knock at the door. Then equally surprised to be taken away from his work for nothing more than that. Returning to the notes he was making from Chen Li's text, all he said was, "A safe journey to them!"

During the night, with the dropping of the wind, the atmosphere had unexpectedly cleared. Sweetened by the stained glass of autumn, the light of the sun had returned to that corner of the country, and fine weather seemed determined to take up residence.

Liliana could now take possession of the hammock again, and she did so without delay, as soon as lunch was over. From the moment she was there, instead of starting to read the books she had brought with her, she lay looking at the sky above the park, where dozens of storks were preparing for the great flight south: a sight with something solemn about it, like a ritual.

"Young child, permit your aged brother to rest his weary bones!" declaimed Ştefănucă, with a ceremonious bow.

Liliana, who had not heard his approaching steps, started and turned around on one elbow. "Now that it's just the two of us, without Mother, who has monopolized you since you arrived, let me hold you to account. What got into you to mess around the whole summer with politics instead of keeping me company? I don't have anyone to go fishing with, to go riding with. Playing croquet's no fun when it's just with Mother. What more can I say? Some brother you are! I can now conclude from your case that age makes one an ass."

Ştefănucă smiled sympathetically. Here, with Mother, with Liliana, with the park still full of the echoes of past games, it was as though he were starting to feel like a child again.

"Well, why did you stay there? First of all, give me a report! What films have you seen? Which girls have you met? Come on, what are you waiting for?"

"Then you should know that I haven't been to the cinema since you left Bucharest, and nor have I had the honor and pleasure of meeting any of your dear classmates."

"You haven't!?"

"I was taking part in the electoral campaign."

"Really, how can you waste your time going around sticking up posters, yelling 'Down with so-and-so' and 'Up with so-and-so' with those hooligans, and breaking heads by the score?"

Ştefănucă smiled again. What did Liliana in her hammock know? And at the end of the day, why should he put her right? She still wouldn't be able to take things seriously. So he changed the subject, with a hint, "Oh, I forgot to tell you, I saw your admirer. Totonel. I met him one morning, on the boulevard."

Liliana stammered with spite the supreme invective, "You're an idiot!"

In fact, since she had started going to the tea parties of her group of friends, that is, since the previous year, in sixth grade, Liliana had not met any boy to her taste. She found them all stupid and full of themselves. Once, at one of these tea parties, Totonel, a boy of Ştefănucă's age, had tried to kiss her during a dance. Her response had been prompt: a couple of slaps across the boy's face. To her chagrin, however, the incident had caused a sensation, and since then all her acquaintances had made a habit of mentioning the name of Totonel whenever they wanted to get her in a rage.

To pacify her, Ștefănucă began with compliments, "Young child, I get the impression that the summer has suited you down to the ground. You've got a tan. Your hair has lightened. And swimming seems to have got you into good form. The eye of your aged brother declares itself pleased."

Liliana blushed again, this time with pleasure. In front of her classmates, she let it be understood that she did not care about her physical appearance. More than that, she took every occasion to mock at displays of coquettishness. In secret, however, she often looked at herself in the mirror, examining herself with a frown.

"Young child, a champion does you the honor of challenging you to a round of table-tennis."

Liliana stepped out of the hammock, affecting sarcasm. "A champion? Ha! Ha! Ha!"

Then the two of them broke into a run, racing each other to the table-tennis table, which was situated at the end of the croquet lawn. There they stretched out the net. As she raised her bat, Liliana spotted Lucian wandering off on his own toward the end of the park. She couldn't stand him. Fond as she was of Ștefănucă, she could not get along with their elder brother. He had never had fun together with them, as though he had been born old. When they were children, playing at Indians with feathers on their heads and painted faces, crawling on all fours through the grass, shooting arrows at the farmyard birds, encircling the castle, which was transformed in their eyes into a white settlers' farmstead, Lucian had kept apart, mocking them with superior airs, until he managed to spoil their inclination to indulge in the fiction together. When they had made a tree house a few years ago, all nicely arranged, he had not even deigned to climb up just to see how they were accommodated. He did not ride with them; he did not accompany them when they went fishing to the meadows by the Prut. No, the gentleman did nothing but think. Even at that moment, Liliana could have slapped him as he passed by, grave and distant, without acknowledging their presence. Instead of going about like Ştefănucă in a simple sports outfit, he was dressed with ridiculous elegance, with a silk scarf, worn under his shirt, long city trousers that might have come straight from the ironing table, and sandals that exposed his feet like ladies' sandals. Puah!

Turning her eyes away from him, Liliana was quick to serve the first ball. "Play!"

Giving his brother and sister a wide berth, Lucian headed along the great walnut-lined path, determined to walk all around the park. Within the family, he was bound by a feeling of closeness and understanding only to his father. Grigore Holban's manner of existence did not seem to him in any way strange, still less deserving of derision. There was no other way for a scholar to live than as a hermit among books. To a certain extent, the son considered himself destined to lead a similar sort of life. Only that he, as a philosopher, was going to prove his value with a different resonance. In the last years of high school and the first years of university, Lucian had concentrated on bringing his cultural knowledge up to scratch, reading with a perseverance that had both made him anemic and damaged his eyesight. His ambition was to be able to make his contribution to the debate over the orientation of contemporary spirituality. The end of his period of intellectual training had happened to coincide with the year in which the Herald movement had started to gain ground, galvanizing the sympathies of the young. Although he balked at accepting any form of discipline, Lucian had not hesitated to join the group of militants at the Faculty, convinced that in the great moral crisis of this moment in history, to have maintained an attitude of neutrality would have meant missing the most interesting chance to make his mark with an idea, the more so as he imagined that he alone was capable of constructing a system of political thought upon the as yet nebulous premises of the "new man."

The days continued to be bright, with a gentle sun. Wisps of cobweb floated in the air. The leaves slowly turned yellow as nature peacefully followed its course.

In the park, there were walnuts to be gathered, with the help of a horde of children from the village: some climbed up nimbly like monkeys and shook the highest branches, while others gathered the fallen walnuts in baskets. However, when they saw Ştefănucă and Liliana at the end of the path, fixing a target of concentric circles to the bark of a tree and then counting the paces back from it to where they each prepared their bow, none of the children had the patience to stay put, and they all rushed up as if to see a circus show.

With a short whirr, the arrow sped from Ştefănucă's bow and hit one of the outer circles of the target. Now it was Liliana's turn to bed her bow: her arrow buried itself right in the black circle at the center.

"Bravo!" cried Ştefănucă, ready to shoot a new arrow.

Involuntarily, however, he felt that the game no longer engaged him as it used to: he was no longer able to take aim calmly or to handle the bow decisively. Moreover, the outcome itself now left him indifferent. Indeed the same thing had started to happen with table tennis and croquet too. He had taken part in them all in a sort of inertia, just to please Liliana.

"I give up!" confessed Ştefănucă, after he had finished the five arrows that each of them had to shoot.

"Really? You just give up, without trying to get your own back?" said Liliana in surprise, her cheeks burning.

"I've got bored. I unreservedly concede your superiority. Look, it would be better for you to give the children some instruction! I'll leave you my bow…," said Ştefănucă, trying to escape and seeing the curious horde standing around.

The unexpected proposal seemed to please Liliana, who immediately put the bow in the hand of one of the bigger boys, while the others wavered between staying there and running off.

Ştefănucă headed toward the gate of the park, turning over the dried leaves with his footsteps. The days of vacation on the estate, which had normally been so pleasant for him, seemed to have lost their charm. He could hardly wait to get back to Bucharest, to be together with his comrades again. The heroic lifestyle, in its most outstanding representations, had always delighted Ştefănucă. When he was around twelve, he had dreamed of being d'Artagnan in Dumas's novel. Together with another three classmates, who had agreed that each would take on the role of a musketeer, he had let his life be guided for a time by the strictest rules of knightly honor. Unknown to his mother, he had even joined a sports club and taken lessons in fencing. Then came the period of detective novels, of Sherlock Holmes. This time, Ştefănucă could imagine himself as nothing if not an amateur detective. With the same passion that others bring to solving crossword puzzles, he had started to follow newspaper reports of murders and enigmatic thefts, endeavoring in his mind to investigate each case. A brass revolver was never missing from his pocket. The adolescent Ştefănucă's last decisive reading had been a novel by Cronin, *The Keys of the Kingdom*, which brought him the revelation of the Christian phenomenon as nothing else ever had. The model of Father Chisholm, complex in such a *different* way in his goodness, understanding, and humor, had made the ideals of virility that had hitherto been embodied for him by the heroes of so many adventure novels seem mere vanity. He could think of nothing finer than to become a missionary, going in his turn to carry the word of the Gospel into the last lands unconverted to Christianity. Aware that in Orthodoxy, there were no missionaries, he made plans to convert to

Catholicism. At the same time, his deskmate, Nicoară, who had previously been Athos in the days when he himself had played the role of d'Artagnan, was secretly organizing the first Blood Brotherhood in the school. Ştefănucă had enrolled from the beginning, out of a feeling of collegial solidarity. And before long, he was truly won over, and it seemed to him that this was precisely what best matched his latest aspirations. Did not the Herald Movement present itself in a way as a group of lay missionaries who proposed to reform contemporary society, which in most respects was Christian in name only? A crusader's struggle awaited him with people right here in his own country, so he willingly gave up the idea of pursuing the same goal in China, South Africa, or the islands of Polynesia....

Outside, in the openness of the rolling steppe, where he had arrived as he walked on his own, thinking of his comrades in Bucharest, Ştefănucă suddenly became aware of being surrounded by the great shadows of the encroaching evening. He had not even noticed when the sun went down, when the herd of cattle turned back toward the village with their bells gently ringing. A light wind was starting to make itself felt from the Bessarabian bank of the Prut, chilling the atmosphere. Ştefănucă made his way back, his hands deep in his pockets.

Chapter III

It was almost nine when Lucian woke from his sleep. He did not leave the bed at once, as he still felt his strength sapped by the dream he had had as day approached. His obsessions in sleep betrayed a sexual crisis that had begun in his adolescence, when he had realized that he was not structured normally. The first symptoms had manifested themselves in the sixth grade at high school in connection with the classmate he shared a desk with, an ephebe type. With some confusion but at the same time aware of a murky pleasure of anticipated sin, he had found himself in love. He exploded in veritable crises of jealousy whenever he got the impression that his friend was nicer to others. He invited him to the cinema. He did his school assignments. He pampered him with the fulfillment of his every wish, especially as the boy did not receive a single penny of pocket money from his parents. It turned out, however, that the state of vassalage imposed by such a strange affection came to have an unpleasant side for Lucian's friend, who lost his patience one day.

"Lay off, for God's sake. You're too clinging!"

These words had wounded the admirer's sensibility so cruelly that, from that moment on, he had taken the decision to repress his inclination, thus starting a muted war with himself.

Rising from his bed, Lucian stopped for a moment in front of the mirror. The angles of premature baldness, whose advance he followed day by day like a catastrophe, made him turn away, even more out of sorts. At the window, he lifted the blinds on the grey of a rainy morning. He pulled them down again quickly, however, with a sensation of repulsion like that of touching a reptile. He had a phobia of colds, of humidity, of the viscosity of ugly autumn days.

Lucian's gaze fell upon his desk, where a good part of the books in his library lay stacked in piles. That way, they were more readily at hand for the purposes of study. He could feel that he was going to produce a monumental work, one that, within the bounds of his country's culture, would be comparable only with Pârvan's *Getica*, Blaga's *Mioritic Space*, or Călinescu's *History of Romanian Literature*. It was at that moment that he first imagined his volume in the windows of bookshops, published in French, no less, in the collection "Bibliothèque de philosophie contemporaine," under the shortened title *L'homme nouveau*. The thought did not draw a smile from him. He found it perfectly legitimate, even if up until then he had never imagined himself being translated into a world language. Although his book was focused on the case of certain local historical coordinates, it was going to bring into debate the very destiny of contemporary man. At the same time, it would offer the solution for getting out of the crisis. Was he not predestined to be the prophet proclaiming the renaissance of spiritualist thought that was bound to come?

The image of the bookshop window displaying *L'homme nouveau* melted away, however, the moment Lucian returned to his bed. As the night ended, he found himself alone, disoriented by the spasms of pleasure, on the shore of the sheet where the illusions of his dreams always ended up. Irritably, he pressed the bell button, letting it be known that his tea could be brought. After the maid had come in with the tray, Lucian first looked hurriedly through the newspaper. He passed over the first page, where panegyric articles about the late prime minister continued to be published. For a week, since the assassination had taken place, it had been impossible to find anything else to read. He stopped only when he reached page 3, at the statements made by Sebastian Răutu, the new president of the Council of Ministers. They were about the decreeing of the state of emergency, about the launch of court proceedings against the leaders of the Herald movement, about the public order measures that were going to be taken in the University.

Lucian began slowly to stir the sugar in his cup of tea with a teaspoon. Adversities did not usually frighten him, though that was not to say that he could easily see himself leading a life of privations. His waverings lasted no longer than it took for the sugar cube to melt in the tea. For the prophets of new eras, the roads are always without return. Lucian drank his tea with a feeling of sadness, which was, however, overcome in the end by the vanity of knowing that his role had a predestined significance.

Ștefănucă hunched down at his desk, where he was only now completely hidden behind the back of the classmate in front. This way, he could talk as much as he liked without being observed from the teacher's desk. Nicoară did nothing to protect himself, although the substitute Philosophy teacher had called him twice to order.

"Look, I tell you, he's turned himself in. For sure."

Ştefănucă was still confused. "All right, but I don't understand why."

"How not? Since the authorities are opening a public lawsuit, intent on establishing complicity at any price, there was nothing left for Toma Vesper but to—"

But Nicoară did not manage to finish.

"Hey, you! You still won't shut up?"

"Who? Me?"

"Yes, you! Trying to play stupid? Come out here!"

Nicoară got out with difficulty from behind the desk and made his way toward the teacher's table, with a slight sway in his walk like a sailor who had just come onshore.

At the sight of the boy approaching with his arms tensed like a boxer, the substitute teacher was suddenly afraid that he might be beaten up in front of the class. With these eighth-grade hooligans, one had to be prepared for anything. He therefore stopped him at a distance of several paces.

"Kindly repeat what I said about Plato's ethics!"

Instead of replying, Nicoară pricked up his ears in the direction of the neighboring desks, waiting for someone to prompt him. However, right at that moment, the door opened. It was the headmaster. The class rose to their feet with the usual rumble. While they were all standing, Nicoară quickly slipped back to his place.

The headmaster went straight to the teacher's table, from which he proceeded to speak in a deliberately sententious tone, "Gentlemen, I have to inform you that I have received a circular regarding school discipline. You must know that pupils who are guilty of participation in clandestine political movements will be expelled, without the right to re-enroll in other schools. I would draw your attention to the fact that this is no joking matter. According to the dispositions, we now have to check that you do not have subversive propaganda material on you."

The headmaster turned toward the substitute Philosophy teacher, who stood petrified beside the blackboard. "You keep watch from here to check that no one hides anything while I search each desk."

The control began in an atmosphere of stifled laughter. Whenever he came upon a packet of cigarettes or an issue of *Sports Gazette*, the headmaster raised his arms in the air and burst out, "You good-for-nothings! Aren't you ashamed of yourselves? Anyone would think you hadn't been raised within the walls of a model high school."

He did not confiscate anything, however, but moved on, his shoes making the squeaking sound that was familiar to all their ears from Mathematics exams.

"Aha!"

The interjection, this time articulated differently to what had gone before, gave way to a moment of silence.

"Not much of a surprise that I should catch you with such a badge! Since you first came to this school, you've always been the same disorderly element from whom nothing good can be expected."

Nicoară bit his lips, scarcely able to refrain from answering back.

The headmaster moved on to Ştefănucă. In his case, he was content with a mere search of pockets, but he could not believe his eyes when he saw the Herald badge slipping out of a handkerchief.

"No! Have you taken leave of your senses? Really, Holban, is this possible?"

Under the gaze of the headmaster and of the whole class, Ştefănucă lowered his head. Unconsciously, he kept fingering the ethics textbook that he was holding.

Annoyed, the headmaster continued his inspection. He had started searching the desks simply as a matter of form, confident in advance that he was not going to find anything incriminating. Now out of the blue, reality had proved him wrong beyond all expectations. What was to be done? If he reported the matter to the Ministry, he would indirectly attract a vote of blame on himself. Moreover, while expelling Nicoară could do no harm, the same could not be said of Holban, whose name was set to feature on the marble plaque of distinguished prize-winners.

The headmaster had no time to weigh the issue further, however, as he suddenly came upon another badge. "So you too?"

"Yes, me too!" confessed Cernat, having no way out.

The headmaster returned to the teacher's table, where he began by noting down the names of the pupils who had been caught with badges. The discovery of an offshoot of the Heralds in his school might prove a good story for the gutter press. No! He had to proceed with tact. To tell the truth, the confiscated badges did not amount to much. Since even Holban was among the culprits, it could be assumed that it was nothing serious. The wisest thing to do would be to cover up the case.

"Gentlemen, I am giving you a final warning! Those of you who do not come to your senses, starting from tomorrow, will face exemplary punishment, according to the sanctions specified by the Ministry. Nicoară, Holban, and Cernat, remember! I shall bring your case before the council of teachers. For my part, I intend to ask this time that your guilt be overlooked. However, you should not take this as a sign of weakness. Communicate to your parents that they are requested to come to my office at four o'clock this afternoon!"

The headmaster made his way to the door, adopting a martial air. In the meantime, the class had risen to their feet again, with the same accustomed rumble.

After their prayer, Ștefănucă did not stay to debate matters any further with Nicoară and Cernat. It was too late. When it was time to go home from school, he always met his sister at the corner of the boulevard, and from there, they made their way home together.

"Come on, brother, I'm drenched!" said Liliana impatiently when they met, although her school cape, with its hood pulled down over her nose, belied this.

Ștefănucă joined her without saying anything. He was worried. With the arrest of Toma Vesper, about which Nicoară had brought him up-to-date, the authorities now had in their hands all the leadership of the Heralds. Once again, an element of doubt, with the presupposition of an atonement, found its way into Ştefănucă's mind. It all started from the assassination. No matter how justified it might have been in the eyes of his comrades, political assassination was still murder. The words of Jesus had a meaning that permitted no equivocation: "They that take the sword shall perish with the sword."[5]

Liliana walked without noticing her brother's silence. She had started to get hungry. Thinking to get home faster, she kept hurrying her pace, stepping, as luck would have it, in every puddle on the pavement. The weather was driving her out of her mind. For a week, it had rained incessantly. She had seen all the movies one after the other so that there was no one left with which she could fill her afternoon. As for studying, she could never do that for more than an hour. All that was left for her was to catch a light music channel on the radio and listen to it till evening with her feet against the wall.

Ştefănucă knew as well as everyone else that at their interrogation, the assassins had declared that they had shot the prime minister on their own initiative, without the knowledge of any other person. They had judged the assassination to be necessary, but after committing it, they had somehow been conscious of their guilt, because they had not tried to run away. Only the third accomplice, Dr. Rotaru, had not turned himself in to the authorities. Of course, this was because he was not actually guilty. The prime minister had died instantly, killed by the first shots fired by Ifrim and Ionescu before he was even within range of Rotaru's revolver. So even though they knew that they were making themselves guilty of murder, that they

---

[5] Matthew 26.52

were sacrificing themselves without any prospect of salvation, the medical students had not flinched from bringing down the prime minister, who had "drawn the sword first" with the launch of the persecution against the Heralds. In the end, Ştefănucă came to see something sublime in their action.

"Oh, I forgot to tell you!" Liliana burst out. "On Saturday, we have a tea party at Sanda's. Nuni is bringing her records. You know she now has the whole Charles Trenet series."

"I'm not going. I'll just come around and pick you up."

"What? Are you crazy?"

"No, but lately, I've got rather fed up with tea parties."

"I understand! The gentleman has become blasé. You must know, however, that I'm not swallowing it. If you don't stay at the tea party, I'm not talking to you."

"Don't then."

"No? All right!" concluded Liliana, ready to cry like a child.

Were the assassins truly sublime? The process of reasoning on which Ştefănucă had started could end in no other conclusion. Then why, deep down, did he still not feel at ease about it?

"I'm just going to make a detour as far as the church."

"What's the matter with you?" wondered Liliana, forgetting that she had decided not to speak to her brother.

Ştefănucă went off at a rapid pace, without answering. He strode with his forehead like a battering ram through the ever-denser web of rain. Prayer would illuminate him fully. How had he not thought of this earlier? In the church, the truth awaited him, and the truth could only be one. Ştefănucă was now running all out. However, he was met by a closed church door.

Crivina…Periş…Buftea….

From Ploieşti onward, the train had not stopped at any stations, rushing through the night with the pulse of its wheels ever more accelerated.

Although he had a place in the compartment, Rotaru was traveling standing. He felt more at the ready alone in the corridor of the carriage. His head, mirrored in the blackness of the window, was almost unrecognizable. Indeed, during the time he had been living in hiding, Rotaru had let his beard and mustache grow and had lost weight, till his cheeks seemed hollowed out, and his eyes had acquired the uneasy look of someone always on his guard.

Chitila.… The train continued on its way, leaving the station with its trees shaken by the wind and a few somnambulant railwaymen. Drops of heavy rain had begun to trickle along the windows, weaving a spider's web over the darkness. The howl of the locomotive rang out for a moment in the emptiness of the night, after which only the pulse of the wheels remained audible, insistent as an obsession.

It was not yet a month since the day of the assassination. Rotaru had not turned himself in to the authorities, as the other two comrades had found it in themselves to do. Why should he answer before a sectarian justice for something that lay far beyond its understanding? The assassination of the prime minister—in other words, the bringing down of a man set against the fulfillment of a historic destiny—constituted a wholly legitimate act, which in the absolute could not be condemned by anyone. Rotaru had fled the next day into the mountains of Buzău, which he had chosen because he originated from that area. He had been sheltered by a forester, who knew little about what was going on in the world. There, in the high solitude of the fir trees, a solemn silence reigned. Not even a distant echo of the power saws at work in the valley could be heard. As the autumn was well advanced, the high pastures were cleared of the summer sheep-folds, so that the whole mountain seemed to have regained its primordial wildness. Rotaru had shared the hut with Old Ştefan, the forester. A hut in which there was nothing but two wooden benches and a fireplace with a cauldron for the *mămăligă*.[6] With the forester, he had learned to recognize the constellations of the sky, to distinguish the tracks in the forest, to understand the bellowing of the stags. After the tense days of the assassination, life in the midst of nature had relaxed him in a way. Rotaru could sleep free of obsessions, could walk with clear thoughts. Just two weeks after his arrival, however, bad weather had wrecked his equilibrium. A cloudy unease had come over him from one day to the next, and it had become permanent with the rain and fog of the late autumn. He had begun to suffer the weight of loneliness. He had lost sleep and appetite. He had been constantly cold, despite his winter jacket: it was something that came from the depths of his being, like rising damp in the soul.

____

[6]Maize polenta—a staple of the traditional Romanian peasant diet. (Tr.)

After ten days, feeling that he was moldering alive, he had no longer had the patience to stay put. Sick of nervous agitation, he had decided to return to Bucharest, another forest in which one's tracks could be lost, but where at least one did not have to cut all connections.

The shunting yard… Dozens of phantom trains packed in parallel lines, all together in their waiting. Here and there the staring eye of a signal cast its red or green phosphorescence over tracks made shiny by the rainwater. The howls of the locomotives crossed one another in the night. Bucharest… In a few moments, the train would be in the station. Rotaru experienced a new feeling of sadness. In the city of all his student memories, he saw himself alighting from the train as a stranger. For as long as circumstances forced him not to drop his mask, he would have to avoid everything that had made up his life until the assassination: the hospital, the medical school, the student residence. For the first time, there would be no Mia on the platform to greet him. Mia…. Their love had been something serious from the beginning. They had got engaged in their first year at university, but the girl's state of health, her tuberculosis, with long periods staying in mountain sanatoriums, had caused the wedding to be continually postponed. Memory suddenly replaced the wet window of the carriage with the window of the confectioner's at the corner of the Botanical Garden, where they used to meet on rainy evenings when they could not go out to walk. The owner of the shop, an Adventist, would be reading his Bible in the corner by the till. The few tables, with red marble tops, seemed never to be occupied all at the same time, which gave the place a special feeling of intimacy. Mia's cake was always a *savarin*, while his was a *sarailie*.[7] The pendulum clock on

---

[7] *Savarin*: cupcake, *sarailie*: Turkish honey and nut cake (Tr.)

the wall, which hadn't worked since God knows when, took the confectioner's out of the temporal dimension, always stuck at the same meaningless time: half-past four.

The pulse of the wheels slowed after passing under the Grant Bridge, and the train finally came to a stop. The light of the platform replaced the darkness, dazzling the eyes. After he had got down from the carriage, more because he was pushed by the passengers behind, Rotaru stood still in confusion. All along the way, he had been distracted by random thoughts so that he had been unable to decide anything. Where was he to go until he could find a purpose? He thought for a moment of Mia, although he was convinced that the police would have found out about the connection between them from the university and would be keeping her under observation. And even if, ridiculous as it seemed, his fears should prove to be exaggerated, the next problem was the opposition of the girl's parents, who had never looked kindly on him because of his political affiliation. To them, he was a madman, an individual with no guarantees of reliability, in the strict bourgeois sense. And now, of course, to them he was a common assassin…

The passengers pouring out of the train caught Rotaru up in their flow toward the exit. Beside the locomotive, the escaping steam covered the bustle of the platform. There seemed to be something chaotic about it all, after the severe harmony of the forests of fir trees in which he had lived alone for almost a month. As he passed the waiting rooms, his tired eyes were met by the posters of the evening papers, with the latest telegrams: "City of Călăraşi Threatened by Floods," "Britain Launches New Warship," "Pope's Health Improves." So these were the issues on the day's agenda?

PART TWO

Chapter I

At the end of the street, Vasia turned his head to take a last look at the imposing building of the student residence, in front of which the platoon of gendarmes was now assembled and ready to march away. Then, taking up the heavy weight of his trunk, he set off through the rain, with no idea where he was heading. In the end, the rawness of the morning drove him to enter the first bar he came to, in order to warm himself up a bit.

The woman at the till raised her wide eyes from the newspaper in front of her only for a moment. She sized up her customer at a glance: a man with no occupation whose order could not be expected to amount to much. She yawned, cradled her jaw with its aching molar in the palm of her hand, and immediately immersed herself in reading about a crime of passion in the Tei district.

After passing hesitantly in front of the counter with its display of ham, salami, cheese, meatballs, and pickled fish, Vasia stopped at a table beside the stove, where he put down his trunk and took off his rain-soaked coat.

A waiter who had detached himself from the window in the meantime approached, dragging his feet. "What will sir have?"

"A hot *țuică*[8]."

____

[8] Traditional Romanian plum brandy (Tr.)

The waiter shuffled away, wiping his nose with the edge of his apron.

Vasia passed his hand over his unshaven cheek, over his high forehead, over his wet hair. He felt worn out. He had spent the last few days in detention again. The first time, he had been arrested at home, in his village in Bessarabia, the day the Heralds were dissolved. This second time, the arrest had taken place after they had done away with the prime minister, when he had been lifted from the residence together with a number of other students. A week of pointless interrogations. They had beaten him several times till they drew blood. He had been pretty much starved. On his release from the police prefecture, he had barely been back at the residence for a full day, and the next thing he knew, here he was thrown out in the street as a result of this evacuation demanded by the gendarmes.

"Your *ţuică*!"

Vasia, who had begun absent-mindedly to crumble a toothpick he had found on the table, raised his eyes and took hold of the hot cup. Only now did his vision take in, as a random detail, the cataract in the waiter's eye. Not realizing that he would scald his insides if he drank hot *ţuică* without waiting a little, he poured it down his throat in a single gulp. He felt pierced by a boiling fluid that burned him till it cut his breath. In the state of drowsiness that followed, his head fell heavily over his crossed arms on the table.

"Ye gods! I'll teach you a lesson!" yelled Commissioner Boian, his eyes as round as onions. And his palm rose, ready to strike Vasia's cheek.

But how strange! With his palm stopped in mid-air, Commissioner Boian dropped to his knees. Behind him, also kneeling, huddled the university cashier, who paid out the scholarships once a month, together with the gendarme officer under whose command the evacuation of the student residence had been carried out.

It was only when Vasia realized that he had a revolver in his hand that things began to make sense. They were all down on their knees before him, begging for mercy.

Vasia took aim first at Commissioner Boian, whose head rolled on the ground, leaving his body as straight as before. The waiter, with cataract in one eye and an apron as dirty as a used handkerchief, lifted the head onto his tray with the skill of a professional. Fired up with enthusiasm, Vasia held out his revolver, ready to shoot a second time, into the still-living headless body. However, he was prevented by a hand from behind.

Waking up in confusion, Vasia found again the table with the cup of *ţuică* and the crumbled toothpick.

The waiter finally let go of his arm, which he had been shaking for a few moments. "Come on, mate! It's getting late! Aren't you going to order something to eat?"

Although the rain outside dimmed the daylight so that, from that angle, Vasia's eyes could not clearly make out the items on the counter, their image nevertheless became quite distinct within him, in a fantastic dilation: ham, salami, cheese, meatballs, pickled fish…. He swallowed several times before giving his answer, "No. I won't have anything else…."

In the large waiting room of the Gara de Nord, where he had finally come to shelter from the rain and to pass the time until the hour of tutoring that he had to do with his one and only pupil, Vasia sat huddled at a corner of the bench, crushing seed husks between his teeth. He had finished the last of the four paper cones he had bought when he got off the streetcar. Below, on the dirty cement, innumerable husks lay scattered around his feet.

The harmonica played by a soldier who was waiting there for some connection or other made the atmosphere even more oppressively sad. The clock on the wall left Vasia with the impression that it was barely able to move its hands; he could almost believe that time itself, no longer feeling that it had any purpose, was ready to stop forever in the greyness of the rainy afternoon. The station seemed dead: no bustle, nothing. In the waiting room, Vasia and the soldier with the harmonica sat far apart, like last survivors.

The empty cone was crushed like the rest and thrown onto the cement. Then Vasia stretched out along the bench with his hands under his head. Thrown out of the student residence, with his scholarship cut off, there was nothing for it but to make do with what he could earn from tutoring in mathematics. However, he would definitely have to increase the number of pupils. As it was, he was thinking of asking Dr. Proca for an advance against the lessons he was going to give his boy. He lived out the scene in its every detail, visualizing himself in Vlad's room, at the table by the window, where they sat during lessons. At that moment, he was alone because he had sent the boy to see if he could speak with his father. His view from the window was blocked, as usual, by the wall that extended along one side of the yard.

"Well, what's the matter? I hear you wish to speak to me about something," said Dr. Proca from the door.

"If you could possibly advance me some money against future lessons... I'm in great need...."

Dr. Proca took his wallet from his jacket pocket, a wallet as thick as a book, with a monogram in the corner. His short fingers, with their nails cut to the flesh, first sought and then extracted a number of 20 lei notes.

"Will this do?"

The soldier's harmonica could still be heard, endlessly rambling on. Agitated by hunger, which was causing him veritable hallucinations, Vasia got up from the bench and started to pace up and down. Through the window he saw again the Station Square, shining with rainwater. The clouds had thinned and it was no longer raining. Turning his eyes to the clock on the wall, Vasia realized that time had not, in fact, stood still. It was half-past three. If he went slowly, with the pauses imposed by the weight of the trunk, then the walk to get to his pupil's home at the agreed hour would fill up the rest of the time.

At the bakery at the corner of the square, which he entered at the very moment they were taking some cheese pastries out of the oven, Vasia bought himself a bread roll with the last small change in his pocket. If he had not wasted money at lunchtime on the cones of seeds, he would have had enough, on top of what he had paid for the roll, to buy a cheese pastry, one of those warm and crisply puffed pastries that filled the trays that had just been brought out into view. He left regretfully, biting ravenously into the roll as if it were a hunk of meat.

When Vasia made to enter the Proca family home, the maid opened the door to him with the words, "The doctor has left word that he has something to say to you, so go to see him first. Master Vlad isn't home yet."

Puzzled, Vasia dumped his trunk and his coat in a corner of the vestibule, and then made his way to the waiting room, where patients were already gathering in large numbers. However, no sooner had he managed to take his place on the only chair that was still free than he heard his name called from behind the door by Dr. Proca: "Voinov, come in, please!"

Under the enquiring gaze of the patients, who could not understand the preference accorded to the last arrival, Vasia went into the consulting room.

"My dear fellow, knowing how conscientious you are, it seemed strange to us that you should miss a week without a single word to let us know."

Vasia lowered his eyes. The wet prints of his boots formed patterns on the linoleum.

"Three days ago, we telephoned the student

residence to find out what had become of you. We were very sorry to learn that you had been arrested...."

Biting his lip, Vasia continued to look at the wet patches on the linoleum.

"I must confess that you have never given us any cause for complaint. You have been the ideal tutor for Vlad."

Vasia clenched his fists.

"Far be it from me to judge your political orientation. As a father, however, I have a responsibility for the education of my son. I do not wish him to fall prey to extremist ideas. In the circumstances of the present day, I cannot leave him any longer under the influence of your example. I'm sure you understand me! Consequently, my wife and I have decided to look for someone else for the boy...."

Doctor Proca suddenly fell silent, sucking and puffing in the attempt to prevent his cigar from going out. When he realized that the danger was over, he took his wallet from his jacket pocket, a wallet as thick as a book, with a monogram on the corner. "Let me pay up what I owe you, the three lessons since the beginning of the month. There you are!"

With the blood rushing to his cheeks, Vasia took the money that the doctor's hand held out. Then, without a word, he rushed out, slamming the door hard behind him.

It was almost midnight when Vasia arrived in the Cişmigiu Garden. When he left Dr. Proca's house, he had first gone to get something to eat as quickly as possible. With his hunger eased, he had then wandered the streets aimlessly for hours. He had not gone back to spend the night at the station, for fear of finding that soldier still there with the harmonica at his lips. In his present state, the rambling melody of the harmonica, echoing in the emptiness of the waiting room, might have driven him in the end to throw himself under the wheels of the next train. With leaden feet and fingers cut from dragging the trunk behind him, he finally sat down on the first bench he found in the Garden. Before closing his eyes, he had the impression for a moment that the stars in the now cloudless sky were all shaking together, ready to fall down on his head.

One by one, the buildings of the city were blowing up. All around, nothing but smoke and whirling rubble. In the streets, the dogs were running madly, whining all the time. Not a person to be seen. It seemed they had all fallen prey to the flames.

At one window, his eye was caught by a waving arm. It was Dr. Proca, almost unrecognizable now, gesticulating like a delirious scarecrow. But no one had any right to survive. No one. At a signal from Vasia, the flames rose high up, engulfing everything.

In place of the last flickers of the fire, great outpourings of blood had begun to cover the burnt walls, while the sky formed a bloody vault above. A splendid scene: for Vasia, it was sublime in an enchanting way. Delighted, he started to applaud.

Vasia woke feeling stiff and clapping his hands unconsciously. Above him, the sky was burning. The sun, red as blood, was bringing in another day. He stood up with difficulty, with the feeling of contusions all over his body. Then he quickly sat down again, slightly dizzy. Once he had recovered, he began to rub himself with his hands to get rid of the stiffness. He could see no way out of the impasse. Now that he had lost his only pupil, there was nothing to do but to leave for home while he still had money for the journey.

Vasia lifted up his trunk and slowly made his way to the gate of the Cişmigiu Garden. At a bakery on the corner of the boulevard, he bought a pretzel. Nibbling it, he went on his way, determined to take a streetcar to the station. After a few steps, he heard someone calling him from the opposite pavement, "Mr. Voinov!"

Ştefănucă came running across the boulevard.

"How do you do, Mr. Voinov?"

Vasia looked at his interlocutor but did not recognize him even close up.

"I see you don't remember me. In the spring, when the Blood Brothers were being set up, you came with the organizational dispositions. Do you remember now? The circumstances were a bit funny, because you happened to be substituting for our class teacher...."

"Yes, of course! Aren't you Holban from seventh grade?"

"Excuse me, eighth grade now. But where are you going?"

"To the station. I'm going home. My scholarship has been cut off. I've been thrown out of the student residence. I don't have any more private tutoring. What do you think I should do?"

Ştefănucă felt choked by a sense of revolt. The wretches! For the first time, he had before his eyes a victim of the persecution unleashed against the Heralds. Voinov seemed to have been reduced to the state of a vagabond. The hallucinating look. The sunken cheeks. The slightly trembling hand, which was hesitating to carry the last of the pretzel to his mouth. The trunk. No. He had to do something for the comrade in distress. It was an elementary duty.

"Listen! You mustn't go! I'll take you to our house. We've got a place for you to sleep. And food, thank the Lord, is no problem! What do you say?"

There followed a moment of silence, in which Vasia lifted the pretzel to his mouth and bit into it with a strange grimness.

"All right, I accept!" came the reply in an unexpectedly quiet voice.

"Come on then!" Ştefănucă grabbed him by the arm and turned him around in his tracks.

Chapter II

Ștefănucă switched off the light and slipped out, careful not to make any sound until he reached the hall door. As he went downstairs, however, the stairs began to creak under his every step. Realizing that at any moment he might be caught, Ștefănucă set caution to the winds. After taking the last three stairs in one leap, he put his shoes on carelessly and made a dash for the door, without a word of answer to his mother, who had come out of her room, wakened by his footsteps, and was fumbling in the dark for the banisters.

In the cold depths of the night, the city seemed dead. No car horn was to be heard, no rattle of a streetcar, no echo of a footstep.

Before going any further, Ștefănucă crossed himself, then he set off quickly as though someone was on his tracks. He did not shorten his route by going along the boulevard but took some back streets, where it was unlikely that he would meet anyone. That night, teams of Blood Brothers were going to cover the walls of the city with Herald posters. Their little group had been assigned the Botanical Garden district. The pasting up of posters had to start after midnight, when there was no more movement on the streets.

As he approached the Cotroceni bridge, Ștefănucă spotted his comrades with a bucket and something that looked like a whitewash brush.

"We've got frozen waiting for you!" Nicoară burst out when he saw his classmate.

"All right, but it isn't twelve yet!"

"Your watch has stopped. Come on now, so we can get finished faster, or there'll be hell to pay!" broke in Cernat, picking up the bucket. "I had to hide twice on the way to avoid being checked by patrols!" In fact, there was no truth in any of this, though that is not to say that it had not taken place in his mind. Every time he experienced any out-of-the-ordinary situation, Cernat was in the habit of imagining reality at its most dramatic, and he knew how to make others see things as he did. Going out into the field to paste up posters could not but be full of dangers.

"Anyone would think you were scared!" said Nicoară mockingly as he started to move.

"Scared! Me? You don't know me!"

The sound of a policeman's whistle, coming unexpectedly from somewhere in the district, made the boys quicken their pace and cut short their conversation.

At the first street corner, Nicoară decided. "Ştefănucă, stay here! And you stand guard at the other end so that I can get on with pasting up the posters in peace."

Ştefănucă stayed where he was, his sense of hearing intensified by the night. All around, the same silence. Thick clouds seemed to form a blanket over the city.

"Hey!"

Ştefănucă started in fear, thinking there was some threat. He ran toward Nicoară, who, however, received him calmly, with a question held out at the end of his brush, "Well, what do you say?"

On the walls around about, there were posters at intervals showing Saint George killing the dragon. Not a word of propaganda. The lines spoke for themselves: the saintly halo, the arm thrusting the spear, the rearing horse, the serpent.

"I can just imagine the faces of the authorities when they see our posters in the morning. As long as they don't manage to rip them down before then...," remarked Cernat, who had also come over, seeing that Ştefănucă had abandoned his post.

"You think the gendarmes can do that everywhere in one night?"

Moving on to another street, a shorter one this time, the boys no longer found it necessary for anyone to stand guard. As they pasted up the posters, they started talking again.

"I wonder if the uproar there's going to be over the posters might not do some harm to the prisoners, especially now, right before the trial!" thought Ştefănucă aloud.

Holding his brush in the air, Nicoară was slow to run it over the poster that Cernat was holding out to him.

"God, what it is to be a gull! The whole point of the posters is because of the trial! We've got to keep the heat up, make it clear that we can still act, even when our leaders are locked away in prison. Do you get the idea?"

When they reached the end of the street, the boys got ready to stick a number of posters along the fence that surrounded the Botanical Garden. But even before they were across the streetcar tracks, they heard the cadenced steps of a patrol approaching down the hill. Losing no more time, they abandoned their bucket on the pavement and quickly jumped the fence into the pitch darkness of the Garden. They did not even notice the voices crying out behind them. The shots that followed moments later, on the other hand, echoed deafeningly in their eardrums. They curled up behind the first tree, out of breath.

Nicoară, who came back to his senses before the others, whispered, "Leave the posters here. If the bastards catch us, at least they'd better not find them on us! Let's scatter now, each by a different route, toward the exit over there...."

Worried about who had slipped out of the house, secretly, in the middle of the night, without paying any attention to her questions, Raluca Holban could not find the peace to fall asleep again straight away. She tested all the hypotheses, one by one. From the start, she had ruled out Liliana, whom she considered to be a good girl. Then Lucian, at whose door she had glimpsed a strip of light, the best evidence that he was in his room. There remained Ștefănucă and the stranger. As far as Ștefănucă was concerned, she had thought it would be easy to check, but when she had tried to enter his room, she had come up against a locked door. For Ștefănucă to leave the house at the dead of night without saying anything, it had to be something serious—in other words, some other accursed political business. On the other hand, the stranger aroused even more justified suspicion. Faced with the *fait accompli* of his having been brought into the house, she had had no option at first but to accept what Ştefănucă had decided on his own initiative. Thereafter, terrified by the stranger's anarchic ideas, she had been able to think only of how to get him out of the house. At one point, she had gone so far as to consider resorting to her husband's assistance, with the plan that he would write from the estate that he was suffering from an attack of appendicitis, so that his study would have to be prepared for his return to Bucharest. In the event of such staged circumstances, there would be no other option for the intruder but to leave, especially as there was no other free bedroom available in the house. It was only as she looked at the blank sheet of paper that she had realized how vain her illusions were. Surely she knew her husband better! Grigore would merely have thrown her request in the wastepaper basket, annoyed at the very idea of being mixed up in the staging of such a farce.

Raluca Holban was determined to seek the truth all the way, to remain awake until the person who had gone out returned. The radiator had long cooled and her unease made her feel the cold all the more. She could hear nothing; even Tan, the Angora tomcat, had stopped purring in his deep sleep.

It was all like back then, that gloomy afternoon. The staffroom. The headmaster of the high school talking about the sanctions to be applied in the case of pupils who would not give up their Herald activity. Those few parents, with their heads downturned. The rain outside....

Rising from the end of the table, which seemed all the longer as there were so few sitting around it, the headmaster beckoned Raluca Holban with his finger to come to the window. From there, she could see Ştefănucă in the garden below, blindfolded, in front of a platoon of gendarmes ready to fire. A scraggy dog, but with the face of Vasia, lay in wait behind a heap of rubbish. Everything was depicted in a dirty grey, like a poor-quality instant photograph.

Raluca Holban made to cry out, but her lips moved in a void, soundlessly.

Beside her, the headmaster's order burst out like a detonation, shattering the window: "Fire!"

Then things became blurred together before her eyes, starting to revolve along with her until nothing remained.

When Raluca Holban woke from her sleep, the first thing that struck her was how the electric light was dissipated in the murky atmosphere of the early dawn. She lifted herself up on one elbow, and looked, still confused, at the familiar details around her. Her eyes gradually picked out the bed, disordered by her tossing and turning in her sleep, the tomcat curled up at her feet, the wardrobe with its oval mirror, the chest of drawers and the armchairs, the shelves of books. It was some time before she came back to herself, fully reclaimed by palpable reality.

God, what a terrifying nightmare! Yet another to add to the many that had been tormenting her almost nightly. Of course their sinister absurdity was never arbitrary. In all of them, the same signs appeared. If this went on much longer, she would go mad.

By the time she had put on a dressing gown, she had gooseflesh under her thin nightdress. She lifted the blinds of the window and was confronted by the first snowy day of winter. There was a blizzard. The street was no longer recognizable in the chaos of drifted snow.

Raluca Holban left her room and went to knock on Ştefănucă's door, but she got no response. Then she went to the bathroom, where she found him brushing his teeth.

"Good morning, Mom!"

"Good morning!"

"What's up with you?"

"I didn't sleep too well."

Ştefănucă did not dare to ask further.

"Ştefănucă, do you love me?"

By way of an answer, the boy kissed his mother on the forehead.

Wiping away with her hand the toothpaste foam that had been imprinted like a seal under the pressure of the kiss, Raluca Holban continued with lowered voice, "If you really love me, I'm going to ask you to do something. Give up politics! Have done with the Herald movement! I don't feel I can carry on anymore with my heart always leaping for worry about you."

In the mirror, Ştefănucă's features hardened, and the toothbrush remained in the air, suspended in the broken gesture of his hand. Did his mother know what his last night's departure had been all about? There was no room for doubt. Otherwise, what was the point of such a request, heavy with undertones?

"Mom, how can I make you understand? For me, the Herald movement is everything. I can't even think of giving it up. But believe me, you have nothing to worry about. I take good care."

Scarcely able to hold back her tears, Raluca Holban left without saying a word. She went straight back to her bedroom, where she fell into an armchair. Her last hope was crushed. Good Lord! No one thought of her. No one. They all lived just as they pleased, without caring if they were treading on her heart. She felt that her cup of bitterness was filled to the last drop. At the end of the day, she was just a poor woman, not a saint who could endure serenely to the end.

Through the spider's web of her tears, Raluca Holban looked around her in a lost way, as if expecting some support from the mute objects. Not even Tan warmed her with his presence; he was far away in a deathlike sleep.

Chapter III

Vasia had not gone to bed yet. He still felt he had to get accustomed to the details of Grigore Holban's study.

The room was large, with a high ceiling. Heavy curtains clothed the windows. The massive furniture, consisting of a bookcase, a writing desk, a chest of drawers, some armchairs, and a sofa, was scarcely sufficient to fill the space. A carpet, on which footsteps were muffled to silence, completely covered the parquet, right to the door. Vasia's rudimentary trunk sat in one corner, looking as awkward as its owner. Several family portraits in gilt frames hung on the papered walls: oil paintings in tones darkened by time.

Vasia got up from the armchair, attracted as usual by the old map of Mesopotamia mounted behind glass in a suitable frame at the back of the bookcase. From the parchment of the map, his gaze then drifted toward the shelves of books. They included, mixed up at random, works of Henry Bataille, Maurice Maeterlinck, Paul Bourget, Henry de Régnier... Almost nothing but French literature of the beginning of the century, from which one could easily reconstruct the literary tastes of the adolescent Raluca Holban.

Vasia turned his back on the bookcase and passed on to the writing desk, where the other curiosity awaited him: the goldfish bowl. He paused a little to gaze at the immobility of the little red fish in the transparency of the water. Just so many knick-knacks, all too little different from the porcelain ornaments in the glass cabinet in the hall or on the sideboard in the dining room. Delicate nothings for the gratification of the eyes, like everything one encountered in the Holban house.

It was all still new for Vasia, starting indeed with the circumstance of having a room to himself. As a child, at home in the village, he had slept crowded together with his parents and the other brothers and sisters. In later years, in the high school dormitory and then in the student residence, he had shared a bedroom with at least four others. Finally, just some ten days before, he had ended up sleeping on a bench in the Cişmigiu Garden. Now his existence had changed, as if under some spell. Although the unexpected turn things had taken came as a relief, he was annoyed at the compromise involved in accepting the shelter of the Holban house. Did his hosts not belong to the bourgeois elite that was to be exterminated in the crucible of revolution? Since he had been living in the midst of the Holban family, he could see more clearly than ever the vanity of the luxurious parasitic existence of such people. To be honest, what did each of them amount to, judged separately? The old man: a maniac who had shut himself up on his estate in the ivory tower of his library. The mother: a lady who killed her time making jams and petting her cat. The elder boy: a self-imagined philosopher, with something artificial, something of the hothouse about him. The girl: the human version of a drawing-room Pekinese. Finally, Ştefănucă, although well-meaning, could not be considered a specimen alien to the family group. The overall impression fitted in with the map of Mesopotamia, with the goldfish bowl, with the wallpaper, the curtains, and the carpets that lined each room. Once he was installed in the Holban family home, in order to feel somehow at peace with himself in spite of everything, Vasia had thought it best that they should all know right from the start whom they were dealing with. And he had taken advantage of meal times to speak openly, starting by confessing that he had joined the Heralds only as a way of arriving with them at the revolution. Unlike the others, he had no inclination toward illusions of any new politico-social organization, considering that there was no one to achieve it and no one to deserve it. He had had the example of his parents before his eyes for long enough. Although they lived like cattle, the same as the other peasants in the village, they resigned themselves to the point of reconciliation to the yoke of destiny, sealing their endurance with the idiotic judgment: "God willed it so!" They never emerged from the inertia of their passivity. If this was reality, a revolution should not even bring reforms in the interests of the people. The only thing to be done was to put an end to the institutions in power, not just the forms as such, but also the people who represented them organically.

When Vasia finally lay down, he was received by the softness of the bed, its sheets rustling in their starchy cleanness.

In the armchair by the window, Raluca Holban sat with Tan on her lap. The fading of the winter's day deepened the shadows around her. Outside, she could not even make out whether it was still snowing.

Stroking the cat in a sort of inertia of boredom, Raluca Holban pondered on her loneliness. There comes a time, between the ages of fifty and sixty, when the life of a woman begins to enter a blind angle of tedium. It is the age when one no longer expects anything from one's husband, when one's children have grown up, when one no longer even cares much about keeping or forming a friendship. The days become mere calendar pages.

Raluca Holban put Tan to one side in order to light the lamp. As she passed the mahogany writing desk, her eyes rested on a black-covered notebook. She picked it up and went back to her armchair. The need to write had unexpectedly come over her one day the previous autumn, and it had made itself felt several times since then, revealing itself to be a struggle with time. Writing was a strictly private activity for Raluca Holban, unconnected with any ambition to publish. She began to read from where she had happened to open the notebook. Each sentence touched piano keys in her soul:

1900. The high eaves of the house in Strada Batiştei kept dripping, disturbing Raluca's ears with the impression that the rain would never come to an end. From the hall, the pendulum clock chimed another hour of sleeplessness: the sound of a zither being struck, making up a curiously disharmonious chord, dispersed in the darkness, leaving the rooms to hear once again only the creaking of the furniture, something like a sighing of the old wood. Then it seemed to Raluca that Gran'mama was talking alone in her room next door, just as she had found her once before, two nights previously. With bated breath, she got out of bed and fumbled her way through the darkness to the other room, where she lit the candle on the night table. As before, she found her grandmother at the head of the bed, with a glassy look in her eyes and the folds of her cheeks purple. She had grasped the walking stick at her side, doubtless with the idea of supporting herself as she got out of bed. However, the feeble legs that had got caught up in the disorder of the sheets kept her immobile, while her bony hand held onto the stick without knowing what to do with it. Her confused words betrayed one and the same obsession, "Come on, Raluca! Hurry up! I have to get dressed…bring me the velvet dress with the frilly collar! Come on, help me! Can't you see they're waiting for me? The coupé is at the gate…." Then, turning toward a corner of the room that was completely submerged in darkness, she said, as though addressing someone, "Just a moment, I'll be right there! Lord, what horses! You can see who the coachman is…."

Trembling despite herself, Raluca took Gran'mama's arm. "Calm down! You've been dreaming about something or other. No one has come for you. Why get dressed? It's nighttime. Go back to bed!" Her grandmother burst out in a thin chuckle, "Hee, hee,

hee! Nighttime? Where do you get them from, my girl? Can't you see? The coupé doesn't even have its lights on. Come on, bring me my dress, or I'll be late...."

From the hall, the sound of the pendulum clock was more muted than in Raluca's room: the echo of the sound of a zither being struck, making up a curiously disharmonious chord.

☓

They were all waiting in the hall. In her great chair, a piece of furniture as out of the ordinary as a metropolitan's throne, Gran'mama seemed finally to have given up asking questions. She had dozed off with her head slumped forward, her hands clasped demurely over her lace handkerchief on the lap of her velvet dress. Uncle Olimpiu, Raluca's new guardian, the man behind the whole conspiracy set in motion to have her grandmother taken into an old people's home, was pacing up and down, his squeaking boots grating on the ear. Her aunt sat at the table, not knowing what to do with her hands: sometimes she would bring them together, the next she would pull on her fingers one by one, then she would spread open her palms and look at them as though seeing them for the first time.

With tears in her eyes, Raluca turned again toward the window. If instead of the coupé that was to take Gran'mama to the home, she had seen the street bathed in sunlight and a hearse approaching, her anguish could not have been deeper. Forced by Uncle Olimpiu, she had accepted the role of helping Gran'mama to get used to the idea of going away, playing on her delirium about the coupé. As things turned out, however, Gran'mama had not had another of these episodes for two days now. She was her old self, fully conscious of what was going on around her. In the morning, when Raluca had tried to persuade her to put on her velvet dress to go in the coupé, she had seemed completely puzzled. "Why the velvet dress? What coupé? Where am I to go? As far as I know, one goes in a coupé to weddings or funerals...."

In the end, she had allowed herself to be dressed with an embarrassed smile, understanding nothing. All decked out in her velvet dress, which gave her an air of solemnity, she had been seated in the hall, with her things packed in a suitcase. To her anxious questioning, Uncle Olimpiu, each time, lifted his finger to his lips. "Shhh! Surprise! The coupé...you'll see!" Then all that could be heard was the squeaking of his boots.

However, before Raluca could move from the window as the black-lacquered coupé came to a stop, Uncle Olimpiu, who had heard the sound of the horses' hooves from the end of the street, rapidly stepped up to Gran'mama, rubbing his hands. "Come on! Cheer up! The coupé has arrived. Let's go!"

Wakened from her torpor, her grandmother curled up in her chair, at the same time lifting onto her knees the silver-handled walking stick that she had never been without since her legs had begun to fail her. "No! Leave me in peace! I'm not moving from here!" Uncle Olimpiu lost his patience. "If she's not willing to understand, we'll need to carry her." And turning to the servants, who were crowding at the door, he lost no time in shouting, "Gheorghe, Anica, come and help me!"

Raluca left the room. She ran up the attic stairs to get as far away as possible. Behind her, the octogenarian's voice, with a high-pitched tone that was strange to her, reached her through the walls. "No! I don't want to! Don't you dare touch me! Raluca, where are you? No!"

Raluca advanced with hesitant steps. At the gate of the iron fence that surrounded the park of the old people's home, no one stopped her. There was no movement anywhere. It was as if the sweet scent of freshly blossomed lime trees had chloroformed everything as far as the dingy, moldy-white walls of the building. The impression became more powerful a little further on, when her eyes came upon the first living being: an old woman asleep on a bench, her mouth wide open like that of a dead person before their chin was lifted.

After stopping for a moment in the hall at the entrance to the home, as she found no one to ask the way to Gran'mama's room, Raluca began to climb the stairs. On the first floor, a sign with the word "Infirmary" led her into the depths of a dark corridor with doors on both sides. She stopped, finally, at one of these, on which was written "Duty Doctor." With her heart in her mouth, she knocked softly: no answer. She tried the door and went in. From a leather sofa of the sort common in consulting rooms, an individual with a thermometer in his hand got up. His white coat left no doubt that he was the doctor of the institution. By signs, he let Raluca understand that she had to wait while he took his own temperature. Embarrassed, she began to let her eyes wander from the bareness of the walls to the fly-paper that hung from the lamp, whose bulb was lit in broad daylight.

"Hmm! 37.3 again. Yes! What do you want, young lady?" uttered the doctor, with a raspy voice.

"You see, I want to know the number of the room where my grandmother is. She was taken in here yesterday at midday."

"Ah, 'Madame Coupé.' The gentleman who came with her told me. Incipient sclerosis of the brain. What can one do? Old age... Some wet themselves... Some sleep all day... Some see the phantom coupé."

Still looking at the thermometer, the doctor talked in a tone that it was difficult to know what to make of.

"Room number eight...."

"Thank you... Excuse me," murmured Raluca, noticing just as she was preparing to shut the door that the doctor had put the thermometer back in his mouth.

Room number eight. With her hand on the door handle, Raluca held her breath. When she finally plucked up the courage to open the door, her eyes alighted first on the velvet dress, which seemed stripped of its bloom there on the basic institutional chair: something quite absurd, a relic of carnival. Gran'mama was in bed, dozing with her head turned on a pillow that was raised behind her. Beside her, on the bedside table, a plate with some boiled potatoes lay untouched. Through the open window, the sweet smell of lime trees in bloom wafted in.

When Raluca sat down gently on the edge of the bed, Gran'mama moved her eyelids with difficulty.

"Raluca... Raluca... Why have they brought me here? Why? Am I to end my days in a home? You have to take me away right now."

Gran'mama's hand, clasped around Raluca's was all trembling.

"I wanted to go away on my own last night. My legs wouldn't carry me...."

Raluca got up slowly. As she had averted her eyes from Gran'mama's gaze, she could not see that with what she was starting to say, she was lifting the mask of anxious torment from her grandmother's face.

"All right...I'll take you away from here. I'll go and talk to the doctor. Don't you worry...."

Raluca went toward the door, barely moving her feet. Once outside, however, she rushed along the dark corridor and down the stairs two at a time. As if stunned, she saw nothing as she hurried past the old woman asleep on the bench, her mouth wide open like that of a dead person before their chin was lifted.

❦

Gran'mama lifted herself up from the depths of the bed, looking wide-eyed at the coupé that had stopped in full view at the door. She started to call out as on other occasions, unaware that she was in the home. "Raluca! Raluca! Come and dress me! My velvet dress...the coupé is waiting for me...."

Sensing that no one was moving anywhere, she tried to get up on her own. Her legs struggled in the sheets, while her hand reached out into the cold for the walking stick that must be close at hand. When she finally reached the edge of the bed, she was breathing with difficulty. She thought of lighting the candle and felt along the surface of the bedside table for the box of matches, but she could not find the familiar spot. In her first attempt at standing on her own feet, well supported by the stick, it seemed to her that the parquet was no longer stable: it was moving under her like waves in water. In her ears, the pendulum clock's sound of a struck zither kept ringing, announcing an unknown hour with its endless chime. Then, through darkness thinned to the point of transparency, the angel who had got out of the coupé came to release her from her stumbling in the void.

಄

"Doctor, the old lady in number eight has died! I've just found her lying on the floor, near her door," said the nurse, still shocked.

The doctor, who had just prepared himself for his morning temperature check, murmured to himself, with his eyes on the thermometer in his hand. "The coupé... the phantom coupé...it came for her in the end...."

Back from the dining room, Liliana did not settle down to studying—or rather to preparing cribs for the next day's history test. She threw herself down on her bed and remained there with her head supported on one elbow. She was so confused that sometimes her eyebrows even rose up in a puzzled expression. Since

Vasia had come into the house, she had lived with the sensation that the universe had reduced to him. She found herself eagerly awaiting mealtimes when she would have the chance to admire him to her heart's content. She was not yet able to tell what disturbed her the most. His metallic gaze, in which there was nevertheless a hint of nostalgia? His harrowed features, so out of the ordinary in a young man? His slightly guttural voice, pitched low like a cello? Or, perhaps, more than anything else, the energy that emanated from his whole being, overwhelming one?

Liliana started and pricked her ears. She recognized Vasia's heavy tread. She leaped up from her bed and rushed out.

"Where are you off to?"

After asking the question, Liliana was about to flee back, frightened at her unprecedented forwardness. However, she could not do it; she felt as though her feet were pinned to the spot.

Vasia, who had blushed again, as usually happened to him when he met Liliana about the house, confessed, caught by surprise, "I'm going for a walk. I like the snow…."

Liliana raised her eyes. This answer put Vasia in a new light. Now there no longer seemed to be anything frightening about him, anything to keep one away from him. The chance was not to be missed.

"Can I join you?"

"I don't see why not."

"All right. Then just wait for me a moment while I get dressed."

While Liliana was wrapping herself up, Vasia

stopped still, puzzled. Her proposal had come so suddenly and unexpectedly and he had no idea what had made him accept.

"I'm ready. Let's go!"

Outside, once she had drawn the cold air with its snowy teeth deep into her lungs, Liliana asked curiously, struggling to keep up with Vasia, "Where are you thinking of going?"

"Somewhere at the edge of the city. I can't stand the streets in the center."

"Why not?"

"You can't understand. Every time I happen to pass in front of a statue or by the walls of public buildings, I feel sorry that I don't have anything with me to blow the whole lot up."

"Why?"

"I told you that you're not capable of understanding!"

"Vasia, I have to confess something…something stupid. But it doesn't matter. Perhaps it will amuse you. The revolution you talk about when we're sitting at dinner makes me think of some nightmares I had when I was little, after one of our governesses, a Baptist or something like that, read the Book of Revelation to us.…"

Liliana watched Vasia out of the corner of her eye. He was not smiling. The rough character of the boy's beauty seemed to be better defined when his hair was whitened by the snow, the skin of his face like a bronze bust, the collar of his coat raised over the determined clench of his chin.

With a warm impulse, Liliana took his arm. "You're a very solitary man."

"Don't imagine that it bothers me. On the contrary! Solitude gives me the consciousness of absolute liberty and independence."

Liliana said no more, for fear of breaking the unity of the atmosphere of walking together.

For his part, Vasia could only wonder at every step at the fact that he was holding Liliana by the arm, that he was setting his mind to her childish thoughts.

The snow was falling lightly but thickly: a fine web of lacework in front of their eyes. Even the pleasure of feeling the blown snowflakes was more complete for Vasia than in the morning, when he had gone for a walk on his own.

As they walked on, they arrived without noticing it far out from the center of the city, in places where Liliana had never set foot. The streets had narrowed and the houses were on the scale of those in some provincial market town. There were no cars to be seen anywhere. As for streetcars, they could scarcely be heard. Out here, the winter seemed ready to envelop everything under snow. If it kept falling much longer, in a day or two nothing would be recognizable anymore.

"Whereabouts are we?"

"Near the Cotroceni Plateau."

After another period of silence, right at the edge of the plateau, Liliana found herself for the first time being asked something by Vasia. "Have you ever had the occasion to go a long distance by sleigh?"

"No, why?"

"You can't imagine how exhilarating it can be to race in a sleigh across a steppe, like a white sea!"

In fact, the memory associated with Vasia's

thought was only partially pleasant. At the time, he had been a child, in primary school, at home in the village. A hard winter, as winters always were on the accursed soil of Bessarabia. His elder brother's first epileptic fit. Out of the blue, the poor boy had fallen to the ground, with bulging eyes, grimaces, and foam at the mouth, and then he had remained unconscious like a waxwork. Their mother, a superstitious woman like all the old wives in the country, rushed horrified to find the priest, thinking that he would free the boy from the unclean spirit. But the priest happened to be out of the village that particular day. The nearest town with a doctor was about ten kilometers away. Their distraught father went to borrow a horse, which he then harnessed to the sleigh. To get away from the house, where the neighboring women had gathered as if for a death, Vasia begged to be allowed to go with him. Their father, all cap and woolen coat, gave the horse no respite from the whip. As the sleigh raced onward, the cold cut Vasia's cheeks. From then on, it was all right. There was no room for a single thought. Vasia had felt like the wind on the boundless expanse of white. An unparalleled sensation of being absorbed into the vastness.

"That's the Russian in you awakening!" joked Liliana beside him.

"Yes. The Russian in me!" replied Vasia like an echo, with his gaze dissipated in the ashen evening.

PART THREE

Chapter I

Lucian left the house without the slightest pleasure. He found winter unbearable. He had always longed for a country that had a warm climate all year round. On snowy days, he hardly ever went out. He would stay in his room, dressed only in his pajamas, just as he had got out of bed in the morning, reading or working, curled up on a pillow, down on the rug, beside the heater. Only rarely did he go into town, when he happened to have a seminar at the Faculty. And when that was over, he scarcely even stopped at the second-hand bookstalls on his way back.

Lucian pulled his hat down over his ears, so that all that could be seen of his tapir-like face was his spectacles. This was the second time he had gone out today, which made it something quite out of the ordinary. In the morning, at the end of the aesthetics seminar, Darie had told him to come to Lică's in the afternoon, at half-past five. He had been given to understand that they were going to debate the issue of publishing a magazine. Vintilă Oprea, known as Vintilică or, for short, Lică, at whose lodgings they were all going to meet, made Lucian feel uncomfortable—in the first place by his physical appearance. The vegetal growth of hair happened, in his case, to be almost monstrous in its abundance, encasing his head in a veritable helmet of curls, giving his eyebrows the thickness of mustaches, spreading over his face with such force that you could never see it clean-shaven, sprouting vigorously even in the hollow of his throat and on the backs of his hands. When they had met in their first year of university, Lică had lost no time in boasting of what he considered to have been the great event of his provincial adolescence.

"It was at the time of the great blizzard, two years ago. One way or another, I can say that life and even death in Piteşti were sunk deep in the snowdrifts. Nothing like it had ever been seen even in the time of the oldest pensioners in the town. I'll be damned if the snow didn't reach almost up to the eaves! For a week, not a single train went through, and that means utter disaster in a provincial town, where only the stopping train arriving on time gives people the illusion of contact with the rest of the planet…. And then what about supplies? Whoever had the odd pig about the place had no option but to slaughter it. I must confess that slaughtering a pig has always seemed to me a grand business, worthy of an epic song, especially if the man that does it knows how to do it well. So I spent a whole morning watching when our neighbors decided it was the time to slaughter their pig. While the dismemberment of the pig was going on in the yard with due attention to detail, the dead body in the house was left lying there alone, with candles lit and sheets over the mirrors. The neighbors' old father had died the day before the blizzard. Four days later, he was still there, impossible to bury as there was no way you could struggle as far as the cemetery on the edge of town. He had started to smell, and the relatives no longer knew what to do with him. But let me get back to the pig. All the meat, from the thighs to the offal, was finally gathered up in a chest. From what I could hear, it was to be put out in the cold on the little first-floor balcony. What was in my mind, when I suddenly decided to carry out the theft, I couldn't very well say. The need for an extreme sensation to break, just for once, the monotony of so many years of boredom—or just to make some money from the clandestine sale of the meat, which had unexpectedly come to be worth quite a sum? I teamed up with a classmate, who was addicted to crime novels the same as me. Around eleven p.m., with masks over our faces, we slipped into the neighbors' yard carrying a ladder with us.

The electric cables that had been ripped out during the blizzard hadn't been repaired yet on our side of the town, so the most complete darkness reigned. We got to the back of the house, put up the ladder, climbed onto the balcony, and found the chest just where we imagined it would be, covered with a sheet. It was all going almost too smoothly, surprisingly simple. Lifting the chest didn't call for too much effort; indeed, it hardly felt as though it could contain a pig that they said had weighed 150 kilograms when it was alive. Then, when we were going down the ladder, which was a bit more difficult, as we made some movement or other, I suddenly saw slipping out of the chest, from under a corner of the sheet, the tip of a foot and a piece of ice. There's no point in spinning things out with how horrified we were…. In the chest, instead of the pig, was the dead body, which of course had been put there overnight so as not to stink through the whole house…."

At first, Lucian hadn't known what to make of his new classmate. All this seemed to be just a joke in poor taste. In his uncertainty, he had asked Darie, to see what he would say about Lică's confession. Darie, who always looked at things with pedantic seriousness, determined to find in everything a deeper layer of significance pointing to a Christian drama, had answered without giving it much thought, "It's said that Dostoevsky once went to see Turgenev, whom he despised from the standpoint of a totally different morality. He found him taking tea, surrounded by some admirers. Without more ado, he began to confess, recounting the ugliest deed in his life: how he had raped a seven-year-old girl. His making this confession precisely to such a man as Turgenev cannot be understood except as an act of Christian humility. *Mutatis mutandis*, who knows whether it might not be something similar in Lică's case…?"

Lucian could hardly believe his ears. This held the record for mystification: Dostoevsky and Lică.

Lucian walked as far as the streetcar stop, where people were gathering in expectation. It was still snowing, slowly and silently. Although the cars did not run now without a snowplow in front, the lines quickly got covered with snow from the arrival of one streetcar to the next.

When he entered Lică's room, Lucian observed that he was the last to arrive. Or not quite, as Victor Stanian was still missing. With their coats on their shoulders, Lică, Darie, and Serafim were sitting around the table, looking as if they were playing poker with a dummy hand. However, the playing cards were there more to serve as an alibi in case of a raid.

After leaving his galoshes at the door, Lucian shook hands with each of them. Then he sat down at the place their host had vacated for him: a rough kitchen chair.

Left with nowhere to sit, Lică set about gathering an armful of books, which he then piled up to support his bottom.

"I say we start without waiting any longer for Stanian. Good Lord, the meeting was settled for five-thirty!" said Serafim, losing his patience.

Lucian pulled his coat tighter around him, penetrated by the cold of this unheated room. His eyes stung and his breath was choked by the smoke of their cigarettes.

"As a consequence of Toma Vesper's acquittal," Darie began, "we can consider ourselves free to act again. From what I told you this morning, you know in principle what it's all about. We've received instructions to bring out a magazine that will reflect Herald ideology, but of course in such a way that the Censorship will have nothing to catch us with. Our message will have to be glimpsed by reading between the lines."

"And funding?" asked Lică unexpectedly, gathering back with his comb the lock of hair that kept falling like a comma over his narrow forehead.

"That's not your concern! What matters just now is to establish the contents of the first issue. The magazine must be out before Christmas."

"Still, seriously, how do you think we can do

anything? It means imagining that the Censorship is an institution of babies. We mustn't take things so lightly or we'll get our fingers burned for sure!"

Darie's fingers began to beat like drumsticks on the edge of the table. He could not stand interruptions. Managing to keep a grip of himself, however, he merely replied drily, "Let's not forget that the new head of the Censorship happens to be an acquaintance of the Holban family."

Although he felt all eyes on him, Lucian remained silent, fingering the ace of clubs. He wondered, puzzled, perhaps for the hundredth time since the morning, how the neighborly relations in the country between Colonel Ioanid and his family had come to be known.

Darie, who in the meantime had taken from his pocket a pencil and a piece of paper, broke the silence, "Well, Lică, what will you write?"

"I don't know."

"Impossible. Think of something! We've no time to lose."

"Hmm, maybe something about the crisis of democracy…."

Lucian lifted his eyes from the ace of clubs. The mere enunciation of the theme, with the blatantly plagiarized title, led his thoughts to a well-known article by the professor of metaphysics. Lică was incorrigible….

"You, Holban, what have you thought of?"

Lucian had not made up his mind yet. However, to pre-empt any trespassing into the sphere of issues that he considered to be exclusively reserved for him, he replied without hesitation, "Something about the moral coordinates of the new man."

Darie went on to Serafim, who was biting his nails. "You?"

"You know that for a long time, I've had in my head the idea of a—"

The sound of footsteps in the corridor interrupted Serafim, and made them all turn to their playing cards.

The knocking on the door brought the blood to Lică's cheeks. He had no option but to go, with hesitant steps, and open it.

The boys were unable to see who was outside, as Lică deliberately blocked the partly open door. All they could hear was how the exchange of whispered words kept growing louder.

At a certain point, Lică pushed the door shut, and made to return to the table. But he was scarcely able to take a step before the door opened again and the head of a woman in a headscarf appeared. "If you don't change your mind before this evening, you'll never lay your hands on me again. Get that into your head!"

Lică exploded, "Get out of here, you Devil's bitch!"

His foot, however, did not hit its target; the woman had quickly slipped back into the dark corridor. Swearing through his teeth, Lică closed the door and this time turned the key. With a slightly trembling hand, he began to comb back the locks of his hair that had fallen loose. Only when he had managed to calm himself did he mumble by way of apology, "Just a crazy woman from the neighborhood who keeps asking me for money…." Serafim could not refrain from winking at Darie. He had found the scene highly amusing. He also considered that it would serve him well to put Lică down a little in their rivalry at the Faculty.

Darie, on the other hand, was left paralyzed. The meeting had gotten off to a bad start with the fears expressed by Lică, and it was threatening to degenerate completely now that everyone's attention had slipped down the slope opened up by the trivial incident. As he had no sense of humor, especially in situations that he was accustomed to invest with a certain solemnity, Darie genuinely felt a sense of profanation. His first thought was to start with a moral, but in the end he realized that he would not be able to change anything that way. Picking up from where things had fallen into suspension, he asked Serafim, as though nothing had happened, "Well, go on! What do you want to write about?"

"Ah, yes, something grand. I want to set aside any feeling of national modesty in order to establish that the responsibility for all the disasters that have damaged our history and culture lies nowhere but in the gelatinous quality of our moral structure. I want— "

When he got worked up over an idea, Serafim generally held firmly to it, so that the polemical verve with which it began unexpectedly to unfold made you forget his gauche appearance and those nervous tics of an idiotic child, like biting his nails.

"And what title should I put against your name in the summary?" asked Darie, interrupting him with an impatient wave of his pencil.

"I don't have anything good enough yet. But by tomorrow I'll think of something that will work."

"So be it. That leaves Stanian…."

Lucian was no longer following Darie's words but was holding his head in his hands. His temples ached. His nose was completely blocked. More than that, he felt a stabbing pain at the apex of his lungs.

Lică tore the sheet of paper in a rage. His state of nerves was a consequence of the scene with Paraschiva, to which the boys had happened to be witnesses. How he had always tried to preserve appearances, lying to the others just as much as he deceived himself, only for that bitch to ruin everything in a moment! If he had had something to hand just then, he would have been capable of killing her on the spot without hesitating. The bitch! As if he hadn't then observed the deliberately nonchalant attitude of Holban, who had humiliated him with the form of a contempt that was even harder to bear than the knowing smile shared between Serafim and Darie. It was easy for the likes of Holban to keep their noses in the air. With everything handed to you on a plate from your birth. With a name to open the doors of the great and good of the country and more money than you knew what to do with. While he.... However, wasn't it the lesson of so many novels and historical examples that the greatest achievements were generally obtained by heroes of the plebs, with nothing but sheer willpower and lack of scruples? That wasn't just a mere consolation. Even his own case was only partly a counterexample. If he stopped to judge things coldly, he had to recognize that indeed, at least in the beginning, he himself had struck a winning blow. After all, he, the son of a wretched clerk in Piteşti, a young man without much going for him, barely out of high school and newly landed in Bucharest, now found himself published in the *Journal of the Royal Foundations* with an article about Nietzsche and getting into the good books of a man like the professor of metaphysics! For all that, he was still obliged to live in a slum, to eat nothing but mashed beans, included in the rent, to be content in bed with a woman like Paraschiva, the laundress next door, who drained him of all his pocket money. Quickly grasping the reality of the situation, he had not taken long to come to the general conclusion that men of letters were destined to die poor in the land of Romania if they didn't somehow have the good fortune to be born with houses and estates. Advancement was only possible through politics, so he had been quick to enroll in the Herald movement, the up-and-coming political formation of the day. Until the elections, he had even gone over the top. An actor by temperament, he had swung between martial and pious attitudes as the moment dictated. And for a while, this too had amused him. In general, in contrast to how things stood in the other parties, the Herald movement was attractive to him because of the lack of favored competitors. Indeed, almost all the members were young and equally unknown in the public life of the country. On the day they came to power, when an elite would be constituted simply by appointment to leadership posts, he would be up among the first to get his hands on something due to the fact that he knew how to push himself forward. He wasn't a mere wishy-washy idealist like most of the others. As a disciple of the professor of metaphysics, he could even say that he had built himself a little stepping stone of privilege toward future promotion. The measures taken by the government against the Heralds had, however, brought an unexpected smashing of his illusions, obliging Lică to review his whole strategy of advancement. First of all, he had changed his attitude toward the professor, who had been arrested and then released soon after—though at the end of the day, his newspaper was still suspended. Moving in the professor's circles now meant compromising oneself in the increasingly circumspect eyes of officialdom, and so Lică had cast him off like the Devil, and even started to speak ill of him. It was only from the meetings of the comrades that he had not yet managed to withdraw, for fear of the revenge of fanatics like Darie.

The plans for the magazine worried him more than he had let it be seen during the afternoon's meeting. Instead of thanking God that none of them had ended up with a criminal record, the boys were looking for trouble. Refusing to provide an article might awaken all sorts of suspicions. On the other hand, to write something was sheer idiocy. After much reflection, he had concluded that he could avoid responsibility by paraphrasing an article of his master's, something full of paradoxical equivocation on totalitarian dictatorship. But how could one write without wood in the stove, with one's stomach turned inside out by the same mashed beans, haunted by the memory of Paraschiva's face as she came muttering at the door?

Furiously, Lică started to tear the second sheet

of paper in two, although he had not even got as far as writing a single word on it. When he got up from the table, his troubled gaze rested on the chromolithograph on the wall, the only item that decorated the bareness of the room. It was an image of Napoleon with his generals, surveying the progress of the Battle of Waterloo. Bought at a fair while he was still in high school, this garish copy took for Lică the place of an icon. Napoleon remained for him the embodiment of the most glorious destiny of an ambitious man. He could not conceive of living anywhere without having the great man before his eyes.

Lică turned the bulb on the ceiling. He was fed up with this little mark of squalor: the absence of a switch with which to put out the light. In the dark, he began to take off his boots and his outer clothes, then he got under the quilt half-dressed so as to keep out the penetrating cold. However, before he could make himself comfortable, he felt something at his throat. He jumped out of bed and turned the bulb again. By the faint light, he crushed a bedbug between his fingernails.

Chapter II

ucian waited for an hour to enter Colonel Ioanid's office. At the first interview, he had enjoyed a more than favorable reception. The colonel had even seemed apologetic about his appointment to the Censorship, confessing that he had agreed to accept the post only for a short period, to please the prime minister. It had almost brought tears to his eyes when he spoke of how he no longer had time to play a single game of chess. Although he did not have too much to do since all that had to be done was entrusted to the officials under his direction, he still found himself detained from morning to evening. Only at the end did the question of the magazine come up. When he heard that it was to be a cultural weekly and that the editor in charge would be Lucian himself, the colonel had given his consent on the spot. However, he had added that the release of the publication authorization would be delayed for a few days as procedures required that a censor should first make a report on the basis of the material presented.

The door of the office opened at last, and a pallid youth invited Lucian to enter. After a handshake, which this time was appreciably lacking in warmth, Colonel Ioanid sat down immediately, coughing with displeasure. Then, without raising his eyes from the dossier in front of him, he began with a certain gravity, "My dear Holban, I couldn't believe my eyes when I read the censor's report. I had understood, when you came a few days ago, that it was to be something of a quite different nature. In order to clarify matters, I set about examining for myself how things stand. And to tell the truth, the conclusions in the report seem to me to be amply justified. Here, if you like, let's take each article in turn. And let's begin with your own: 'The Man of Tomorrow: A Moral Archetype.' You start at a distance, with the man of Greek Antiquity, of the Middle Ages, of the Renaissance, of the French Revolution…. It's when you come to our own century that you betray your propagandistic thesis.

Take this: 'In absolute terms, what is the meaning of democracy and mechanical civilization? Nothing. There are no longer even grounds for seeing a new type of man taking shape. Our contemporary, who believes himself to be free and emancipated, the master of the planet, supplied with all the inventions of modern technology, appears only as the protagonist of a pitiful dumbshow. In spite of thousands of years of evolution, the basic need of our social existence remains the same, but it awaits its resolution. We need serial Christs, nothing else. The moral archetype of evangelical man must become a collective reality….' I stop here. Hat upon a single leg: guess, what's the mushroom? The 'new man' of the Heralds, a ruffian well known to the officers of the Siguranţă! How do you expect us to continue tolerating the mystifications that have brought you where we know only too well?"

And the short arms of Colonel Ioanid, reminiscent of a penguin's wings, flapped his puzzlement in the air.

"Let us pass over the nebulous diversion of the article 'Understanding Kierkegaard.' What is the point of this interest suddenly manifested out of the blue in a Danish mystic, who I see does no more than wax delirious about 'existence,' 'nothingness,' and 'despair?' I fail to understand.... With the article 'Let Us Rehabilitate Ourselves in History,' however, things become clearer. Judge for yourself, without bias! How can a Romanian, and one who has pretensions to be a patriot too, curse the history of his country in such a manner? Just listen a little: 'The Romanian people do not yet have a true history. We have always limited ourselves to living a vegetal existence, in its inertia of circumstances, without conceiving for ourselves a heroic destiny. We have endured all the foreign yokes with a resignation that passes for our supreme wisdom. We have slipped through time only by humiliations and betrayals. Revolutions have not shaken us, nor have we fought any war in a grand style. The excuse of the chronicler Miron Costin—"Time is not subject to man, but poor man subject to the times"—cannot be admitted as an inexorable principle of history. We are the victims of our own psychological voids, not of any fatalities of a different order. To change our destiny in the world, to take the leap into history, all we have to do is to take the path of restructuring under the sign of a new messianism.' And the nonsense carries on for another three pages. Well, what do you say?"

Seeing that Lucian gave no answer, Colonel Ioanid

continued after a moment's pause: "The article 'Fulfillment in Religion' is sliding down the same slope. Take this, at random: 'A people defines its spirituality according to the level of its religious fervor. Now, if we stop to judge ourselves by this standard, we must recognize that we are completely sterile. The Romanian is not a mystic, whence too the lack of any dramas of religious consciousness in our history and culture. And yet a national messianism cannot be conceived without a mystical fulfillment in religion.' Finally, the article 'The Ultimate Consequence of Democracy,' which peddles self-evident sophisms, is also revealing of the waters in which your magazine is eager to bathe. Listen a little to this reasoning: 'A political party must be dogmatic, exclusivist, and intolerant. If it makes deals with its adversaries, it loses the very reason for its polemical existence. In politics, fanaticism is the only attitude with an ethical value. Those liberal minds that see the formula of happiness in democracy generally condemn extremists for fear of absolutism.

No man with an intuition for the historical phenomenon can fail to see that totalitarian ideologies bring to perfection the very process of the evolution of democracy. Dictatorship is not necessarily imposed through coups d'état. The day a party wins power by the vote of the majority, in other words, through something equivalent to a plebiscite, the system of plurality of political parties is virtually abolished, due to the fact that it is no longer felt to be necessary. An elementary judgment is enough to understand that normal political life leads by its very nature to dictatorship....' There you are. Now say something!"

Lucian kept silent. He had shifted his gaze to the portraits of the royal family, who reigned all-powerful on the wall facing him. The foolishness with which he felt Colonel Ioanid had been crushing him for half an hour had from the start taken from him the courage to take any kind of attitude.

"My dear Holban. Stop playing with fire! You were lucky that it happened to be me here. Otherwise, the imprudence of these articles could have cost you. Believe me!"

"Well, what news?" asked Lică, grabbing Lucian by the arm to stop him.

"They're not giving us the authorization… I've just come from the Censorship."

"What are you saying?" Lică slapped himself across the mouth. "Didn't I tell you from the beginning that nothing would come of it? See what happens when you deal with madmen."

The thought of mocking him suddenly took root in Lucian's mind. With a perverse pleasure, he found himself distorting a truth that, in any case, had no way of being verified. "You should know that it was your article that upset the Colonel more than all the rest."

"Mine? Impossible!"

"The Colonel said that the others were just empty rambling, but yours gave the impression that it was trying to pull the wool over the reader's eyes with a show of apparent logic. He also found your source in an article of the professor's—"

Lică felt as though his feet were being cut from under him. This was too much! And for Holban of all people to be the one to let him know, almost with a smile of jubilation on his thin lips! Implicitly acknowledging his plagiarism, he exclaimed in spite of himself, "All right, mate, but no one expects an old brass hat to spot—"

"Ah, but there's an exception to every rule. Colonel Ioanid is a subtle intellectual. And on top of that, he also happens to be a subscriber to the professor's newspaper."

"You're joking!"

Lucian hesitated for a moment. Then, intending to carry his lies through to the climax of the final blow, he added casually, "I believe that as of today, we too are entered on the list of suspects."

"His mother's funeral! Holy Communion!"

Lucian did not wait to hear more but pretended to be in a hurry to go into the lecture room. Left alone, Lică did not know right then what to do. Swearing offered too little release of tension. He bit his lips and passed from the Faculty entrance hall into the street to cool himself in the cold that had set in as evening fell.

After a few steps, he was met by the increasingly intelligible cries of the newspaper sellers coming from Calea Victoriei. "Latest! Toma Vesper is on trial! Latest!"

Lică rummaged in his pockets for a one leu coin. Then he rushed to snatch the paper from the hand of a boy who kept on shouting with all his might. By the illuminated window of a florist's, he began to read.

In the last two weeks, as a result of raids made in the Capital and in other cities in the country, the officers of the Siguranţă have found a whole stock of subversive propaganda, arms, and ammunition, which shows that the former Herald movement is carrying forward its criminal activity of undermining the order of the state. Faced with this situation, the prosecution service has reopened the public action against Toma Vesper, the leader of the Heralds, who was acquitted two months ago in the trial of the assassins of the previous Prime Minister.

Lică stuffed the newspaper into his pocket. He understood that the government was determined to suppress the movement at all costs. Toma Vesper's being put on trial could only mean the beginning of a new wave of terror. It seemed that he himself could no longer expect to get off lightly, especially if it was true what Holban had said about the lists of suspects. He considered it totally absurd to suffer any inconvenience when he had not even managed to get any advantage out of the movement. How could he have calculated so badly? He was left with only one way of escape. And the plan which some time before had begun to take root under a crust of shame suddenly grew into decision. He was going to become an informer.

Relieved, Lică continued on his way under the snow that had again begun to fall thinly.

In the building where Stanian had his rented room, the steps of the staircase could barely be made out in the darkness. When they got to the end of the fourth flight, almost gasping for breath after fumbling their way up so many stairs, Darie and Serafim stopped at the first door on the corridor, then knocked gently.

"Who is it?" Stanian's voice resounded from inside.

"It's us, folks!"

"Come in!"

The studio apartment was roomy, although it did not give that impression at first sight due to the clutter of things that filled it. In one corner, a piano with peeling varnish, Mariana's only dowry. On the first chair, a basin, surrounded by a bucket and several mugs. Then there was a wire cupboard, which served as a larder. Then stacks of books as far as the table by the window, on which there was a scattering of plates and cutlery, together with Stanian's writing things. In front of the cupboard stood the child's pram. On the edge of the bed, Mariana sat breastfeeding Victoraş. Beside her, a paraffin lamp stood in for both heater and cooker. In the only armchair in the room, Stanian was smoking, stretched out with his feet on the chair by the table.

For Darie and Serafim, the picture was nothing new, so they sat down without feeling any embarrassment, one of them pulling the chair from under the feet of Stanian, while the other reclined on the bed next to Mariana.

"What's up with you, mate? You've been making yourself scarce all week," asked Darie.

Before Stanian could give an answer, however, his wife got in first. "What do you think's up? I've told him to look for a job. We're not making ends meet. Lately, at any rate, all the money from his gymnastics lessons has been going in doctor's fees. I don't know what's the matter with Victoraș. It's one thing after another. Now he's got something in his eyes...."

Serafim caught himself letting his eyes rest on Mariana's uncovered breast, and quickly turned back to Stanian. "Well, to be honest, I can't really see you in an office! But who knows? You might make an 'experience' out of wearing out your trouser seat at a desk."

"Instead of supporting me, you make fun of him. That way he's certainly not going to settle down to anything!" Mariana burst out, a dusting of freckles suddenly showing itself like a rash as her cheek reddened.

Darie joined in. "Wouldn't it be better if you took the pedagogical seminar too? Look, in the autumn, there's the Capacity exam. If you're going to do teaching work anyway, why shouldn't it be in your own field? How long are you going to waste time taking gymnastics classes as a substitute?"

"Just let me be, in God's name! I'm big enough and ugly enough! I know what I'm doing!"

Then, to change the subject, Stanian asked in a quieter tone, "You didn't tell me what the word is about the Censorship."

"Ah, yes! That's what we came about. We're

not getting the authorization. They're smarter than we imagined."

Mariana rose from the bed, detaching the child from her breast. "And a good thing too! I guess you'll quieten down now. Can't you see it's no longer a joking matter? If even Toma Vesper—"

However, she had no chance to finish, thanks to Victoraş, who had started to cry himself blue in the face.

"My wife is incapable of appreciating the beauty of *vivere pericolosamente*!"

"Hmmm…*vivere pericolosamente*…," muttered Mariana. The words stuck in her throat as she continued trying to calm the child.

At first, before they were married, she too had enjoyed thinking in the same spirit as him. The reality of marriage, however, had brought her down to earth with a bump. What did Victor understand by "*vivere pericolosamente*"? Apart from the tedium of daily existence in squalor, the threat of prison? This?

Meanwhile, Stanian had moved on to something else for fear of adding fuel to the fire. "Anyway, what's new at the Faculty?"

"Nothing!" replied Darie, leafing through a book by Shestov, *La Nuit de Ghetsemani*, which he had spotted earlier among the volumes on the floor.

"How do you mean nothing?" said Serafim in surprise. "What about the morning seminar?"

"Oh, yes! Indeed! Lică presented his paper. You can imagine the show!"

"What paper?"

"'The Psychology of Woman.' Nothing special when all's said and done. The first to offer criticism was

Holban, who excelled himself. He was right enough, but he might have been a bit less rough about it. In my view, it doesn't do to bite one another in public—us, I mean, members of the movement...."

Mariana did not hear the rest. Her ears were ringing. Everything was going around in her head, randomly, in a cloud. And it was as if a feeling of nausea were taking possession of her. Could she be pregnant again? That was all she needed right now! She would only know in a few days. Leaning over the child's pram, now that he had fallen asleep sucking his thumb, as she rocked and whistled, she could feel the exhaustion rising from the small of her back up her spine to her neck and along her arms.

> *I would not even now be writing this line to you*
> *but the rooster crew three times in the night—*
> *And I had to cry:*
> *"Lord, Lord, whom have I denied?"*

> *I am older than you, mother,*
> *but still as you know me:*
> *a little slumped in the shoulders*
> *and bent down over the questions of the world.*

> *Even today I do not know why you sent me into*
> *the light*
> *Just to wander among things*
> *and to do them justice telling them*
> *which is more true and which is more beautiful?*
> *My hand comes to a stop: it is too little.*
> *My voice fades out: it is too little.*

The lines made Mariana start momentarily. It was something from Blaga. She recognized at once the solemn, sibylline phrasing, orchestrating the usual grand disquietudes and metaphysical uncertainties. What thread had led from Lică's seminar paper to Blaga? And when had Victor started reciting? Doubtless, the boys had put him up to it as they always ended up doing. Victor was a passionate reader of modern poetry and knew by heart a great many lines, which he was happy to produce at any time without needing much persuasion.

Why did you send me into the light, Mother,
why did you send me?

Mariana's attention scattered again into the void of her great tiredness. Her eyelids sat ready to close. The words continued to penetrate her almost completely dulled hearing as though from far off.

My body falls at your feet
heavy as a dead bird. [9]

Then nothing could lift Mariana out of her slumber anymore. Not even the movement of the boys as they left, much later.

Out in the corridor, at the head of the stairs, taking care that he could not be heard inside, Darie said quietly to Stanian, "Thursday afternoon, five o'clock, we're holding a meeting at my place. I can't accept your absence again."

---

[9] Lucian Blaga, "Scrisoarea" (The Letter), from his volume *În marea tre-cere* (In the great transition), 1924.

"Have no fear."

"By then, I'll finish your Shestov book."

"You can keep it as long as you like! Listen, I didn't want to ask you in front of Mariana, but how are things with Toma Vesper? Does anyone know anything about him?"

"He's still in Jilava,[10] in the instruction phase of the trial," replied Darie, trying to push the borrowed book into the pocket of his coat.

"The orders that he has sent to us from prison instruct us not to make any move. However, his attitude now, so they say, is completely different from last time," broke in Serafim, shivering in a coat that had barely fitted him since his final year of high school.

"Yes!" agreed Darie, although he gave the impression that he spoke with difficulty, as if reluctant to go any deeper into the matter. "Can you imagine that he refuses to defend himself? He's determined to remain silent from start to finish. I've heard a rumor that, if he survives the sentence that's in preparation for him, he's thinking of becoming a monk."

"A monk?" exclaimed Stanian, scarcely able to believe his ears.

"Come on, it's getting late! Good night!" said Darie, closing the conversation as he pushed Serafim ahead of him down the stairs.

Stanian went back into the room, where he found Mariana asleep, sitting with her head slumped forward. He threw himself into the armchair, with his hands in his pockets, cold from the length of time he

---

[10] A village adjoining Bucharest to the south, site of a prison where many political prisoners were detained in the inter-war period and many more under communism, including Dinu Pillat himself. (Tr.)

had stood outside with the boys. Toma Vesper. What a man! Before the elections, or after the dissolution of the Heralds, or even later, following his acquittal in the trial over the shooting of the previous prime minister, he could at any time have launched a coup d'état, the more so as it was clear that the most dynamic element in the ranks of the country's youth would have supported him whatever the cost, to the end—the messenger of Saint George, as he himself believed, without a shadow of doubt. Instead, he had folded his arms and waited to be thrown into prison. What then was the meaning of his decision to keep silent? Not to speak at the trial that was going to be staged for him was to recognize his guilt, to seek at all cost for atonement in the harsh sentence that was waiting for him.

And in the end, if he should survive, a monastery…. Why? On the dingy white of the wall in front of his eyes, no answer was written.

Chapter III

ucian managed to secure a place right at the front of the lecture hall, which was quite something at the metaphysics professor's course. Soon, in a quarter of an hour at the most, the audience would have poured in a compact mass into the last free spaces in the room, lining the walls, encircling the rostrum, blocking the entrances. Already the coats discarded on the deep ledges of the windows were piling up on a scale worthy of a theater cloakroom.

As he sat and waited, Lucian set about warming himself up by doodling in his notebook. His signature, which gave the impression of being written in gothic letters, multiplied itself down whole columns till it ended up filling the void of the page. Tired as if from an effort, Lucian let go of the pencil and raised his eyes. Darie was trying to get through to the seats at the back of the lecture hall, obviously seeking to reach the group of students who stood out from the crowd in their national costumes. Serafim, Stanian, and Lică had remained below, pushing their way among the latecomers toward the door and the rostrum. The Jews, however, seemed to suspect nothing of what was being set in motion against them. In Lucian's row, for instance, the third student to his right, Juditha Nachmanson, was sharpening her pencil, getting ready to take notes just as at every other lecture. Why didn't he warn her before it was too late?

Lucian's gaze turned uneasily back to the rostrum. Rosner, who had just come in the door, was looking around for a place somewhere. Why not at least warn him? After all, they had been friends in high school. It was on Rosner's gramophone that he had been initiated into the music of Stravinsky and Honneger. It was from him that he had borrowed Spengler's book *Untergang des Abendlandes*,[11] from which he had spent a whole year taking notes. By virtue of what inertia was he now sitting still, letting things take their course? Even cowardice has its limits.

From the back of the lecture hall, Darie's voice suddenly boomed out, thrilling as a trumpet. "The Yids had better get out of here!"

For a moment, the hall stopped still in frozen silence. Then, as if to order, the chanting began from every corner of the lecture hall at once, "Down with the Yids!"

Imperative, dramatic, absurd. With each passing moment, the chorus gained volume, charging the atmosphere. The whole crowd was now vibrating, in unison, "Down with the Yids!"

Lucian resumed writing his signature and filled the last column.

"Let me past."

Lucian made way for Juditha Nachmanson, not daring to look her in the face. Only after she had gone did he raise his eyes and catch a glimpse of her squeezing her way toward the door, her head downcast. She was not alone. In her wake, another ten girls and two boys hurried to get out of the room. Had all the

---

[11] (The Decline of the West)

Jews gone? Hundreds of eyes were on the lookout, as if at a hunt.

Beside the rostrum, this time with his back turned to the room, Rosner stood immobile, perhaps imagining that he could lose himself there in the dense group of latecomers. Good Lord, what was he waiting for? Watching with bated breath, Lucian had scarcely managed to formulate the question, when the answer was confirmed on the spot, right before his eyes. Deafened as he was by the unanimous chanting, he could hear nothing of the exchange of words opened by Stanian. However, before it all ended in a melee in the doorway, he caught a glimpse of the Jew's face, his spectacles pushed off his nose, grimacing under a hail of fists.

Lucian left his place, pushed his way out of the room with difficulty, and found Rosner at the head of the stair. "I was meaning to tell you—" The words got stuck in his throat, even before Rosner's answer spluttered through his broken teeth, broke all connecting bridges: "We have nothing more to say to one another."

What was the beaten Jew to say, with his hair tousled over his forehead, his myopic gaze fumbling in the void, his nose and mouth smeared with blood, his tie pulled to one side? What was he to say? Any word of excuse or sympathy could mean nothing but yet another humiliation for the poor man.

As Rosner went down the stairs with rapid steps, Lucian turned around, biting his lips. From the lecture hall at the end of the corridor, he heard the round of applause with which the auditorium always greeted the professor on his arrival. He stood outside the door, no longer able to get back in. His ears caught sentences at random, his attention as distracted as his conscience.

"What I am telling you here is the parable of the Publican and the Pharisee. The attitude of the Pharisee was that of the saint who claims that he does not give way to sin, that he is strong. Well, being too strong is a more grievous sin than being too weak, because being too strong can lead you down the road of challenging God, while being too weak cannot lead you down that road. Being too strong can take you out of the domain of transcendence, and can move you into pantheism, into immanentism, with completely different images and a different equilibrium… For me, there is, metaphysically speaking, no possibility of finding equilibrium apart from the formula of transcendence; there is no possibility of finding equilibrium except through something outside your own self. Any attempt to find equilibrium through your own self leads nowhere; it is, as I was saying, like the snake that eats its own tail, or as much of it as it can eat…."

Lucian turned his head to the left, and his eyes fell on Stanian, who was also listening, squeezed in the doorway. Unable to endure his position anymore, he signaled to him with his hand over the shoulders of two classmates, indicating that he had something to say. Then, outside in the corridor, he asked him angrily, "All right, man, what did you all have against Rosner? So many against just one!"

Stanian, who seemed tired, answered without looking him in the face, "What were we to do if he didn't have the sense to get out of the room?"

"From Lică, let's face it, anything's to be expected, but you—"

"What do you want? It was a moment of anti-Semitic frenzy throughout the whole room. How could I stay out of it? You know very well that I see no point in going by half measures, that when I live something, I live it unreservedly, to the end. I admit that I was cruel in a way, because the others got their fists in after me. But that's the way it had to happen. My blows fulfilled a historical function." Stanian was gradually getting warmed up. "The professor's right when he argues that it's necessary that the Jews should always suffer. Their race lies under the seal of a curse, since they crucified Jesus. They can't be assimilated among us because on every level, we find an utter 'incompatibility of humors' between Jews and Christians. The Jews are destined to remain aliens, irreducible ferments of decomposition for any community on earth where they may happen to be, and we Christians have the task of reacting according to the circumstances—of being the instrument of their damnation until the end of the world...."

The only relative that Lică had in Bucharest was an aunt on his father's side. Aunty Miţa, as they called her in the family, had done well for herself early on by marrying a man who traded in quality groceries in the Flower Market. Only a few years after the wedding she had seen him to his grave, inheriting everything as his sole and uncontested heir. The woman had sharpened her commercial acumen with age, teaching herself how to put the money she made at her shop into lucrative investments. In this way she had got her hands on some vegetable gardens at the end of Șoseaua Vitan, which brought in a good rent. However, her stinginess had increased along with her wealth. She lived frugally, scarcely spending a penny.

It was to visit her that Lică was now going, as he did regularly, obsessed with the idea of becoming her heir. He walked calmly, in no hurry. The ejection of the Jews from the classroom, the blows rained down on Rosner, had filled him with a feeling of satisfaction that was utterly new. Although for the past week he had been in the pay of the police, he had been unable to hold back from joining the boys in the anti-Semitic disturbance that they had set up. What a triumph to see Juditha Nachmanson, Angelica Goldstein, Idda Avramescu, and all the other Jew-girls in their year leaving the lecture hall like bedraggled turkeys! They, who always played the clever ones, claiming with unparalleled cheek a monopoly on all the ideas in their seminar discussions or in exams…. What a triumph to have driven Rosner out with their fists, while the whole room looked on. Rosner, the ultra-decadent aesthete, who despised them as retrogrades and obscurantists. Damn Yids!

In the Boulevard, Lică came upon a funeral procession, obviously someone of importance, since there was a band, too. His mouth watered at the sight of the koliva[12] borne solemnly on large silver platters. The garb of the attendants, with their two-cornered hats and black frock coats, gave him a thrill as usual. To him it was the strangest of uniforms. The hearse,

---

[12] Funeral cake made of wheat, sugar, and nuts (Tr.)

drawn by four caparisoned horses, allowed no glimpse of the casket, as it was completely covered with floral wreaths. Lică fell into line with the convoy, feeling a sort of pleasure at making his way toward the Flower Market to the rhythm of the funeral march, following the gently swaying hearse. However, he could not restrain his curiosity and asked the gentleman closest to him, "Excuse me, who is the deceased?"

Showing no surprise that there might be someone in the cortège who did not even know the name of the person being taken to his grave, the man broke off the conversation he had entered into with some acquaintances concerning the estate the dead man had left, and replied casually, "Tase Popescu."

Lică gave a grimace of disappointment. Tase Popescu. He had never heard of the man. Such koliva, such flowers, such music, all for some ordinary, unknown guy!

A little bell tinkled rapidly as Lică pushed open the door of the shop in the Flower Market. As usual around closing time, there was no movement inside. Aunty Miţa was closing the till, gathering the money in rolls, while Niţă, her only shop assistant, the son of a distant cousin, was weighing some cheese for a customer.

"Hello, Aunty! I see business is booming. Won't you give me a loan? You'll have the money back in a week, upon my honor!"

Aunty Miţa started as if confronted by a thief, and quickly covered up the rolls of money. "What business? Can't you see the empty shop? What little trickles in goes out on stock and to the taxman. I'm hardly left with anything at the end of the day."

With greedy eyes, Lică weighed up the laden

shelves, taking no notice of what Aunty Miţa was saying. He had launched his request on the off chance, like a fisherman casting bait, well aware of how difficult it was to squeeze a penny out of her. He helped himself in passing to a handful of raisins, then hurriedly spoke to pre-empt any comment, "Come on, you're talking nonsense! With stock like this, you can't be strapped for cash...."

Aunty Miţa, who began to feel uncomfortable every time anyone alluded to wealth, found herself obliged to make conversation, "Well, what's new in politics?"

Her nephew spared her the need to buy newspapers. Through him, she always got to know how things stood in the market, what murders had been committed in the capital, how long the government was going to last.

"The Yids are done for! Today we threw them out of classes. If it carries on like this, tomorrow we'll see they're pushed out of trade, the next day out of the banks, the day after that out of the press."

"What's this you're saying? Is it true?"

"It isn't going to be quite so easy, because the government is in the pay of Jewish high finance. But in the end, things still change as the hour dictates. Can't you see? Humanity is moving to the right. Anti-Semitism provides the solution to get us out of this crisis." Lică turned unexpectedly from Aunty Miţa to Niţă. "Cut me some slices of salami, please. But make them on the thick side." Then, before Aunty Miţa had a chance to object, he got back to the subject. "How long will we still have the Yids on our backs? You can't move in your own country without bumping into them. They make fools of us in every field with their experience in trickery." Lică scoffed a slice of salami, then approached Niță with authoritative familiarity. "It's all right if you go to pull down the shutters. I can help myself."

Aunty Miţa ran out of patience. "But just you put an end to this habit of nibbling all the time, before you leave me out of stock. Or if you must nibble, then pay for it!"

"So, to get back to the Yids. What would you say if you saw me around these parts one day in the Romanianization Office of the Lipscani stalls?" asked Lică, slipping a lemon into his pocket.

Stanian could not get to sleep. He lay on his back with his eyes open in the darkness. He could make no movement, as he was blocked on one side by Mariana, who had fallen asleep as soon as her head hit the pillow. A smell of frying still hung in the room from their evening meal. It seemed all the more unbearable now that his attention was no longer engaged by anything. One by one, the last noises had died away: the sewing machine in the seamstress's room next door; the quarreling of the couple that lived above them; the accordion playing of the strange lodger at the end of the corridor, the survivor of a recent suicide attempt; the footsteps of people coming home late sounding on the stairs.

Stanian had sat up for a long time re-reading

something by Kierkegaard, and for the first time had come to understand him on the problem of marriage. Why had he not had the sense to stop in time, in the moment of intuition of the absolute, when everything still had the value of a miracle? What depth there was in Kierkegaard's gesture of breaking off his engagement to Regina Olsen just when the two of them loved each other most! Even if the Danish philosopher had gone on to suffer all the rest of his life from the obsession with what he had done as a presentiment of the incompatibility of his "essence" with the model of marriage, he could find consolation in the knowledge that the ideal identity of love had been preserved. For Stanian, love remained the chapter of a failed experience. To start things over again from the beginning sometime, with another woman, seemed to him completely pointless. It would still end up in the same deterioration. Even the mere practice of the sex act had always enclosed for him a seed of suffering, from the perspective of that *post coitum triste*. The sensation of the flesh turning to ashes after burning in the supreme spasm made him decide in favor of ascesis every time. If he had not yet been able to achieve this, it was due solely to his scruples regarding Mariana, who must not in any circumstances know what was happening to him. In the zigzag motion of his thought, he reconstructed word for word one of the sentences he had heard that morning in the lecture: "Any attempt to find equilibrium through your own self leads nowhere; it is, as I was saying, like the snake that eats its own tail, or as much of it as it can eat...."

Stanian felt his right hand going numb on the

pillow and drew it from under his head. As he tried to move his fingers, he recalled the blows given to Rosner. Had these blows fulfilled a historical function? Perhaps. But the Christian conception made abstraction from history. Of course, nothing happened without the will of God, but that did not mean that man was not answerable for whatever he chose to do. Judas's act of betrayal, for example, which led to the crucifixion of Jesus, fulfilled the prophecies of Scripture, but Judas was no less guilty, barring himself from the right to salvation. The Jews must continue to suffer for their refusal to accept Jesus. Yet how could you deliberately make yourself the instrument of their damnation, if you knew that in so doing you contradicted the very principles of love for your neighbor on which the whole of Christianity rested? While he was beating Rosner, he had stopped thinking of anything. He had fallen on him, followed by the crowd of others, striking like a madman. He had understood what his blows meant only when he had tried to find a higher purpose for them in front of Holban. Stanian felt the need to light a cigar, but he was stopped in the end by the fear of disturbing Mariana's sleep. Preyed on by his doubts, he had the impression that he was like a broken compass. His experiences of life, on the authenticity of which he generally insisted so much, suddenly seemed to him arbitrary and sterile. In order to be able to lie no more, to live the truth in itself, no matter how terrifying, he concluded that there was nothing for it but to wait for the hour of the Last Judgement, when the meaning of all things would be made clear, once and for all.

In the void of the darkness, the stars fell all together, not just here and there as in late summer nights. The foundations trembled from the depths. The angelic trumpets resounded from all around, their voices rising all-encompassing above the clamor of breaking waves. It all lasted no more than a moment.

Time drew back into the mold of the present, revealing the anticipatory experience to be a mere hallucination. The room submerged in darkness was the same as before, and the muffled crying of the baby in his perambulator bound the web of reality with the sure thread of life.

Stanian fumbled his way out of bed, his skin chilled all over. When he got to the side of the perambulator, he found Victoraş sleeping peacefully. He was not even sucking his thumb. He felt the little boy's diaper to check if he had wet himself, then quickly slipped back into bed beside Mariana, who was still asleep.

PART FOUR

Chapter I

As soon as he was outside, Rotaru looked around to check that there was nothing to fear. Then he set off quickly up the street, his face hidden behind the raised collar of his raincoat.

Since coming back to Bucharest, Rotaru had changed lodgings three times, obsessed with the idea that everywhere he was watched by suspicious eyes. He usually presented himself as a teacher at a school with evening classes to explain why he only went out after nightfall. The last time, following up a newspaper announcement that specified a preference for a "poor young professional," he had landed a low-ceilinged but clean attic room. The landlady, a woman in her fifties, whose face made up to the point of stridency betrayed her efforts to conceal her age, had welcomed him with a familiarity that boded well, and the rent she asked for was derisory. It was only later, after he had been settled in his new dwelling place for a week, that he was surprised one night to find her imposing herself on him in his room and realized the hidden aim behind the announcement in the paper and the low rent. Having no alternative, he had resigned himself with disgust to being a "kept man." The days passed oppressively, with nothing to distinguish one from another. Although he had got hold of identity papers in another name, by way of a comrade infiltrated into the Police Prefecture as a clerk, Rotaru dared not go about town in broad daylight. Shut in his attic room, he spent his time sprawled on the bed reading thrillers in installments. He could read nothing else. When it so happened that he had finished what was to hand before evening fell, until he could go to buy the next installment from the tobacconist's, he would circle around his room restlessly, smoking heavily, sometimes a whole packet.

Then, later, when he got dizzy, he would wait with his elbows leaning on the window ledge for the darkness to come like a friend and take him out into town. For as long as he had been in hiding in Bucharest, Rotaru had found it impossible to sleep without the use of narcotics. And even then, sleep was far from giving him ease. Almost nightly, he was haunted by one and the same nightmare, with only a few differences in detail. First he would hear footsteps climbing up the stair to the attic. Then he would see the door starting to shake as it was battered from outside, until there he was with the police inside the room. Curled up at the head of the bed, he would let himself be riddled with bullets, putting up no opposition. He woke up every time in a cold sweat, his hand reaching out for the revolver on his bedside table. And it took him a while to come back to himself again; in any case, he stayed awake until daybreak, with his ears pricked in the heavy silence.

After getting the latest installments of *The Adventures of the Submarine Dox* and *The Man with Five Masks* from the nearest tobacconist's, Rotaru headed for the Boulevard, where at a prearranged time he was to meet a comrade. Since his return from his mountain refuge, he had gradually resumed contact with some members of the movement, although they had agreed, as a prudent measure, that he should no longer be known except by a false name. To them all he was therefore "Comrade Sandu."

On the Boulevard, Rotaru spotted some gendarmes checking the identity of passers-by. He quickly turned back, even though his papers could not have unmasked him. After a detour through several backstreets, he came out into the Boulevard again, this time a little further down. Twice he noticed vans passing with police in them. Then, outside the University, there were several patrols walking around, as if to pre-empt a demonstration. What could be the point of all these measures?

As he was preparing to change direction for the second time, Rotaru heard cries of "Special Edition!" close to the statue of Michael the Brave. He hastened his step in that direction, in a state of dull unease. When he managed to get his hands on a newspaper, it was with difficulty that his eyes began to pick out the words:

Press Release:

During the night of February 25th–26th, on the occasion of a transfer of prisoners from Râmnicu Sărat Prison to Jilava Prison, an escape while under escort took place. Taking advantage of the fact that they were being transported in an open van belonging to the Prefecture of Police, the convicts jumped out of the moving vehicle while it was passing through the Ţigăneşti forest. After their warnings had been ignored, the accompanying police officers were obliged to open fire, fatally wounding Toma Vesper, sentenced to ten years correctional imprisonment for conspiracy against state order, and Dumitru Ifrim and Valeriu Ionescu, sentenced to hard labor for life for the assassination of the late prime minister...

With tears filling his eyes, Rotaru could barely follow the text. He was unable to take in the truth, although the words forced themselves on him in black and white, the printing ink not yet fully dry. Prey to conflicting feelings, he moved away. It seemed to him a pity that he had not fallen alongside the comrades with whom he had laid plans for the attack. By living on, he had the impression that he had broken solidarity with their destiny, and that almost meant betrayal. On the other hand, he knew well that if he had turned himself in after the attack, his name would have appeared there, in the newspaper, among the corpses. He could not help but feel a dull sense of joy, organic in nature, at the mere fact that he was alive. Strangely, the very movement of his steps suddenly seemed to him something extraordinary, unique!

When he got out of the streetcar, Stanian did not go in the direction of the National Theater. On the way, he had read over a gentleman's shoulder the press release in the "special edition," and he felt he had no room left for anything else. At that moment, he could not have cared less about his role as an extra in *Vlaicu-*

Vodă,[13] which brought in a little bit to supplement what he earned from the gymnastics classes, and he had also completely forgotten Mariana's request to buy some aniseed tea from the pharmacy for Victoraş's cramps.

At the entrance to the Faculty, Stanian was stopped and his identity checked. Had it not been for the doorkeeper, who was ready to put in a good word for him, he would have remained outside, especially as at that hour there were no more classes to provide a pretext for entering the building.

Out of breath from climbing the steps two at a time, Stanian arrived at the psychology class library, where he found Serafim and Darie.

"Well, what do you two say?"

"I, for one, don't believe a word of it!" replied Darie, who was sitting on the corner of a table, stubbornly clinging to his first reaction.

"To tell the truth, this escape while under escort does look to me like a bit of a stitch-up...," admitted Stanian.

"It's all nothing but a maneuver by which the authorities imagine that they can deprive us of all hope. Listen to me! I'd wager they haven't dared to kill Toma Vesper."

"I don't know what to believe anymore...," confessed Serafim, pausing from biting his nails, but from his confusion, they could sense that this time he did not share Darie's point of view.

"Come on, be realistic! How can we doubt that Toma Vesper has been done away with, when it's being

---

[13] A historical drama by Alexandru Davila, first performed in 1902, based on the story of a fourteenth-century prince of Wallachia. (Tr.)

publicized the way it is, with the government openly assuming the risk of any consequences?" Stanian argued, becoming more agitated.

"Listen to me! You'll see!" was all the answer Darie was prepared to offer, sure as ever of his intuitions.

"In the meantime, there has to be some sort of reaction! A challenge like that can't remain without a response!" said Stanian, who had now lost his patience and was pacing up and down.

"Yes, but not just anyhow, as each thinks fit. Nothing should be set in motion without an order. If we don't remain disciplined, we're done for."

"Of course! Especially now, when it's become a life and death struggle!" agreed Serafim, and he started to bite his nails even more determinedly.

Stanian had understood that he had nothing more to discuss with the boys. It seemed to him that both Darie and Serafim were merely hiding their lack of daring behind statements of political tactics. If, with the news of Toma Vesper's death still hot, some of them could take that attitude, then all hope was lost.

Without a word, Stanian left the class library, slamming the door in their startled faces. He went down the stairs as fast as he had climbed them just a quarter of an hour earlier. Outside, when he observed how quiet the street was, his indignation reached its peak. He felt the need to discharge it in some gesture that would remove him from complicity in the general cowardice. The sight of a patrol of gendarmes, he believed, offered him the occasion he needed.

With a hoarse voice, as if it were foreign to him, and without further choosing his words in the fiery state that was tormenting him, Stanian cried out in the gendarmes' faces, "Assassins! You'll pay us for the death of Toma Vesper! Long live the Herald movement!"

The three gendarmes stifled these last words by jumping on him. In the meantime, several passers-by had stopped, ready to gather at the spot. But more gendarmes, arriving at a run, gave them no chance. "Move on, move on...."

Mariana lay down on the bed, worn out. Until shortly before, she had kept trying to soothe Victoraş, who had been writhing since the beginning of the evening, tormented by cramps. Now that the child had finally fallen asleep, she could relax a little too. Stretched out on the bed, she waited for her husband to come back from the theater. What an idea to be an extra on the stage! Instead of finding serious work, he would always end up with something offbeat, where one would least expect, to the point that he was becoming a real laughing stock among his classmates. What kind of security could one feel alongside such a man? Of course, Victor had his paradoxical justifications: "Life must be lived in the unpredictability of adventure," "To live like any clerk, knowing that you're insured for everything, up to and including your funeral, means failure," "We must live life freely and authentically, or else it has no value." Mariana had come to know all these sentences by heart, together with many others that played variations on the same theme, as she was forced to live their sad pointlessness day by day. Reality made her unable to see clearly anymore. She had even lost her sense of humor, which had constituted her little personality. She felt old. She could no longer console herself except with the thought of sleep. The child tired her so much, on top of everything else, that she could not even attain the sense of fulfillment associated with motherhood.

Outside, the pulse of the city sounded faintly. Certainly, it was not yet too late, if so much traffic could still be heard. For a moment, Mariana's attention focused on the night with its cars and streetcars, with its restaurants, theaters, and cinemas, as though she were suddenly puzzled that beyond the walls of the room, which enclosed the exhaustion of one more day, there might still be something else.

At twelve, she had to feed the child again. The thought made her feel painfully weak. Breastfeeding was a veritable torment for her every time, and afterward, she was left enfeebled to the point of losing consciousness. For some time, everything had taken on oppressive proportions. In the few nights when she happened not to be in deep sleep, she had dreams in which she was exhausting all her strength trying to stop the collapse of boulders of immense size.

Footsteps could be heard on the stair. However, as she did not recognize them as Victor's, Mariana took no notice of them. She started only at the sound of blows on the door, which woke Victoraş up too.

"Who is it?" asked Mariana, with a stifled voice.

"Siguranţă! Open quickly or we'll break in the door!"

Mariana saw black before her eyes. It was only with difficulty that she found the strength to raise herself from the bed. As she opened the door, her hand was all trembling.

Three sturdy young men pushed their way into the room, each making for a different corner, where they started to rummage through things at random.

Mariana looked on blankly, with her hands crossed over her chest, not hearing the screams of the child forgotten in his perambulator. So in the end he had not been able to escape what she had feared so many times. The search could only be a consequence of that *vivere pericolosamente* that Victor had always been going on about.

"Where have you hidden the weapons? Tell the truth, or we'll beat it out of you!" snapped one of the agents, fed up with searching in vain.

"What weapons?" stammered Mariana.

After a moment, however, realizing that she truly had nothing to hide, she tried to stand up to them more firmly, "I don't know what you're looking for. My husband isn't involved in politics. He's got troubles enough of his own. He minds his own business, teaching gymnastics lessons and playing as an extra at the National—"

"Really? That's a good one! Maybe that's why he got it into his head to start a disturbance in the street over the shooting of Toma Vesper!" said the agent in amusement as they went through the piles of books.

All the blood drained from Mariana's cheeks. With dry lips, she repeated what she was unable to comprehend, "Disturbance in the street…shooting of Toma Vesper…."

Meanwhile, Victoraş kept yelling till his voice was hoarse.

"Come on, lady, pull yourself together. Can't you see the kid's getting into a state?" said the oldest of the agents kindly. He stood by the side of the perambulator, awkwardly making shushing sounds.

Chapter II

hey sat huddled together in Ştefănucă's room, where they had rushed as quickly as they could. Although the dead man was not actually lying there with candles at his head, the atmosphere was that of a funeral vigil. Only the little lamp on the bedside table was lit, and they spoke in lowered voices, almost whispering.

"I can see how it all happened as if it was right before my eyes," said Cernat, distressed. "The van that's mentioned in the press release hurrying along the highway, with the circles of light from the headlamps, then, suddenly, stopping at the edge of the forest…the gendarmes shove Toma Vesper and the other two out… the officer shouts at the prisoners to make a run for it, while the guards prepare to open fire… the salvo of rifle fire echoes through the forest…the fugitives fall in a heap…Toma Vesper's arms, with his hands cuffed, lie stretched out on the tarmac, unable to reach anyone…."

"No!" objected Nicoară. "Toma Vesper couldn't have played along with their staged escape while under escort. I'm sure he stood to face the bullets without flinching."

"But how come Saint George abandoned him? I don't understand. There could have been a miracle…," said Ştefănucă with his confusion showing in his face.

Neither of the other two answered him.

"What a man!" murmured Nicoară after a pause, shaking his head. "When I think that I had the chance to live alongside him, day by day, at the seaside camp, when we started building the church...."

"What a pity we weren't there with you!" interrupted Ştefănucă.

"Let me tell you something that happened then, something that still affects me. In our camp program, we had sports lessons: volleyball, shooting. Although I was maybe the youngest of all, I managed to make a name for myself as one of the best marksmen. On one occasion, with a revolver borrowed from one of the students, I brought down a seagull that was flying foolishly over the beach. Holding the bloodstained bird by a wing, I took it as a trophy to Toma Vesper. He looked me straight in the eye—Good Lord, the weight of that look!—and said to me, 'Why should you kill a seagull? The bird is innocent. Your act of cruelty must be punished.' In the evening, during the usual ceremony, he cited my case before everyone, and as a punishment it was decided that I shouldn't work for a day but should remain confined to my tent, with nobody talking to me."

"Strange!" said Ştefănucă, profoundly amazed. "Such severity for shooting a seagull, when a year or so later, in the trial of the assassins of the prime minister, the same man would not denounce the accused as murderers!"

"The prime minister was guilty!" replied Nicoară bluntly.

"But I think Toma Vesper also has to be understood another way, in the case of the assassins,"

Cernat broke in. "Even if deep down he might not agree with political assassination, it would have been out of keeping with the code of honor of comradeship for him to have distanced himself publicly from men who had risked all for the Herald cause."

In the silence that followed, the clock downstairs in the dining room could be heard striking ten times.

"Let's go!" said Nicoară, standing up.

"No, wait a bit," begged Ştefănucă.

"No. It's late."

Ştefănucă saw his classmates out to the street. The sky was overcast. In the distance, the rattle of a streetcar died away.

When he went indoors again, Ştefănucă found his mother waiting for him in the dining room. "Come and eat. We all finished dinner a long time ago."

"No, I'm not eating anything!" replied Ştefănucă, as he started to climb the stairs slowly, his shoulders drooping.

The atmosphere in the Cişmigiu Garden belied the season in preparation. Clouds rested in the treetops, ready to cover everything in ashen grey. There was something about the water of the lake that suggested the gaze of a blind person. Hauled out on planks, the boats lay abandoned and rotting.

Ştefănucă had set out for school, but halfway along the road he had had second thoughts and had stopped in Cişmigiu. The emptiness in his soul seemed to find its correlative in the dismal morning. Since the previous evening, when he had learned of Toma Vesper's death, he had remained with the same sensation of drowning. One day on holiday at the seaside, he had swum out from the beach without realizing how far he had gone, so that on the way back, at a certain moment, he had found that he no longer had the strength to reach the shore. Out of the whole incident, what he remembered above all was flapping his arms at the moment when he started to sink to the bottom. With a supreme effort, he had grabbed at the surface of the water as though at something substantial. On the verge of drowning, the loss of any point of support had been his last conscious sensation, before a boatman had managed to reach him and pull him out of the water. Since he had enrolled in the ranks of the Heralds, he had come to believe that the realization of their program was dependent on a man who, even if he had ended up on the accused bench and then in prison, was still there somewhere as a cardinal point. Yet now the man that he and the other comrades had considered almost a saint, whence their secret faith in the immunity of his being, was no more than a bullet-riddled corpse. Ştefănucă had tried at first to console himself with the thought that the triumph of any spiritual revolution had at its base, as the unit in which sacrifice was measured, death. And yet the drowning sensation did not leave him. He had never had much of an idea of how strong the Heralds were across the country. Whether, in spite of the persecution unleashed against them, they could still do something. He had imagined, however, that in every town, if not every village, there must be countless other young people who thought the same way. Now, with the death of the leader, it was as though he could no longer feel the presumed multitude of fellow adherents of the movement standing shoulder to shoulder.

"Excuse me, please. Have you got the time?"

Ştefănucă looked in puzzlement at the governess with a child who had stopped him on his way.

"Excuse me, please. Have you got the time?" the governess asked a second time, more emphatically.

"Yes… half past nine."

"Thank you!"

Ştefănucă stopped at the first bench and sat down next to a park attendant who had fallen asleep there. He was not properly settled, however, when, to his surprise, he saw Nicoară and Cernat emerging from the path that led to their high school. Both were nibbling sunflower seeds, equally lost in thought.

Ştefănucă stood up. "Good morning! What's happened? Why did they let you go?"

"Two days holiday for disinfection. Mateescu's gone down with scarlet fever!" replied Cernat, leaving off gnawing seeds for a moment.

Before they parted again, Nicoară informed Ştefănucă of the disposition received, "You've to be in Andronache forest this evening at nine. The place where we met in the period before the elections. We're doing a night march. I guess you still remember how to get there." Ştefănucă brightened up. A march. There couldn't be a better idea! It was only fitting that the fallen leader should be honored with something more than feeble tearfulness.

The evening had dispersed some of the clouds of the day. Here and there, the sky was even clear enough to allow the glimmer of the occasional star to show through.

Ștefănucă walked quickly, periodically looking at his watch. The low, squint-walled houses crowded along the edge of the road seemed never to come to an end. From behind the fences of the close-packed yards, dogs kept barking at him. Outside, on the road, there was no one.

Ștefănucă reached the signal box, and could not believe his eyes when he saw that the forest began right there. Since last time, he had remained under the impression that the long part came after the level crossing. He continued for about a hundred paces on the other side of the railway and then turned off into the forest, feeling less and less sure of himself. He recalled that from the main road, a path branched off to the right at a certain point, leading to the clearing with that immense oak tree that had astonished him as a natural phenomenon the first time he saw it. He therefore had no option but to cut across in that direction, feeling his way through the terrifying undergrowth.

"Halt! Password!"

"Long live Toma Vesper!" replied Ștefănucă, startled.

"Come on, brother, you're the last one!"

Cernat, who had been left on guard duty until fifty individuals had been counted in, the full complement of the Blood Brothers of three high schools put together, set off rapidly. While he had been standing there, demanding the password of anyone who approached the meeting place, his mind, which always became heated in unusual circumstances, had led him to see himself confronting death itself. The fact that he had been given a revolver had made him imagine that danger must be imminent. If the boys hadn't been lifted one by one in the street, that must mean that they were all going to be challenged together during the march, from some direction or other in the forest. However, their column would advance without hesitation. Under machine-gun fire, they would fall row by row, honoring Toma Vesper to the end. The sublimity of the heroic scenes he dreamed up filled his eyes with tears of emotion.

In the clearing, the boys hurried to take their places at the end of the marching column, next to Nicoară. A short command rang out, and their bodies stiffened as they stood to attention. At the second command, the column was set in motion, past the oak tree and then along the path that went deeper into the forest. For reasons easy to understand, they walked without singing. Their unity was achieved only by the rhythm of their steps.

As if by magic, the frost of sadness was shaken from Ștefănucă's soul. Not a doubt, not a care, not a fear could persist any longer in the tight ranks that had begun their march into the void. He had Cernat's shoulder by his side. And Cernat, in his turn, had Nicoară's. Together they all felt one and the same step. Their hearts beat to the same rhythm. They breathed the night air with the same lung.

To Ștefănucă, a new certainty became ever clearer. Toma Vesper had not fallen riddled with bullets in the forest of Țigănești, the victim of a staged escape while under escort. He lived. He walked with them in the night. His footsteps led them all like a wave.

Chapter III

lear as a pool of water, the morning bathed the city in a new light, all the more enchantingly fresh for coming after the indeterminacy of so many cloudy days. In the almost empty streets, the sweepers were completing the work that they had begun well before it was light. The street traders from Oltenia, yokes balanced on their shoulders, shouted out their cries in counterpoint, beating the rhythm with their bounding steps—"Get your fish, fish, fish!" "Scallions-and-garlic, scallions-and-garlic!" "Brăila cheese, cheese!"—adding something of the air of a Balkan market to the atmosphere.

At windows, sheets hanging out to air fluttered like white flags.

Lucian, who usually walked immersed in thought, taking no notice of what he met along his way, now caught himself resting his gaze on every detail. It seemed to him that he was starting to display the psychology of someone condemned to death, his attention being claimed with absurd intensity by all the little nothings of the everyday scene. To tell the truth, it was not what might happen to him during the strike that made him uneasy so much as the ridiculous spectacle he would make. He could not in the least picture himself scuffling with the police in the clashes that were more than certain to take place, and nor could he see himself yelling like one out of his mind, caught up in the frenzy of a raging crowd. He was experiencing a sensation of nervousness such as he had never known before any examination in his life. Since the shooting of Toma Vesper, Dumitru Ifrim, and Valeriu Ionescu, the student body had been in ferment. The leadership committee of the movement's organizations in the University, of which Darie was a member, representing the Faculty of Letters, had agreed to debate the proposal of a protest strike. After much consultation, the conclusion had been reached that the strike could only succeed if it were unleashed unexpectedly, at a certain distance of time from the date of the government's criminal provocation, that is to say, when the authorities were least expecting it. The date of the strike had been fixed as the day of Saint George, the patron saint of the Heralds. It only remained for the plan that had been worked out in detail to be translated into action. Lucian had hesitated all night over whether to take part in the strike. In his view, the initiative was not politically opportune in any way. The instigators of the strike, who were also the best activists, were preparing to unmask themselves with a complete lack of concern. By evening, they would all be under arrest, due to the imprudence of a totally gratuitous gesture. In politics, romanticism led only to folly. And yet, in spite of his reasoning, Lucian had always felt that he was going to maintain solidarity. Had he fallen victim to a phenomenon of mystical contagion? Of course not, since he had kept his lucidity whole, right to the end, and had not let himself be carried away by the emotionalism of Darie, who had addressed them at the last meeting as though from the barricades.

Lucian stopped outside a confectioner's and stood for a while looking at the trays of cakes, although in truth, he had no appetite. Then he moved on to the window of the drugstore next door, where he paused again, admiring the decorative arrangement of the toiletries. He considered buying a lotion to stop hair loss, a lotion that he had not yet tried and that he had been reminded about when he saw the bottles with the familiar advertisement, there between the soaps and the toothpastes. There was still a while to wait until it was time for the shops to open. At the corner by the Faculty, he came upon a Gypsy woman sitting on the pavement with a basket of snowdrops and violets, and he delayed for a moment to ask, without knowing for sure why he was doing so, "How much for a bouquet?"

"Five lei, mister."

Lucian went on his way slowly, with his hands behind his back, followed by the voice of the flower-seller, who had started haggling, "Four lei! Come on, yours for three! How much do you want to pay, then? Two lei! First sale of the day!"

Outside the Faculty, there was no movement to be detected, leading Lucian to presume that the authorities did not know anything yet. To be ready for any eventuality, the organizers of the strike had at least had the wisdom to show some foresight, and the evening before, they had left a number of students hiding in the lavatories so that they would have a secure foothold inside the building.

When he entered the Faculty, the first person Lucian met was Lică. Among the others there, he did not seem to recognize any of those that he knew were to make up the picket of strikers at the main door. Before he got as far as asking, he felt a blow to the top of his head. As his hand leaped toward his spectacles, in a reflex gesture of self-defense, his body collapsed limply into the arms of two officers, who each grabbed him under one armpit.

At the canteen in the basement of the Faculty, Lică drained his glass in one draught and smacked his lips emphatically. It was a long time since he had felt in such good spirits. He still could not forget the sight of Lucian's head as he had collapsed under the blow of the rubber baton. Everything had fallen into place admirably. Tipped off by him the evening before, the agents of the Siguranţă had made a raid on the Faculty during the night and had got their hands on all the students who had remained there. Then, at dawn, the officers had gathered around him at the entrance. Whenever one of the boys designated to form part of the picket of strikers had stepped inside the Faculty, the individual in question had been met with a blow of the baton and taken out by the back door. Out of all of them, it was Lucian that Lică had been determined to knock hardest. From the beginning, he had brought it to the officers' attention that when the one that he was going to indicate with a particular gesture entered, they were to strike him from behind too, on the grounds that the individual was capable of defending himself with a revolver.

"Hey, how come you're free?"

At the sound of Elvira's voice, Lică started, "I don't understand. What do you mean?"

"Come on, stop pretending!"

"Damned if I know why you're asking!"

"Ugh, a bit thick you are! I'm surprised you've escaped because I heard that Darie and the others were arrested this morning, even before they could stop classes taking place."

"So what? What have I got to do with them?"

"Stop hiding behind your fingers! As if I didn't know you're one of their lot."

"Me, one of their lot? Well, a while back, in my younger days...." And to change the subject, Lică quickly added, "Honey, tell me, how about us going out this evening to a cabaret?"

Elvira was wide-eyed, "To a cabaret?"

"Yes, why are you surprised?"

"Hey, what's up with you?"

"How do you mean?"

"Well, lately, you're no longer recognizable. You've put on a tie, at last. And not just any old tie: natural silk...," observed Elvira, fingering the material. Clothes: top-notch! You've stopped wearing those awful sergeant major's boots. How did you strike lucky overnight to have money even for cabarets?"

"Stop trying to know everything, or you'll grow old before your time," replied Lică, trying to joke as he kept combing his abundant hair. "Just tell me where we're to go this evening."

"Let's go to the Colorado. Dinu Şerbănescu's singing."

"The Colorado it is," consented Lică with a blasé air, although he had never set foot in any Bucharest cabaret before.

"But do you think your money will be enough?" asked Elvira, with a final doubt.

"I beg your pardon...."

"Oh, don't be so stiff about it! In the meantime, right now I could do with a starter. I still don't feel like going to Italian."

"My pleasure. Look, we've got a table at the back."

Lică followed Elvira in a state of excitement. The heavy perfume of her hair, the play of her hips as she walked, the shortness of her dress, which showed her legs to advantage—each and all intoxicated him. Then there was the girl's change of attitude. From barely paying him any notice, from hardly listening to him, and keeping her eyes on others even if she did, she had now, quite out of the blue, shown herself to be much more inviting. The bitch had sensed that he had money— so much the better! He liked her lack of scruples, the shameless ease with which this slut from Ploieşti with her luxurious ambitions knew how to get around.

Lică sat down at the table and rubbed his hands contentedly.

"Well, what shall we have?" asked Elvira as she searched in her handbag for her mirror.

"I suggest—"

However, Lică was interrupted by a girl in their year who stopped at their table, coming with news from town, "Have you heard what's happening at Medicine?"

"What?" Lică was eager to know.

"The students have barricaded themselves in since yesterday evening. The police are laying a full-scale siege. A column of other students who tried to come and help those inside the Faculty has been scattered with tear gas. Even here, next door, at Science, the students have stopped classes being held by blocking all the entrances. But for the time being, I see they're still being left in peace."

"Fiddlesticks!" exclaimed Elvira, who all this time had been applying a fresh layer of red to her lips.

Choked with disgust, the other girl left them without even saying goodbye. "Wow, what a great pair we make!" Lică burst out, striking his palms together.

"You think so? Why?"

"I just do! Well, what shall we have?"

Turning his head, Vasia observed that the officers had given up following him, so he stopped running, gasping for breath. He had run as though aiming to break the record for the hundred meters, the same as when he had managed to be champion of the Residential High School. After resting for a moment, he continued on his way up the boulevard, this time at his usual walking pace. As he thought over all the events of the strike, his bitterness could not but come back to him in a feeling of shame. He had had great illusions at the beginning, although the strike had been conceived by the organizing committee in a temperate spirit, with the recommendation to avoid provoking the ethnic minorities. He had always counted on the unpredictability of events, especially as, in such circumstances, one never knows how far things may go.

Evening had fallen, and Vasia had remained in the Mathematics Faculty with a team of comrades. They had started by locking the cleaners in their rooms in the basement. Then they had taken the first strengthening measures. The main door, at the corner of Strada Edgar Quinet, was made of solid wood and at the same time provided with a sufficiently secure system of bolts, so it looked as though it would be hard to force from outside. The entrances from the courtyard and the doors on the upper floors that connected with the neighboring faculties, on the other hand, were more of a problem, so it was necessary to barricade them with some desks brought from classrooms. Once that was done, the waiting began. Apart from Vasia, who had lain down peacefully in the staffroom, even managing to fall asleep on two armchairs placed front to front, almost all of them had spent the night smoking, talking, or doing guard duty together. Much later, Vasia had been woken up by a comrade who had rushed in to inform him that the police were at the main door. After the boys' refusal to evacuate the building, the officers had beaten a retreat. Then, until morning, complete silence had reigned. Strangely, however, at the Faculty of Letters, classes did not seem to be interrupted. The boys' anxiety had really grown when they had seen that entry was being attempted via the blocked doors on the upper corridors. However, after their warnings had been rejected for a second time, the police had withdrawn from there too. Puzzled at how their comrades next door had come to be beaten, when no pressure had been detected from outside, the boys had ended up in a state of ever-lower morale. Toward the end of the morning, the observers at the windows had announced that things were starting to move: cordons of gendarmes had lined up at each end of the street, while a police cistern had stopped close to the Faculty entrance, right at the corner. Vasia had rejoiced for a moment, imagining that the authorities were going to change their tactics. He hoped that something would happen to get the boys out of the inertia of their vegetative state: doors broken down, tear gas, at the very least a gunshot. But still nothing happened. After the chanting of the "Hymn to the Fallen Heralds!" from the top-floor windows, an act which had resulted in traffic being stopped all around the whole University, the waiting had become even more oppressive.

Toward noon, the megaphones in the street had issued an appeal. After informing the insurgents that the strike had been ended on terms of mutual understanding in the other faculties, they were ordered to open the entrances of the building if they did not want any punitive action to be taken. Persuaded by necessity, almost all had inclined in the end toward capitulation. If the strike had been compromised from the start, as seemed to be the case, at least from what could be seen at Letters, there was no sense in maintaining their position any longer. Vasia alone had not been ready to back off. Feeling that the others were preparing to do as they wished, he had slipped out at a certain point from among them. Without sharing his intentions with anyone, he had set himself on watch, revolver in hand, at the window of one of the classrooms, determined that it would not all be over before he had managed to shoot at the uniform of a representative of the authorities. To his surprise and delight, he had identified at that very moment, down below in the street, the flabby presence of Commissioner Boian, the man whose blows and curses he had been forced to swallow when he was detained at the Prefecture during the persecution in the autumn. Taking careful aim, Vasia had fired three times through the window. Having had the pleasure of seeing his victim laid low on the pavement with one hand pressed to his chest, he had hurriedly slipped out of the lecture hall. He had gone into the lavatory at the end of the corridor and had dumped the revolver there behind the door. Then he had climbed onto the window ledge, ready to jump from there into the courtyard of the University. He had not had much time to size up the drop of over three meters, as the sound of voices inside betrayed the fact that the police had been allowed to enter. Once on the ground, he had felt his brain shaken, but apart from that he had not landed badly. He had made off at a run, as far as his legs could carry him. Despite there being some officers nearby, who had followed on his trail, he had finally managed to lose them in the distance.

Instead of rejoicing that he had escaped unscathed, Vasia could not resign himself to the general failure. So the day of the strike had not been destined to be the long-awaited day of revolution either. It had all taken a lamentable turn. Even his flight through the lavatory window, an ending worthy of a farce, had been in keeping with everything else. Only the shooting of Commissioner Boian gave him some sort of satisfaction, although the day should have ended with a hecatomb of corpses, not just one. Above the city, thick clouds swelled like strange waterspouts, which in Vasia's imagination could very well represent the apotheosis of an apocalyptic fire. Once more, he bit his lip. In reality, the spectacle was still just that of a storm rapidly building up, just like so many others that since the beginning of spring had regularly shattered the peace of the day.

PART FIVE

Chapter I

The moment's sensation of freshness turned Rotaru's thoughts back to walks with Mia. In the spring, after their classes at the University, the Botanical Garden had been their usual place of refuge. There they finally escaped from the everyday, time took on a different fluidity, and happiness began, naively and solemnly. The leafy boughs of the trees, closing together over the deep pathways, made one believe one was in a great vegetal cathedral, where the sky could barely be glimpsed through the luminous ogives of the high foliage. They walked with their thighs pressed together, each with an arm over the other's shoulder, their footsteps beating an idle rhythm. Once again Rotaru's hand could freely enjoy the rounded details of the girl's body, released by the season from the heavy clothes of winter. For a time, they had finished up seated on a bench, one of those countless public-park benches, engraved with lovers' names and pierced hearts. Chewing a blade of grass, she would begin to make plans, leaning her head back on Rotaru's shoulder. They would never give up fencing…. Every summer they would set out on a journey, somewhere, far away, starting with the Norwegian fjords…. Back at home, the provisions in their larder must include the greatest delicacy of all: Sibiu salami. Strangely, it was there and only there, in the Botanical Garden, that Mia dared to speak of their future! She broke off only when from some corner or other of the Garden the cry of the peacock, like a hysterical woman, burst out. They would rise from the bench with a shiver and slowly lose themselves in the ever-deepening shadows on the pathways. There followed fiery kisses, perfecting their bodies' embrace. Later, when they left the Garden and reached the stop at the end of the streetcar track, they would dizzily rediscover the city. The phosphorescence of the sky brought Rimbaud's line to Mia's lips like a personal confidence: *Mes étoiles au ciel avaient un doux frou-frou.*[14]

"Good morning! I thought you weren't up yet. What are you waiting for?"

"Good morning…"

"Get dressed, and I'll go and make some coffee! Here's your newspaper and your cigarettes…."

"Fine, fine…"

"I'll be off then. See you're not late!"

"Fine, fine…"

Left alone, Rotaru turned from the window, his conscience again tarnished. He was utterly fed up with the attentions of his landlady, who took on the air of mother and lover at the same time. As soon as she had entered the room, the reality of the present had extinguished the May sunlight, just as it had turned all his memories of the Botanical Garden to cinders. It was the start of another day like any other. There would be the same walking up and down, after the same reading of novels in installments. The same dozens of cigarettes chain-smoked till he was choking.

---

[14] "My stars in the sky had a sweet rustle." (Tr.)

Rotaru lay back on the bed with the paper in his hand. He skimmed over the first pages. Never anything new. Then when he was just about to close the paper, his eye was caught by Mia's name among the funeral notices. Just a coincidence, of course. All the same, with a chill, he started reading the details: *With hearts crushed by pain, forever without solace, Alexandru and Teodora Streiu announce the passing of their beloved daughter Mia, at the age of 24. The funeral will take place in Bellu Cemetery, Thursday, May 6th, 5 p.m.*

The paper dropped from his suddenly enfeebled hands. Mia was dead. Mia was dead. Mia was dead. But along with the mechanical articulation of the thought, he could hear in the room the bubbling laughter of the girl herself. More than that, his eyes could now glimpse her somewhere, all around him, like an image fragmented by countless mirrors. She was wearing her evening gown of white muslin, which Rotaru had last seen at a wedding. Pirouetting, in an absurd waltz, all on her own. Mia was dead. Mia was dead. Mia was dead. As usual, she had her hair in loose curls, that playful look in her badger's eyes. Her restlessness prevented one from perceiving the image of death, just as the blue void of the sky seen from the window could not at the same moment be imagined as occluded by clouds. Mia was dead. Mia was dead. Mia was dead. The thought failed to take on any substance. Only tears had begun to trickle slowly down his rough cheeks.

Close to the stranger's grave next to which Rotaru had sat down, the Vale of Tears opened out, where the new cemetery was. Almost nothing but plain crosses, graves of the less well-off, with none of the baroque architectural pomp of the tombs on this side. Beyond, in the distance, the city disappeared into greyness, outlined by factory chimneys, church towers, and brick walls. Rotaru, however, had eyes for none of this. With his chin resting on his fists, he looked into the void….

"Everlasting be her memory!"

The words slowly chanted by the priest came to him, together with the smoke of incense, carried on the odd breath of wind. Each time, Rotaru felt the same shudder. He could not get used to the reality, although it gripped him ever more tightly. From a medical point of view, he had understood from the start that Mia was not a straightforward case who could be expected to recover after a few years of treatment. The girl had tried first the therapeutic course offered by a sanatorium. A year later, she had agreed to an induced pneumothorax, and for this to succeed, she had been forced to undergo the two-stage Jacobaeus operation. But collapse therapy had not produced results either, and the cavern had remained open. As a last resort, she faced the radical solution of thoracoplasty, a mutilation to which she had never consented. And all the same, only someone familiar with radioscopic examinations could have realized that Mia was ill, so much did appearances belie reality. She did not cough, or have an altered complexion. And she did not live a dulled-down life, like a tuberculosis patient conscious of their condition. What had brought on this sudden end? Rotaru had no way of knowing. Perhaps she had been overwhelmed by the sensation of loneliness, without any immediate prospect of change. For a victim of tuberculosis, morale often counted for more than an effective pneumothorax.

Rotaru took out Mia's letter, the only thing he still had from her. It was a letter sent from the sanatorium during the summer, when he was still on his rural placement. The letter had lain forgotten in his coat pocket. He had found it the night before and had reread it several times, seeking through it to escape the reality that refused to be understood. Mia's hurried writing filled the page with disorderly lines:

My darling,

I am back in the sanatorium, driven away by the heat in Bucharest. The same hours of treatment in bed, with the windows open onto the stone-still grove of fir trees. The same overfeeding, portioned out five times a day, reducing you to your stomach functions. The same white walls, blindingly white in their bareness. The same companions, even if their identities change, that I have been bed-to-bed with in all my spells in a sanatorium. Merry girls, who play boarding-school pranks and have heads full of rubbish. Strange how I don't come to be like them, although my structure is a sthenic one, with life pulsing in me with the same unthinking exuberance! I don't know why, but the sanatorium depresses me like nothing else. It's only here that I start to feel ill. The laughter of the other girls, their jolly mood, seems to me strident, although I know well that it's nothing of the sort. I can't even read. I sit absent-mindedly, with no past and no future. I regress to the vegetative state. Good Lord, how can plants live? I don't even come to miss you. Word's going around that they put bromide in the tea to calm sensual impulses... Good Lord, what nonsense! I have a feeling I'm going to run away soon. You know very well that I could never put up with any sanatorium for longer than...

Rotaru stopped reading. An airplane had flown over very low, shaking the cemetery with its deafening whine. Now it was shrinking into the distance, swallowed into the panorama of the city.

"May God forgive her and give her rest."

So it was all over. All that remained was for the earth to fall on Mia's coffin. Rotaru rose with difficulty, folded up the letter, and slipped away quietly between the vaults, lest any acquaintance should bump into him on their way back from the grave.

It might have been midnight when Rotaru arrived home and climbed slowly up to the attic. After the cemetery, his steps had carried him along countless streets, right to the other side of the city, to the Botanical Garden district, which he had avoided since his clandestine return to Bucharest. There he had found the confectioner's where on rainy days he used to go with Mia after their university classes. It seemed that nothing had changed. The owner, the same old Adventist, was still reading his Bible in the corner by the till. At the few tables, topped with red marble, there was no one sitting. The cakes waited in rows on trays, Mia's *savarins* and his *sarailies*.... The clock on the wall was stopped at the same meaningless time: half-past four. Pulling himself away from the confectioner's window, Rotaru had walked around the outside of the Botanical Garden, all the way running his fingers over the bars of the iron fence. From inside, the sound of the hysterical woman's cry of the peacock reached him. He had not for a moment dared to raise his eyes to the sky: all their stars had fallen. Even the sweet evening air had made him suffer, like a reluctantly accepted glass of champagne, just when he felt in most need of invigoration. At the end of his tether, he had thought of turning himself in to the authorities, just to get it all over with, once and for all. Ultimately, only the fact that he was too tired had stopped him. The thought of a night of interrogation, recounting his clandestine existence in all its multitude of details, had seemed even more overwhelming than the life sentence itself. Later, he had stopped on the banks of the Dâmboviţa, looking over the balustrade at the viscous water crawling along below him. He had resisted the impulse to drown himself, stopped by his disgust at the filthy water. He had arrived at the door of the building where he had his lodgings with the confused sensation of a sleepwalker unexpectedly awakened. After slowly fumbling his way to the stair, he had taken off his shoes so that his feet would make no sound on the wooden steps.

The moment he opened the door of the attic, Rotaru felt a shudder of horror as he heard the voice of the woman who was waiting for him in the bed, with the lamp on the bedside table lit.

"What's up with you? Where have you been wandering?"

In the tone of the question, he could sense the unease that came from waiting on tenterhooks, but there also seemed to be something of a threat.

Rotaru dropped into the chair, looking incredulously at the woman with her dyed hair in curlers, with her puffy face that took a gelatinous shine from the cream she put on it, with her neck misshapen by an incipient goiter, with her sagging breasts visible through her nightdress. On the banks of the Dâmbovița he had hesitated to drown himself only because the water had seemed to him like a tank of filthy slops. And now, as though it were at all cleaner, he would continue to endure his life with this old bitch always in heat.

"Come on, what are you waiting for? Won't you get undressed? I wasn't going to wait with dinner for you till midnight, was I? If you will go off on your own, it's your choice to go hungry."

And, after a moment, with a slightly muffled voice, the woman continued, "Come one, what are you doing? Won't you come to bed?"

Chapter II

For several nights, Liliana had barely been able to close her eyes. She only fell asleep toward daybreak, and even then it was no more than a tentative semblance of sleep, or rather a numbing of the nerves, such as one has on long train journeys or during a night of funeral vigil. When she had first realized she was in love, Liliana had contemptuously considered herself a goose, no different from the rest of her classmates. Then, gradually, the vaporous state of her sentiments, which had at first made her feel somehow disqualified, had condensed into a need for physical closeness that was overpowering to the point of obsession. Before falling in love with Vasia, she had in principle regarded with repulsion the materialized representations of love—what she imagined it would mean to kiss a man or to sleep with him. Lately, however, although still every bit as chaste, she had come to sense instinctively that only by resolution in the act could love take on its full meaning. The ferment of her desires had come to show in her feverish gaze, in her endlessly moving lips, in the unease of a body that had lost control of its movements. And so she had adopted the habit of keeping herself hidden, fleeing from others like a guilty person.

Liliana got out of bed with the blood pounding in her ears. She felt that she was incapable of carrying on any longer. She was going mad. At the end of the day, shame or fear was pointless. Why should she not be honest with herself? Why not? The darkness of the night urged her on like an accomplice, instantly weakening her last resorts of modesty.

Not bothering to look for her slippers, Liliana fumbled with trembling hands for her dressing gown. She pulled it hurriedly over her nightdress. Then she opened the door slowly, so as not to be heard, and went out into the corridor. The parquet floor was cold under her bare soles. From downstairs in the dining room, the long-drawn-out chime of the clock began to sound. Liliana did not wait for it to finish, but crept along to Vasia's room, her heart ready to burst out of her chest.

Immersed in following the demonstration in *Mathematical Gazette*, Vasia did not notice the dining-room clock, although at night its chime was particularly resonant. His thoughts had caused his forehead to wrinkle slightly. As always happened when his interest in the discovery of a solution took possession of him to the point of complete self-forgetting, he had begun to chew the end of the pencil in his hand. Only at the third knock on his door, which was louder than the others, did he lift his eyes from the page of *Mathematical Gazette*.

"Who is it?"

By way of answer, he found Liliana standing in the doorway.

Vasia got up from his writing desk, thinking he was hallucinating. Liliana, in nothing but her nightdress and dressing gown, barefoot, here in his bedroom, in the middle of the night! He stretched out his hands, feeling the need to acquire certainty by tactile means.

Liliana stood with her eyes shut, trying to recover her daring in the darkness under her eyelids. When Vasia's hands gripped her shoulders, a thrill ran through her whole body. Without opening her eyes, she tilted her head back, her lips half open, while the pulsing of her blood gave a heightened rhythm to these moments charged with expectation. She felt Vasia ready to take her in his arms, his breathing thrown into disorder and his body tensed like a spring by the goad of his male desire. But just when she least expected it, the young man's hands dropped from her shoulders.

"Please, go back to your room!"

Liliana's eyes opened fearfully, suddenly seeming cloudy and grey. Her lips moved with difficulty, wishing to say something but unable in the end to do so. Her chin began to tremble slightly.

So much Vasia was able to observe before he lowered his gaze. He heard the rustle of the dressing gown and the door opening and closing again. Then the moments took on once again the identity of those before the girl had come, as though nothing had happened in the emptiness of the room.

Vasia sat down again, turning his distracted gaze on *Mathematical Gazette*, the fishbowl, and all the other familiar details. He held his forehead firmly in his hands in an attempt to control the throbbing in his temples. He had never slept with a girl. He considered the sex act a form of servitude, a chaining of the flesh that could only reduce the potential of his anarchic readiness. Right from the time of his adolescence in the boarding school, when sexuality had begun to be everyone's greatest obsession, he had opted for ascesis.

In the deep silence, the clock downstairs rang out, its single chime signaling that it was half-past something. This time, Vasia heard it well enough, though he had no idea what the time could be. His hands, which in the end had come together for a few moments, as though soundlessly struggling with one another, took hold of the *Mathematical Gazette*, while his eyes picked up again from the beginning the thread of Barbilian's paper on the periodicity of commutative operations: *But A, B, C, being a primitive system for the congruence nX=0, it must be that: av=Mn=MSv.* However, he could no longer understand a thing. In his nostrils, he could still feel the young animal scent of Liliana. His palms still kept the imprint of her round shoulders, and the presentiment of her svelte nakedness, with the specific anatomy drawn in rough embryonic forms under that dressing gown that was scarcely thicker than her nightdress, persisted like an inflaming sensation, right to the last pore.

With her head buried in the pillow, Liliana wept. She sobbed without a break, shedding tears like the rain of a summer thunderstorm. Her weeping shook her through and through, making her flesh tremble. With the floodgates broken, her whole being poured out in cascades. When the tears came to an end, she was left drained of all her strength, groaning feebly, her thoughts like mortally wounded birds. Then the darkness enveloped her. A road through a tunnel with no exit. A dive into a tar-black sea. Utter loneliness in the last night of the world.

When she woke in the morning, Liliana at first felt a sense of confusion at the realization that the ringing of her alarm clock was not the trumpet of the Last Judgement and that the sun had risen as usual, its light falling on the uncovered soles of her feet. A new day of school was beginning, one more just like any other. Her apron, her schoolbag, and all the other things were waiting for her just as they were any morning. Down in the dining room, her coffee with milk was sure to be in preparation.

After leaving Vasia's room, Liliana had been so overwhelmed by the humiliation she had suffered that she had been unable to judge matters. She had burst into a veritable fit of weeping, and then drowned herself in a deep sleep that had taken from her the memory of all that had happened. Only now, as everything began to come together again in a mind that was slightly dizzy from the shock of the previous night, were her thoughts little by little becoming clearer. Why had Vasia rejected her? From a man like him there was no reason to expect bourgeois prejudices. So why? On the other hand, she could not believe that he did not feel anything for her, for she had had the opportunity to feel how agitated he was when he had grabbed her by the shoulders. So why? Her judgment, like her gaze, began to cloud over again, confronted by the answerless void.

From the chest of drawers, Mormor the teddy bear, the lone survivor of the menagerie of her childhood, looked at Liliana with his round porcelain eyes. It was a long time since he had known how to help his mistress.

Chapter III

Raluca Holban was one of those beings to whom spring brings a slight diminishing of vitality, as though it were thinning the blood in their veins. She languished all day, doing nothing in particular. Now that the children were no longer to be seen at home, caught up as they were in the flow of the new season, she almost never went into town. Only toward the end of the day, as the sun was setting, did she go downstairs, into the garden, to sit under the chestnut tree. Now she was there again, sitting in one of those ample chairs of pleated straw that she had inherited from her grandmother. She had with her, on her lap, her black-covered notebook. However, she just kept yawning, and her fingers seemed not to know what to do with the pencil. Nothing that could correspond to the ocean depths of her memories. Not a thing. She could see the shadows beginning to take over the whole corner of the garden and she could hear the din made by the children kicking a ball in the street. Merely sensations limited to the perception of immediate realities. Could it really be she herself who had set down the words that filled the black-covered notebook? She opened it at the latest pages, with the strange sense of disorientation that one feels when trying to find oneself again in a person that one no longer is:

Dinu Pillat

1920. Raluca had left the beach earlier than usual because of Lucian, who was complaining that he had a headache. They were climbing the cliff path slowly under a sky bleached by the sun. Everything was melting and nothing gave any impression of movement. Her eyes turned back for a moment, to the sea below, trying to find a contrast that would free her from the blinding sensation. But at that hour the sea was no more than an immensity of asphalt. Finally reaching the clifftop, they made their way to the hotel, along a row of dust-covered acacias. The rattle of the sand molds in the bucket swinging in the boy's hand was the only sound she was still aware of. Nowhere was there the least spot of shade. Nowhere.

"Raluca! Hey, kids, stop a moment!"

Raluca stopped with a start, unable to believe her ears: a voice ringing out so loudly in the torpor of the street and addressing her of all people!

Through the dry shrubs on a mound near the hotel, behind which the railway wound toward the station, a tall, well-built man was approaching with a trunk in his hand. Good Lord, if it wasn't Ioachim Holban himself, her brother-in-law, whom no one for the world would believe to be the brother of Grigore!

Raluca pulled her beach robe around her the moment she realized she was being closely eyed. Lucian, who had pulled his hand out of hers, stood with his mouth slightly open and looked at the man who had stopped in front of them like a tower.

"Hello, kids! Why the surprise? I haven't dropped out of the sky. I've just not long arrived by train. You have my word...."

Yes, it was Ioachim. The madman of the family, or so they all considered him, apart from his brother Grigore, whom nothing could ever surprise.

Raluca's parents-in-law had firmly disowned such a son and had removed all photographs of him from the house, leaving the empty frames wherever they had happened to be placed. After completing their secondary education, each of the boys had received an estate. Ioachim, however, had scandalized the landowners of the day by dividing his among the peasants, keeping not the slightest piece of land for himself. Then he had been one of the first Romanian immigrants in America. His parents had felt compelled to tear up a photograph from across the ocean in which he appeared as a worker in the largest abattoir in Chicago. Since his return to Romania, he had only once crossed the threshold of his brother's house, on Lucian's fourth birthday, when he had brought a capercaillie that he had stuffed himself, an exceptional example, which he said he had shot in the forests of the Barnar massif.

"I'll come with you. Wherever you're staying, I'm sure they'll find a room for me too. I thought I'd spend a few days here before my ship sails from Constanţa. I'm joining the Foreign Legion. This time next month, I'll be in Africa...."

He spoke with his usual voice as though about the most everyday things. As he finished speaking, he took Lucian by the hand and hurried ahead with him.

Raluca suddenly felt the need to breathe more deeply, but the burning air was not enough for her.

ଓଃ

After the night's storm, the heavy clouds still remained, giving a gloomily oppressive air to the morning. Waves kept breaking, starting far out from the shore, so that the darkened blue of the sea was hemmed everywhere with white foam. The roar of the sea filled one's ears deafeningly, forcing the few holiday-makers who had gone down to the beach to raise their voices in order to make themselves understood.

Raluca had spread her beach robe under her on the still wet sand. A little further on, Ioachim, on his knees, had almost finished making Lucian a castle with towers and crenelated walls. After watching him for a while, without helping in any way, the little boy had come to sit on the edge of the beach robe, where he remained without a care, his eyes fixed on the rolling waves.

"Well, what do you think of it?" asked Ioachim after a while, as he got up and shook the sand from his hands.

"Most impressive!" Raluca was quick to respond, at the same time giving Lucian a push from behind with her foot to make him shift from his place, but without any success. "Ugh, I don't know what to do with such a child! He never plays, neither on his own nor with others. He barely opens his mouth, although he's able to speak normally for his age. He just sits and watches...."

Ioachim was the first person before whom Raluca felt a kind of shame that she did not have a more robust child. She fell silent with a knot in her throat, taking her eyes from the slightly rickety body of the boy at her feet. At the same moment, she saw that something had happened at the other end of the beach, near the fishermen's shelter: a boat was struggling to get out to sea, while a number of swimmers had gathered on the shore, pointing at something.

"I fear there's been a drowning," remarked Ioachim, sitting down beside Raluca with that ungainliness in his movements that excessively tall people tend to have.

"Yes, a terrible thing, if you think what the body of a drowned person can look like. On the other hand, their soul has already attained eternity. It is with God. I imagine death as the most perfect ecstasy."

The hash cries of some seagulls mixed with these last words, and then were lost over the waves that continued to break into foam.

⅓

After the last bend in the coastline, the Tuzla lighthouse, toward which they had set out to walk along the clifftop, began to rise taller and taller before them, upsetting eyes that had so far been used to a composition of plane surfaces: sky, sea, open field.

They walked in silence, with the chirping of countless crickets in their ears. Almost all the way, Raluca bent down to pick poppies at the edge of the wheat fields, but this was more to give the impression that she was not thinking of anything else. She lagged behind a little, refusing firmly when Ioachim, holding Lucian by the hand, waited for her to catch up.

The sea was still, its rise and fall barely detectable along the line of the cliff. Only its color seemed to have something unsettled about it. A light breeze rising from the beach brought with it the pungent smell of the seaweed cast up by the waves of the last few days. The sun was going down toward the other side of the world; soon it would be as red as a poppy on the horizon of the wheat fields.

When they entered the lighthouse yard, Raluca felt herself being clasped around the shoulders by the powerful arm of Ioachim, who asked softly, "Aren't you tired?"

"No! No!" Raluca shook herself clear and hurried on toward the tables where kefir was served.

When they were seated, Ioachim raised his glass of kefir with a slight smile on his sunburnt face.

"Cheers!"

"Cheers," replied Raluca feebly, hesitating to drink.

"It looks as if neither of you likes kefir very much."

Lucian, who could barely reach the level of the table with his chin, screwed up his face as though to confirm Ioachim's supposition, pushing aside the glass in front of him with both hands.

"And are you really determined to leave tomorrow?" asked Raluca suddenly, articulating the words with difficulty and not taking her eyes off the sea, whose green was now turning toward grey.

"Yes."

"Why won't you stay in Romania?"

The moments broke like waves.

"What would I do here? I'm a man that can't settle anywhere."

Where the sea met the sky was emptiness, all along the horizon.

❧

The beach was left far behind her when Raluca took a break from her long swimming strokes and rolled onto her back, spreading out her arms as if to embrace the sky.

She floated there, eyes shut, barely rocked by the slight swell of the water. Her body began to lose the sense of its materiality. Ioachim had once said that death meant coming to feel yourself in God. Was this now not something similar to death, or perhaps even to what she had experienced for the first time when she had been left alone, floating in space, in her bed in the hotel, after Ioachim had closed the door forever behind him?

The thought of Ioachim at once shook Raluca out of the peace of motionlessness. A brief shudder went through her body and she began to swim hard as though fighting a battle.

Her eyes could read no further. In the garden, under the chestnut tree, darkness had fallen. Raluca Holban put the notebook down on her lap, then pressed her cold palms to her burning forehead. She started for a moment at the sound of the gate onto the street. It was Lucian. He approached slowly, with that way he had of walking as though on stilts. After a few steps, he stopped awkwardly, surely just because he had seen her there. He mumbled a "good evening" and turned around, entering the house by the back door. The boy's gesture of avoiding her brought home to Raluca once again the extent of his alienation. Perhaps this was her fault too. To tell the truth, she had never given Lucian a share of the affection she felt toward Ştefănucă, Ioachim's son, although in every other respect she had always cared equally for both.

The gate creaked again, this time behind Liliana.

"Where have you come from?"

The girl's movement showed her surprise. She had not expected to find anyone in the garden. When she had recovered, she lied casually, "I've been at Sanda's."

Then, similarly twisting the toe of her shoe around in the sand of the path, she prepared her withdrawal with the excuse, "Mom, I'm going into the house because I still have some studying to do."

Left alone, Raluca Holban began to think about Liliana. Up until the autumn she had more or less managed to be friends with the girl, but since then, out of the blue, all bridges between them had broken. The change was not just regarding herself. Liliana seemed another person toward them all, even toward Ştefănucă, with whom she had always got on so well. She had stopped going to her friends' tea parties. At school, she had begun to get bad grades. She kept losing weight. If she was asked anything that touched on what was happening to her, she would lose her temper, blush all over, and slam the door behind her.

Raluca Holban suddenly noticed Vasia, who seemed hesitant about entering the house. Obviously the gate had remained open, since it had not creaked as usual. She was used to seeing the young man with his forehead raised, sure of himself, ready to thunder away at the slightest opportunity. Now he was slouched, which made him look shorter, while his footsteps, as he walked alone in the darkness of the garden, seemed those of a man defeated.

Poor children! A feeling of compassion, which she had never before experienced toward them, suddenly took hold of Raluca Holban. Involuntarily, she had caught each one of them in the intimacy of their loneliness. What dramas were they all concealing? Two out of the three were her own children. And yet they were as hard for her to understand as was the stranger. What did life hold in store for each of them?

Raluca Holban wearily leaned her head back. Above her, through the branches of the chestnut tree, her eyes met a faintly twinkling star.

Since regaining his freedom, following the May 10th amnesty, Lucian could no longer be at ease in the house. In the morning, after his seminars at the Faculty, he had begun again to do the rounds of all the secondhand booksellers, and in the afternoon, having given up attending lectures, he would go out to the Băneasa lakes, seeking the tonic effect of the sun like a convalescent. Although the material for his book was almost completely assembled, he now hardly did any work on it. His notes were checked more and more seldom and the red pencil he used for annotations was generally lost among the books scattered on his desk. Lucian always walked alone, for he had no real friend. With Darie, Serafim, or Stanian he was a comrade, in the sense that they shared the same political ideal and experienced history from the same position, but there was no more than that. An intimacy on a different level had been established between him and Rosner, the only person to whom he had so far dared to speak openly about the drama of his sexual complexes, although he knew well that Rosner was not a fellow invert. However, since he had been beaten on the occasion of the anti-Semitic reaction at the Faculty, Rosner had turned his back on him. Lucian had sought the friendship of Vasia from the moment the latter had come into their house. It was as though there were something magnetic that attracted him to the newcomer, and yet at the same time paralyzed from the start any effusion of closeness. And so he had failed to bond with Vasia either, and more than once he had caught himself feeling jealous of Liliana when he saw how unembarrassed his sister could be with the peculiar stranger.

Returning upstairs from the garden, where he had come upon Raluca Holban, Lucian was in no hurry to light the lamp, but stayed in the darkness of his room, leaning on the window ledge, his eyes fixed on the iridescent glow of the newly risen moon. No. He could no longer wait for dinner as usual. It was too beautiful. He went out quickly, without saying a word in the kitchen.

The phantomatic light of the moon had always attracted Lucian. It exerted a strange fascination on him. As a child, on nights when the moon was full, he had tiptoed out of bed to look out of the window. In the first years of his adolescence, the moon had made a sleepwalker of him. When she found out, his mother had called the doctor, who had cured the boy with difficulty by means of a psychological treatment. During holidays on the estate, he would walk in the moonlight till dawn, to the shocked astonishment of peasants staying out in the fields to guard the harvest that they had gathered for threshing.

The passage of a truck, which shook the street, spoiled the unity of the atmosphere for a moment. Then the sensation of unreality came back. The occasional passers-by maintained the solemnity of their step, as though they too were sharing in the same all-embracing mystery, while the walls took on a strange aspect, quite different from their familiar daytime appearance.

In the Cişmigiu Garden, where Lucian eventually arrived, the spectacle was truly magical. The vegetation no longer had definite outlines, but formed great dilutions of shadow. The lines of Mallarmé, the foremost of poets in Lucian's view, spontaneously came to his lips from memory as though echoing the atmosphere:

La lune s'attristait. Des séraphins en pleurs

Rêvant, l'archet aux doigts, dans le calme des fleurs

Vaporeuses, tiraient des mourantes violes,

Des blancs sanglots glissant sur l'azur des corolles...[15]

On the path that he had taken from the entrance of the Garden, Lucian met no one. He was alone with his shadow, among branches that in the glow of the moonlight seemed like reflections in water. From all around, however, out of hidden corners he could hear a rustle of whispers. In vain did Lucian try to escape the biological. The moonlit night no longer led him as it usually did to the perception of the cosmic mystery, to metaphysics.

He walked tensely, unhappier than ever at his lack of a partner.

---

[15] "The moon saddened. Seraphims in tears dreaming, their fingers on the bow, in the calm of the misty flowers, drew from dying violas white sobs that slid on the azure of their petals..." (Tr.)

Turning toward the lake, Lucian came upon the foamy outpouring of a newly flowering lilac. As he bent down to better take in the scent of the bush, he suddenly spotted two shadows through the branches. They shifted away from his gaze, dashing hurriedly into the depths of the darkness, but in the momentary glimpse, Lucian thought he recognized his former deskmate, the boy he had been in love with at high school, there with a soldier. The blood throbbing at his temples, he stopped there by the lilac bush, standing in agonizing wait.

As classes had come to an end early for eighth grade, Ştefănucă and his classmates had taken to studying together in the mornings in a corner of the Holbans' garden, preparing for their baccalaureate.

Sitting on the edge of the table-tennis table, where he had made space for his textbook and notes, Cernat was currently reveling in the honor of representing the examination board. Pointing with his index finger toward Nicoară, who was sitting in the basket chair, eating sunflower seeds in the shade of the chestnut tree, he adopted the familiar gestures and tone of voice of their history teacher: "Now boy, talk to me about 'The Phanariot princes of Moldavia, 1711 to 1744.' With dates. Short and succinct. With me, you know you can't get away with—"

"What, are you crazy? What's the point of this quizzing on details?" Ştefănucă burst out as he got up from the lawn, although the question had not been directed at him.

"The question is included in the course program. Look, here, if you don't believe me!"

"That's enough for today! In the end, the exams are a matter either of luck or of string-pulling," muttered Nicoară, and gave a loud yawn.

Ştefănucă wanted to contradict him, especially as he could no longer study except with the companionship of his classmates. But before he could say anything, Cernat jumped off the table-tennis, decreeing, "Five-minute break!"

The haste with which he stepped out of his role was due solely to the fact that he had spotted Liliana at the window of the room above them.

"Won't you come down for a round of table tennis?"

"No!"

"Why not?"

"It's too hot."

"You're telling me! If you stay inside and stew…. Out here, under the chestnut tree, it doesn't feel hot."

"I don't feel like it! And that's that!" Liliana cut him short and left the window.

Cernat, who in the meantime had picked up a table-tennis bat, made a serve into space. He had been in love with Liliana since he had first met her through Ştefănucă. He had composed verses for her too, on hearing which the girl had burst out laughing. But he did not give up hope as long as he did not know that he had any rival.

"Look, guys, I've got an idea! How about a trip to the Făgăraş mountains after the baccalaureate? The three of us…and maybe Liliana too, so we have someone to make fun of…."

"Yes, that's not a bad idea!" Ştefănucă feebly consented.

"What about you? Nothing to say?' Cernat looked in puzzlement at Nicoară, who was still nibbling seeds.

"To tell the truth, the mountains leave me cold. I don't know, it's as if they close you in. The sea is quite another matter. I came to realize that when I was at our voluntary work camp. When I think that now...."

In the silence left as Cernat's words broke off, Ştefănucă's thoughts returned to a reality that for some time had been giving rise to unease of a different degree of gravity compared with the baccalaureate. Nothing more had been heard. It was as though everything was stuck still. Even the occasional night marches, which had kept them shoulder to shoulder and at the same time had given them the feeling that they were in action, had been stopped since a group had fallen into the hands of the gendarmes in Băneasa. The dispositions, which were taken as orders, were beginning to refer more and more to an issue that made it hard to keep up morale. They kept being advised to be suspicious of one another, to identify traitors in time. That was the state of things now....

"Listen to the dream I had last night," Nicoară began unexpectedly. "It was as if we were at the seaside, just like back then, in the camp. It was toward evening. Everyone was singing, '*God with us. Know, ye Gentiles, and be conquered.*'[16] After the very last

---

[16] Isaiah 8:8–9, Brenton Septuagint Translation, 1884, https://biblehub.com/sep/isaiah/8.htm. (The Greek Septuagint is the source text for the Old Testament in the Romanian Orthodox Bible. The equivalent passage in the KJV and other Bibles translated from the Hebrew text is slightly different.)

verse of the prayer had sounded out full and deep, we didn't get up making the sign of the cross as usual. We kept on kneeling, stock still. Suddenly we felt the air turning bad. A smell of decomposing corpses. And the darkness, which fell on us as the night came on, seemed all made up of crows...." Nicoară cracked the husk of another seed between his teeth. Then, seeing that the others said nothing, he added, "I guess it all came from eating too many cabbage rolls last night."

Cernat sat still on the edge of the table-tennis table, among his textbooks and notes, looking distantly at his slowly swinging feet, but Ştefănucă got up from the grass. "I'm going into the house for a drink of water. I don't know, I feel stifled."

In the peace of the garden, there was no sound to be heard other than someone beating a carpet in the neighbors' yard, over the fence.

PART SIX

Chapter I

After forcing himself to finish the mug of milk, Lică got around to washing. He felt his beard and remembered that this was his shaving day. But before facing the broken piece of mirror propped up on Negulescu's *History of Contemporary Philosophy*, he opened the window wide to freshen the stagnant air.

Outside, in the sun, the long johns and shirts of Mr. Păpurică, the pensioner in whose home he was a lodger, were drying on a rope. By the rickety fence separating the yard from the street, Bombonica lay curled up shamelessly with the butcher's hound. Closer to the house, some hens were picking through a week's accumulated rubbish.

Lică wasted no more time looking out of the window, but turned to the shard of mirror and began to lather his face vigorously. When it came to shaving, however, he noticed to his annoyance that the razor blade scarcely cut anymore, with the result that it left his skin raw and irritated but pretty much as rough as before.

Every detail humiliated him like a mockery. The smell of burnt milk.... The yard that epitomized the atmosphere of a district on the outskirts.... Shaving without hot water, with the last of a bar of clothes soap and a blunt razor blade.... He had foolishly imagined that he would strike lucky by becoming an informer. In fact, the money he had earned, the bulk of which he had been given as a premium for his denunciations on the eve of the strike, had failed to match up to even a quarter of his expectations. He had bought a suit of clothes, a pair of shoes, and some ties, and he had been able to afford the luxury of giving Elvira a shock with a sudden invitation to the Colorado. That was all. What was worse was that he could see no chance of any fresh premium taking shape. He had tried to appear just the same as before in front of the boys in order to find out the political tactics that they were thinking of for the future, but he could sense that they no longer spoke openly in front of him. Could they have got word of his treachery? If he stopped to think about it, he really could not see how, especially as in order to maintain his cover, to be able to continue to play the role of informer, he had been forced to appear several times among the accused at the Prefecture, on which occasion he had taken his share of blows and verbal abuse on the part of the interrogators along with the others. On top of that, he had kept well away from the Faculty until after the amnesty, to make everyone think he was under arrest.

Lică left the room, leaving everything in a mess. In the passageway, he came upon his landlord preparing his rods and lines. So as not to pass without exchanging a few words, especially as it was through Mr. Păpurică that he generally managed to get an extension when his rent was due, he asked with a forced smile, "Going fishing?"

"Yes, indeed, dear boy. It would be a shame not to make the most of this fine weather. Even if I'm not lucky enough to catch much, at least I can enjoy a day in the sun, on the banks of the lake. You've no idea—" But before Mr. Păpurică could finish, he was suddenly interrupted by his wife, who was washing clothes in the kitchen, "Never mind your damned fishing! You'd do better to ask Mr. Lică what he means to do about the rent. It's two weeks since the first!"

"Have no fear! Surely you know me by now. Just one more day."

Outside in the yard, Lică spat heavily and then hurried to catch the first streetcar, eager to get out of this wretched slum as fast as possible.

When he reached Calea Victoriei, Lică began to walk up and down the pavement between the Palace Square and Capşa's restaurant. He went slowly, on the side of the street that was bathed in sunlight. He enjoyed letting his eyes wander over the windows of the big shops, choosing something from each one, but of course only in his thoughts. Each time he arrived at the Julieta studio, he stopped to look at the photographs on display, high-society women one and all, whose names were given too. That was the world he longed to break into, the world that he had to conquer. From the photographs, his gaze drifted toward the women on the pavement. Now, with the advance of spring, there was something provocative about them. In their light clothes, the outline of their breasts showed more clearly, which for him was the most disconcerting detail. As for Corso, Café de la Paix, and Capşa's, he never passed one of them without going in for a moment. With the air of a regular, he would cast his eye around as though looking to see whether someone was waiting for him. As in fact, he never entered with the intention of consuming anything, there was never any question of meeting anyone. He just wanted to satisfy his curiosity by spotting who was at a table with whom, especially as he had learned to recognize the greater part of the pillars of Bohemian café society. Then, once outside, he would enter into conversation with the first stranger he met about this or that artistic personality, whose table he would let it be understood he had just left. All this to give the impression that he had connections.

Toward lunchtime, Lică interrupted his walk so as not to be late at the canteen that had opened a week before in the Faculty basement. At the crossroads at the end of the University building, he recognized the car of the president of the Council of Ministers, with Sebastian Răutu in it. He only just managed to wave a greeting. The prime minister, who happened at that moment to be looking in the direction of the pavement on his side of the street, gave a casual gesture of acknowledgment. After the car had gone, Lică remembered that while he had been walking in the sun on Calea Victoriei, he had completely forgotten his sociology seminar, and he was suddenly sorry that he had further attracted the professor's attention.

In the great entrance hall of the Faculty of Letters, all was in motion as students poured out of their classrooms. Lică, who knew all his female classmates, managed to exchange a word or two with each. A charmer by nature, he kissed their hands, pecked their cheeks, took them by the shoulder.

When he finally went downstairs to the canteen, Lică bumped straight into Darie, whom he had not expected to see free. From under wrinkled brows, the hard look in his classmate's eyes drove into him like a drill. Trying to recover his composure, he stammered, "I'm so glad! Now there's no one missing anymore. The old guard…. When did you get out?"

Lică's confusion scattered any last trace of doubt in Darie's mind. All the time he had been detained, he had agonized over which of them might have been the traitor. Every time, it was on Lică that his suspicions had settled. After his release from the prefecture two days before, the last of the group to be freed, he had found that his opinion was shared by the others.

Instead of shaking the outstretched hand, Darie responded with two slaps across Lică's face, pouring into them all the force of the disgust he felt.

"What was that for?"

Darie, who was preparing to go on his way, stopped for a moment.

"You know fine well! And let this be clear: from now on you have no place among us!"

Left on his own, Lică began to feel his cheeks. It occurred to him that all the same, he had got off lightly. Surprisingly lightly. What if Darie, who had learned, like so many other members of the movement, to consider that any traitor should be shot without hesitation, had fired on him, right there at the top of the stairs? Lică could see himself lying dead on the ground, with everyone gathering around. The girls sobbing, the dean and the other professors who were still in the Faculty at this late hour trying to clear a way through to him…. Then the newspapers, with his photograph under titles in bold letters: "Revolting murder in the Faculty of Letters," "Apocalyptic beasts claim another victim," "Decent student shot for trying to escape Heralds' demonic snares." The sensation in Piteşti, in the high-school staffroom, at the confectioner's, in the street. The majority, who hitherto had never heard of this son of their hometown, suddenly boasting that they had known him since he was a child. Black flags at the door of the Faculty. Instead of going down to the canteen, Lică went back out into the street. He walked slightly stiffly, with something ceremonious in his posture, imagining that he was taking part in his own funeral, after his body had been lifted from the catafalque on which it had been on public display for two days in the great marble hall.

In the translucent twilight, Lică slowly made his way home. After being struck by Darie, he had lost any taste for food, so he had eaten nothing more all day. He had mulled over one plan of revenge after another, but had finally been forced to accept that there was no way he could silence his classmate. On top of that, he might come out of the whole business worse off if the people he was serving found out that he had been unmasked by his comrades. Wishing he could think about something else, he had walked up and down on Calea Victoriei, but without any of the pleasure he had felt in the morning. Then he had turned into Bulevardul Elisabeta and had ended up wandering around the Cişmigiu Garden. Later, he had turned back again. Although his lodgings were over in Obor, he did not take the streetcar but made his way on foot.

As he walked along, now immersed in his thoughts, Lică caught himself starting to judge things differently. He had been furious with Darie, instead of realizing from the start that he himself was the guilty one. One is entitled to behave as badly as one likes, if at the end of the day one gains something by it. But he had betrayed his comrades for no apparent gain, so he could have no excuse. From Darie's blows, not to mention his words, it was clear to him that in the eyes of the Heralds he was as good as dead. On the other hand, he could not expect to enjoy the protection of the police for much longer, given that he was only tolerated in their service to the extent that his informative notes demonstrated that he had a close knowledge of how things stood. A hidden thought urged him to change sides again. To admit his guilt before his comrades in a pathetic Christian confession. To continue as an agent, but in the future to play false to the police. After all, surely a traitor restored to his true loyalties might inspire more confidence than an adept who had been honest from the beginning but had never known the bitterness of self-deception.

As he entered the yard, Lică caught up with Mr. Păpurică, just back from his fishing, with his rods over his shoulder and a basket in his hand.

"Good evening! Well, did you catch anything?"

"Yes, indeed, dear boy. Should be enough for

a decent meal. You'll get a taste yourself, this very evening."

"No, thank you."

"Why not?"

'My stomach's a bit upset…."

"Never mind, we'll save it for you for tomorrow."

As he entered his room from the passageway, Lică caught the rough voice of Mrs. Păpurică suddenly raised in the kitchen, "What's this?! You must be crazy staying out till evening for this little scrap of fish!"

Back in his room, as he fumbled to switch on the bulb on the ceiling, Lică found himself muttering in conclusion, "What a hell of a life!"

Before undressing, he paused for a moment to look at the chromolithograph on the wall. Waterloo. Definitely Napoleon, even on the verge of defeat, was overpowering! Before his image, all the miseries of the day suddenly seemed to Lică mere trifles. All were wiped clean away.

Chapter II

After stopping to drink a lemonade at the corner, Darie continued on his way along the shadowed side of the pavement. Despite the torrid weather, he was still wearing the thick felt jacket of his only suit, from a country boy's prejudice against going into town in shirtsleeves. As he also happened to be somewhat overweight, he suffered from the heat like all fat people, sweating profusely and continuously. His sticky fingers were stained with ink from the lithographed course in General Pedagogy that he was carrying to the examination.

As he took a shortcut through the garden of Saint George's Church, Darie came upon Stanian sitting on a bench, with the child's pram in front of him. Beside him, two older men, obviously pensioners, were sharing the pages of the newspaper *Universul*.

"What do you care? Instead of fretting over exams, you're sitting back playing the nanny—"

"Shhh! Keep your voice down! You'll wake the baby."

Darie looked at his classmate. He had not seen much of him lately, as Stanian came less and less often to the Faculty. While he had been in detention, Mariana had been forced to find a job and had left the child in her parents' care. Now, during his wife's working hours, Stanian had taken over the role of a mother, a role that he seemed to have thoroughly entered into and played with great conviction. For Darie, the joy of their meeting again gradually clouded over. He considered his comrade irredeemably lost, if even at the eleventh hour, with the year ending, he had failed to be conscious of his true duty and found it more fitting to be walking with the perambulator than to turn up for an exam. And on top of that, he still could not forgive Stanian for his act of gratuitous heroism on the day when the papers had spread through the city the news that Toma Vesper had been done away with. In Darie's view, the act had been nothing less than a breach of discipline, and discipline was the only thing capable of giving cohesion to the Heralds. From the case of Stanian, his thoughts returned to his own obsession with the general way things were going. There were periods of stagnation, which were hard to pass through, but hard in a different way from those in which one was struggling face to face with a known adversary. One started to feel betrayed. The road seemed to lead through a swamp. At every step, one had the sensation that the ground was slipping from under one's feet. One no longer knew what to believe. Doubt took possession more and more, reducing one's morale to that of a deserter. The slough…. Another way in which one's endurance was put to the test. History was a process of selection on moral criteria, even if this was not apparent at first sight. One just needed the right perspective on things.

Darie began to wipe his face with a handkerchief the size of a towel. Then, so as not to fall into the torpor that the heat had brought down upon all the benches in the churchyard, he spoke, "Come on, lad, what are you thinking of doing? You can't live 'experimentally' all your life."

Stanian drew the perambulator out of the sun into the ever-diminishing circle of shade and replied calmly, "I've decided to become a monk."

Darie slapped his thigh in a gesture of wonder. "What? Impossible! After all, you're married.... you have a child...."

"You know well that the call of Jesus overrides family ties."

As he spoke, Stanian turned to take a Gospel book from the pocket of the jacket he had thrown over the back of the bench. He opened it at a page marked in red and began to read.

He that loveth father or mother more than me is not worthy of me: and he that loveth son or daughter more than me is not worthy of me.

And he that taketh not his cross, and followeth after me, is not worthy of me.

He that findeth his life shall lose it: and he that loseth his life for my sake shall find it.[17]

"You've gone completely out of your mind!" exploded Darie, who in the meantime had stood up and was continuing to wipe his face with the handkerchief.

The two pensioners left the newspaper pages on their laps and began to follow the exchange of words wide-eyed.

"I'm sorry that you of all people, who also did a year of theology, can say such a thing."

"To be a monk presupposes a mystical vocation. You must understand. It is unforgivable to conceive of

---

[17] Matthew 10.37-39

withdrawal to a monastery as just another 'experiment.'"

"Have no fear! I'm done with 'experiments,' with life in the ephemeral. It seems so strange to me, now that I have begun to realize the true dimension of things, that I could have felt I was experiencing the absolute in so many things that are nothing but vanity: my love for Mariana, what I found in a few books of literature and philosophy, the political activity of the Heralds...."

"How can you judge our political activity to be vanity?" Darie broke in, flushed with anger. "We, who want to raise these Romanian people out of their inertia, to make them live at the high tension of Christian spirituality! Not even the brutality we are accused of belies the authenticity of our apostolate. Think of Charlemagne, who Christianized the Germans by the sword!"

"If we go down that road, then we end up with the Catholicism of the Inquisition. We had better speak no more."

"There's no winning the argument with you! But I believe you'll think again. I'm going now, or I'll be late for the exam."

Their hands met in a handshake, without either of them saying another word.

As the two pensioners returned to scrutinizing the pages of *Universul*, Stanian's eyes followed Darie, who was slow to depart. Once the latter was out of sight, he closed his eyes. He tried once more to step out of the pattern of things. Only now did his last thought, in which he had caught himself judging Darie, bring to his awareness his lack of true Christian humility. He felt a knot in his throat for himself, for Darie, for all of them. First his lips, then his mind, to the rhythm of his breathing, began the continuous articulation of the prayer *Lord Jesus Christ, have mercy on me*. In his ears, the noise of the city in motion gradually ceased to resound, as though the bench had imperceptibly been moved further and further away. As he entered more deeply into the prayer, a state of transparency came over him, something between the fluid and the airy, a sense of peace in a great light.

Mariana turned away from the window, where she had stood for a while looking at the boulevard with its streetcars, cars, and people endlessly going this way and that.

"Wouldn't you like us to go out a little? We can ask Madame Ana to watch over Victoraş while we're gone."

Stanian seemed not even to have heard the question. He remained in his armchair with his eyes almost closed.

Accordion music began to become audible, as it so often did, coming from the room of the tenant at the end of the corridor. It was only in the first few days after the man's suicide attempt that his accordion had been mute, releasing Mariana's ears from the obsessive sense of a musical timbre of loneliness and ugliness, hard indeed to endure.

"He'd have done better to have died then!' Mariana burst out, thinking aloud.

Only at that moment did Stanian open his eyes and turn his head toward her.

"Ugh, if they would all just die for once! No more sound of Madame Ana and her sewing machine. And—"

Mariana stopped suddenly as she met her husband's eyes. A blush came to her cheeks, making her freckles stand out like a rash.

"Why do you look at me like that? I feel like those insects caught on flypaper. And you don't help me in any way. You sit all day with your nose in the Prayer Book or the Gospels...."

With surprising speed, Mariana snatched the Prayer Book from her husband's lap and flung it across the room.

Stanian immediately jumped to pick it up from the corner where it had landed. The book had opened in its fall. Returning with it in his hand, he began to read aloud the verse on the page where he had found it open.

My God, make me know how slight are the good things of earth and how great are those of heaven, how short is the time of this life and how boundless is eternity.

Help me always to be ready for death and not to tremble at Your judgment, to escape the—

Hearing Mariana's muffled sobbing, Stanian raised his eyes from the Prayer Book. The woman was still on her feet, but she had turned toward the window with her head in her hands. When he made to approach her, he too felt a knot in his throat, so he spoke with a slightly choked voice, "Calm yourself! Please calm yourself! Don't be bitter about anything anymore!

What is essential is quite different. Look at me, until I—"

But he was interrupted by Victoraş, who had woken up in his pram and was wriggling and starting to cry.

Mariana wiped her tears without looking at her husband. She took the child in her arms and sat with him on the edge of the bed. Then she took out her breast. She felt very hot. The feeling of weakness that always came with breastfeeding gradually took hold of her. It seemed incredible to her now that just a few moments before she could have wished death on the neighbors, could have flung the Prayer Book on the floor, and could have felt an impulse to throw herself from the window at the sound of Victor reading the verse.

When she lifted her head from her chest, Mariana's eyes fell on the flypaper hanging from the ceiling, right above the bed, black with all the flies that had got stuck to it. One, apparently only recently caught, was still struggling, buzzing feebly.

Stanian sat by the edge of the ditch in the slender shadow of a solitary tree that happened to be growing there. His feet felt hot and swollen; he had been walking along the highway since the first light of day. Now the sun was high in the sky and the mountains of Moldavia were starting to come into view, floating on the liquid horizon.

Certainly the journey to the monastery could have been made much easier by taking a train to the nearest station and continuing by cart or even in one of the local forestry companies' trucks. However, Stanian had thought it better to go on foot, to suffer all the hardships of such a journey, in the conviction that a life in Christ was not to be begun in comfort. He had taken nothing with him, not even his raincoat. In his wallet, he had kept only his identity papers so as to avoid any trouble with the authorities, to whom he could easily have passed for a vagabond.

Stanian lay back, with his hands under his head, on grass discolored by the dust of the road. In the foliage above him, some sparrows were hopping about. Those "fowls of the air" that Jesus offered as an example to the people. As he fixed his eyes on them, Stanian partook of their joyful lack of care for the morrow. But an invasion of ants made him shake himself rapidly to his feet, beside the anthill that he had failed to notice when he lay down on the grass.

The highway was deserted; it was almost unbelievable that there should be such absence of movement in the middle of the day. It was straight, as though drawn with a ruler, and it did not ultimately disappear from sight among houses or trees, but gave the impression of continuing as far as the horizon and then on into the heavens. For Stanian, this was no mere optical illusion. The road on which he had set out, casting off the world, could lead him nowhere else. A strange shiver of unease came to him out of the blue. What if the end foretold by Jesus should happen to catch him on the road, before he was able to prepare himself at the monastery for the eternity of the Kingdom of God? Stanian took the Gospel Book from his pocket, feeling yet again the need to plumb the troubling text, a text which he was amazed to see did not keep the soul of all humanity in a state of alarm:

For as the lightning cometh out of the east, and shineth even unto the west; so shall also the coming of the Son of man be.

For wheresoever the carcass is, there will the eagles be gathered together.

Immediately after the tribulation of those days shall the sun be darkened, and the moon shall not give her light, and the stars shall fall from heaven, and the powers of the heavens shall be shaken:

And then shall appear the sign of the Son of man in heaven: and then shall all the tribes of the earth mourn, and they shall see the Son of man coming in the clouds of heaven with power and great glory.

And he shall send his angels with a great sound of a trumpet, and they shall gather together his elect from the four winds, from one end of heaven to the other.

Now learn a parable of the fig tree; When his branch is yet tender, and putteth forth leaves, ye know that summer is nigh:

So likewise ye, when ye shall see all these things, know that it is near, even at the doors.

Verily I say unto you, This generation shall not pass, till all these things be fulfilled.

Heaven and earth shall pass away, but my words shall not pass away.[18]

---

[18] Matthew 24.27–35 (KJV)

A truck heavily laden with crates rattled past on the highway, leaving Stanian enveloped in a cloud of dust. It was a few moments before his eyes could make out the words that followed:

But of that day and hour knoweth no man, no, not the angels of heaven, but my Father only.[19]

Stanian closed his Gospel Book at once. The truck was out of sight. The highway was deserted; it was almost unbelievable that there should be such absence of movement in the middle of the day.

---

[19] Matthew 24.36 (KJV)

Chapter III

Imperceptibly, evening took possession of the attic room. Rotaru left his bed and went over to the window. His gaze rose calmly to the stars that had begun to come out above the sea of roofs. He was seized by a sensation of power such as he had never known before, not even when, with his revolver at the ready, he had been master of the prime minister's destiny. Since he had taken charge of the regrouping of all the still active elements, he felt like a different man. He had taken the decision at the end of the hardest month of his clandestine existence, the month in which almost all those comrades with positions of responsibility who had one way or another managed to remain at liberty had ended up falling one by one. It had been easy to believe that the Siguranţă had up-to-date information about what the last remaining militant cadres were doing. The fear, rising to the level of psychosis, that they might be betrayed at any moment, had had the effect of paralyzing any initiative. Sitting still and suspecting one another, the Heralds were bringing on their own liquidation. To stir the organism of the movement out of the inertia of inevitable decomposition, Rotaru had realized that something had to be set in motion. The remedy he had found was to pass from static vegetation to action regardless of the risk. Rotaru's appointment to the leadership had enjoyed unreserved support. Vasia had, from the beginning, also been among the most fanatical adepts of the terrorist strategy. Only that, unlike Rotaru, he had advocated freedom of personal initiative in the new orientation of the clandestine struggle. In the end, it was the opposing point of view, calling for the disciplined organization of anarchy, that had prevailed: in other words, the subordination of all acts of terror to a common plan drawn up by the leadership of the movement. Then, the divergence of conceptions had deepened further with regard to the elements to be utilized. Rotaru was keen to appeal to the high school student members of the Blood Brothers, who had so far not attracted much attention on the part of the authorities. Vlasia had walked out of the last meeting in disgust, after predicting that such an approach was unlikely to yield any results. He remained of the opinion that attacks could only succeed with the help of trained people, structurally anarchic and yet lucid in their action, not using children who might lose their cool at any moment.

"What are you doing? Aren't you coming to dinner? I've been calling you." His landlady's voice resounded through the half-open door.

Rotaru left the window, surprised at this return to his enforced destiny as a kept man. All the same, he felt none of the usual revulsion. How could humiliations of this sort touch him now?

"I'm sorry, I didn't hear."

"Where in God's name do your thoughts take you, that you can't hear even when I shout myself hoarse?" asked the woman, ever suspicious.

Rotaru merely shrugged.

The landlady looked at him with a restless unease. He was done with pacing up and down like a caged lion, and with chain-smoking dozens of cigarettes. Gone were his habitual long, gloomy silences, punctuated by incomprehensible shudders. The way she saw it, the only cause could be a woman with whom the boy had secretly found his happiness. Stifling a sigh, she ended up saying in a tired voice, "Come on, the macaroni will have gone cold."

Rotaru followed her down the stairs, treading firmly, sure of himself.

The dining room of the little apartment downstairs, which served also as a sitting room, betrayed a bad taste that was quintessentially petty-bourgeois. Everywhere there were embroidered cushions, knick-knacks of all sorts, dozens of photographs of the landlady with her late husband, paintings of fruit and Gypsy women bought at backstreet exhibitions, jars of preserves lined up as though in a confectioner's.

Before sitting down at the table, Rotaru first hurried to switch on the radio. The cadenced chords of a march at once filled the room.

"Find something else! I can't stand march tunes," said the landlady with a start, unpleasantly surprised,

"Not likely! I enjoy them!' replied Rotaru, his mouth full of macaroni.

The sounds of the march gave shape to a new reality. Rotaru could see himself on the rostrum, his hand outstretched. Column after column marched by in serried ranks, saluting as they passed him. Beyond them, lining the pavements and at every window, the whole city was acclaiming the conquering army of the Heralds. Silence. The march was finished. And in the moment's pause, Rotaru thought he could hear a murmur like the sound of the sea in a shell as the crowd frenetically chanted the name of the new tribune: Ro-ta-ru! Ro-ta-ru! Ro-ta-ru!

Rotaru sat with his head leaning on the carriage window, letting his thoughts flutter together with his hair in the draft as the train sped on. In spite of the sunglasses with which he masked his eyes, he felt overwhelmed by the strength of the light. The sunlight of a summer noon gave a watery glitter to the crops in the fields that faded into the mists of the horizon. After so many months of clandestine existence, in which he had got used to hiding from the full light of day and to moving within the enclosed space of a city, this journey provided him with the opportunity to discover God in all the transparencies of natural being. A sort of pantheistic revelation came over him. If at that moment he could have given way to his deep impulses, unimpeded by any sense of the ridiculous, he would have got off at the next station, gone out into the field, and started to cross himself and to say his prayers. But instead, when the next station came, all he did was to get a lemonade at the buffet. The sensation of the miraculous faded with time, just like anything that ceases to astonish when one has got used to it, and from Roman onward, Rotaru started looking repeatedly at his watch to see how long it would be before they reached Iaşi. The vacuity of his thoughts soon gave way to the preoccupation that was the very reason for his journey. His visit to Iaşi was to be the first in a tour of the country that he had resolved to make after taking over the leadership of the Heralds. Andriţoiu should be waiting for him at the station, alerted in advance by a courier. They had not seen one another since the previous summer when the gravely wounded theologian had been lifted into an ambulance and taken to the city for an operation. Rotaru tried for a moment to recall his comrade's appearance, but he could only visualize him as he had looked after being shot in the stomach: a lost look in his eyes, the blood drained from his cheeks, his lips turning blue. For the Heralds' organization in Iaşi, which was weakened more than any other after the endless succession of arrests, Andriţoiu was one of the last reliable elements in student circles against whom the authorities had not yet managed to bring a criminal accusation.

"What a fine harvest! The wheat's almost as tall as a man."

Rotaru emerged from his thoughts with a start, and turned his head toward Gheorghiu, the comrade he had chosen to accompany him, who had imperceptibly joined him at the window, after spending most the journey at one end of the carriage, where he was better positioned to watch out for any activity.

Short and chubby, with his back deformed by a hump, the man had nothing about him of the humble and awkward air of an invalid. He had been a brilliant student of medicine and had quickly made his name as one of the best specialists in diseases of the nerves. Although he had not played any special role in the Herald movement, Rotaru had since his investiture made sure to have him among his closest collaborators. He liked Gheorghiu's anarchism, which resembled some extent that of Vasia but with the difference that it was disciplined. Since Rotaru had taken the initiative of turning to action, the humpbacked doctor had kept trying to get his support for a plan of exceptional daring. It consisted of digging a tunnel from the basement where Gheorghiu lived, in a house in the immediate vicinity of the Patriarchate Hill, to right under the Parliament building. In Gheorghiu's opinion, which he maintained was based on the reliable calculations of friends at the Polytechnic, the work could be completed in the space of a single month by teams supplied with the necessary equipment and working day and night in shifts. Once the tunnel was ready, on the occasion of the first sitting of Parliament, when all the political elite of the regime would be gathered in one place, the building would be blown up with TNT placed in its foundations.

"Yes… a fine harvest… ," replied Rotaru, beginning once more to take in the view before his eyes.

When he was discussing something, Gheorghiu could not stay still. He would get up from his chair and start walking through the room, with gestures that drew attention to his pair of arms too long for the reduced dimensions of his humpbacked body.

"I can't understand! It's an absurdity. Why should suicide be the gravest of sins, excluding one from salvation more than a murder or some other such infamy?"

Andriţoiu answered calmly, in a tone that contrasted with Gheorghiu's, "It's impossible to conceive of a greater sin than to kill the likeness of God in yourself. If you commit a murder, the way of remorse and penitence still remains open to you. While…I think of Judas. His suicide condemns him irremediably, as certainly would not have been the case with the act of betrayal alone. If he hadn't hanged himself after he sold Jesus, Judas would have found the occasion to redeem himself somehow, perhaps ending up as one of the first Christian missionaries and martyrs. He might have come to be seen as another Paul of Tarsus.…"

While Andriţoiu went on speaking, Rotaru looked at his watch. The others had only been invited to the meeting starting from eleven o'clock, so there was still a little to wait before they started debating things that mattered to him in a different way than the problem of the salvation of suicides, which Gheorghiu had got onto as he jumped from one topic to another. Their journey had ended well. On their arrival in the station, they had met Andriţoiu and the other theologian, a friend of his, whom Rotaru had also not seen since the previous summer. This other man was not at present there with them, as he had been posted on guard duty outside in the yard. They had set off together, making their way on foot to Andriţoiu's family home in the Tătăraşi district. Rotaru had immediately received an update on the local situation. As in all the university towns in the country, it was hard for the clandestine activity of the Heralds to pass unnoticed, especially as the primary distinguishing mark of provincial psychology consisted in the need to find out and to pass on whatever was happening around one. In the restricted circle of the provincial environment, almost everyone played the role of an informer. In Iași, things also stood badly because of the large number of Jewish inhabitants, who were always in a state of alarm with regard to any phenomenon suggestive of anti-Semitic reaction. The house where Andrițoiu lived lay at the end of a yard of overgrown grass between a few scattered walnut trees. Of his parents, only his father was still alive, an old man with paralyzed legs, whom one would not expect to be a source of indiscretions. As for Andrițoiu's sister, through whose room they had been obliged to pass when they entered, they had not found her at home. While they talked, it had got dark. It had been some time before their host had turned on the gas lamp. By its light, Rotaru's eyes were now becoming more familiar with the objects around him. On the eastern wall hung an icon, certainly an old piece, to go by the primitive style in which the crucifixion of Jesus was represented. The wooden bed, without pillow or mattress, covered with a rough blanket, gave an impression of monastic austerity. On the table before the window that opened onto the yard, he could see the outline of a pile of ecclesiastical books, and a little closer lay a French edition of Dostoevsky's *Brothers Karamazov*.

"Theological sophism! It's my belief that—"

Gheorghiu, who was speaking in a standing position, the shadow of his humped back grotesquely enlarged on one of the walls, did not manage to finish, as he was unexpectedly interrupted by the hurried entrance of a young woman of about twenty, tall and slim, with black hair falling over her shoulders.

"My sister Ana," was all that Andriţoiu said. He did not introduce the boys to her.

"Are these the friends you were expecting from Bucharest?" asked the girl, visibly troubled.

"Yes," replied Andriţoiu, getting up from his chair.

"I don't know, I fear I've done you harm, out of foolishness."

Andriţoiu grabbed his sister by the shoulders, while Rotaru went over to the window, his ears attentive in the night, and Gheorghiu began to reduce the wick of the lamp until the room was almost in darkness.

"Tell us! What are you waiting for?"

"Well, you see…I let slip a word in front of Mihai. You warned me from the start against him, but—what do you expect?—you know we're in love…. What does it matter that he's in the Siguranţă! I've always been convinced that he protects you indirectly. If he pursued you like he does the others, he knows very well that he would lose me, so—"

"Enough of this nonsense! Say quickly what you have to say!' Andriţoiu urged her in a choked voice.

"Toward evening I met Mihai in the Copou Park. I told him that I could stay overnight with him because you were expecting some friends from Bucharest and you were keen for me to sleep at a classmate's. I felt him give an involuntary start, although at that moment I didn't give it any importance. It's strange, all the time I got the impression that his thoughts were somewhere else, as if he were in a hurry to get away from me as fast as possible. After night fell, instead of us going back together, he gave me the key to his room and told me to wait for him at home, because he still had something to finish at work, some report or other. It was only once I was alone that my suspicions began to grow. That's why I came straight away. I only calmed down when I came into the yard and met Anghel. Still, it's not good to — "

"Where do we get to from the back of the house?" asked Rotaru, interrupting the girl.

"Into another yard. The fence is broken down. Then, by going from one yard to the next, it's easy to get to the edge of the district. I'll guide you!" Andrițoiu offered, ready to step over the window ledge before the others.

"No! Let's not complicate things. Gheorghiu and I will go alone. In the meantime, you and Anghel go to the window of the front room and open fire to cover our flight—only if it's necessary, of course. For two weeks or so, we'll break off all contact. God be with us!"

They embraced briefly. Then Gheorgiu jumped first through the window, immediately followed by Rotaru.

Outside, in the patriarchal peace of this district in the outskirts of Iași, there was no sound but the chirping of crickets. The walnut trees with their leafy cover intensified the darkness of the night.

After making their way through the broken fragments of the fence at the back of the house, Rotaru and Gheorghiu almost crawled across the end of the neighboring orchard, which was planted with numerous fruit trees. Behind them, from one side, there suddenly came a muffled sound of running boots. That must be the gendarmes beginning to encircle Andrițoiu's home. A new fence, whose planks were firmly fixed in place, impeded their passage into the third yard, especially for the humpbacked doctor. The fugitives had scarcely managed to jump over it when they found a big unchained dog barking furiously at them. Having no other option, Rotaru fired his revolver at it. The shot instantly woke all the dogs of the district, and at the same time triggered an uproar of shouts and whistles from the direction of Andriţoiu's house. Before pushing their way further on, Rotaru and Gheorghiu both raised their eyes to the heavens.

PART SEVEN

Chapter I

Ștefănucă hurried to his meeting place with Rotaru, a little church hidden away on one of the cul-de-sacs on the slope of the old Bucharest district that stretches from the Antim Monastery to the railway station on Spirei Hill. He was late. Indeed, he had lost more time than he had expected waiting in the queue to get tickets for the football match on Sunday. Then, on the way, he had met his high school headmaster, who had held him up with a whole string of pedantic trivialities. Finally, the streetcar that he had jumped into while it was moving had got stuck at the second stop because of a power cut.

Their meeting was to be the third within a week. If he stopped to think about the impression Rotaru had made on him, Ștefănucă had to admit freely that it was nothing special. With his undistinguished features and average build, this individual did not seem made to hold one's attention. He definitely lacked the look of a prophet! All the same, the moment one knew that one was standing before one of the assassins of the previous prime minister, now himself the leader of the Heralds, this grey man, who seemed at first sight to have nothing special about him, at once took on another dimension and really made one feel rather in awe. Ștefănucă could not understand, however, what need there was for a figure of Rotaru's importance to contact him personally, disregarding the most elementary rules of prudence imposed by a clandestine life. One evening, after their last meeting, he had been surprised to be asked by Vasia if by any chance he had met Rotaru. In spite of the trust he had in Vasia, he had hesitated to confess the truth. Vasia seemed not to notice his silence and merely added with a grimace, "Take it from me that he's a fool. Don't let yourself be influenced by him...." Although Ştefănucă was used to not putting too much value on Vasia's outbursts, he had been left slightly perturbed, like water after the fall of a stone.

Walking at a running pace, Ştefănucă had got very hot. He took off his coat and opened his shirt collar above his tie with a quick tug that broke the chain of the cross around his neck. He had to stop so as not to lose it inside his shirt. Although he was not superstitious, he remembered, though he would have preferred not to, that every time the cross came loose from his neck, it so happened that he went through some bad experience. One time had been when he nearly drowned at the seaside, barely escaping with his life. Then in the country, when that restive horse had kicked him and he had been knocked unconscious for more than an hour. Who could tell? Perhaps this time it was going to be something to do with the baccalaureate.

The sloping street greeted Ştefănucă with an atmosphere of provincial quiet. As the daylight faded, the shadows lengthened on the cobbles and the tufts of grass between them. Here and there, in front of a yard, a dog dozed, stretched out in the middle of the street, confident in the knowledge that it would not be disturbed by any vehicle. The church came into view only when one reached the point where the street curved for the length of several houses before continuing in a straight line.

With his crucifix stowed safely in his pocket, Ștefănucă proceeded on his way at a run. No longer looking around him, he entered the church garden, where he was enveloped by a tumult of plant life.

In the dim light inside the church, there was little to distinguish the boys' faces from one another. Leaning with his elbow on the end of a pew, Rotaru looked at them and hesitated a moment longer before finally bringing up the issue of the assassination. His fingers crumpled the streetcar ticket with which he had come from the city center.

"By means of the reorganization measures adopted lately, we have re-established cohesion. Today, reports from all over show that we are strong again. This being the case, I believe that the time has come for us to proceed to action. Any postponement can only be to our disadvantage. We must resort to violence. To the shedding of blood, we have no alternative but to respond with the shedding of blood."

His tour of the country, starting with Iași, where he had narrowly escaped being encircled by the gendarmes, and continuing with Craiova, Timișoara, Cluj, Brașov, and Constanța, had made Rotaru acutely aware of the true situation, which was very different. However, he considered that this mystification was necessary to keep up the boys' morale.

"The struggle to overthrow the regime must be launched with the assassination of the prime minister, who bears the principal guilt for the persecution we have been subjected to. The plan is made down to the last detail. Sebastian Răutu will be attending a gala performance on Sunday evening at the National Theater. Perhaps you have heard…. It marks fifty years since the first staging of *A Lost Letter*. You know the layout of the auditorium. You must obtain tickets for a box close to the stage, opposite the box where the prime minister will sit. I am thinking particularly of the one at the extreme right of the second row above the artists' box. Holban, I understand the director of the National Theater is a relative of yours…."

"Yes, my uncle…," replied Ştefănucă feebly, lowering his eyes, which caught the fall of the crumpled paper in the very moment that Rotaru's long fingers let it drop.

"Good! Let's assume we have the box."

With his eyes still fixed on Rotaru's hand, Ştefănucă saw him clenching his fist.

"You will position yourselves in such a way as to have maximum freedom of movement. After the start of the first act, at the agreed moment, one of you will throw a grenade into Sebastian Răutu's box. To make sure, it will be good if the other two then do the same thing. I myself shall teach you how to handle grenades."

Ştefănucă raised his eyes and blinked several times. Above the pew around which they were gathered to listen to Rotaru, it was just possible to make out in the shadows the image of the angel on the stone rolled back from the tomb of Jesus.

"Immediately after the assassination, a shock troop of armed students will enter the theater and come to your aid. Meanwhile, numerous other groups, to be designated in good time, will take control of institutions of strategic significance—in the first place, the radio station, where their mission will be to interrupt the program and announce the taking out of the prime minister. For organizations across the country, this has been established as the signal to launch a general insurrection...."

As he spoke, Rotaru almost felt himself convinced of the truth of everything he was telling the boys in order to build up their hopes again. Only at the end did he feel a moment's remorse. He persuaded himself, however, that the end excused the means. In fact, the boys were not going to receive any assistance, as, in the present political circumstances, the movement was less ready than ever to attempt a revolution. All the same, through their reckless heroism, something important would be achieved. The assassination would create an illusion of the Heralds' power, thus contributing, on the one hand, to spreading fear among decision-makers in the government, and on the other, to restoring the courage of the demoralized comrades. The myth of the movement must be maintained at all costs.

"Think well! Do you feel capable of avenging the death of Toma Vesper and the sufferings of all the comrades who have been thrown into prison?"

As Ştefănucă again lowered his eyes, he heard Nicoară hastening to reply, "Without question!"

"I'm ready to receive orders too!" came Cernat's voice, slightly hoarse with emotion.

Only Ştefănucă remained silent, his mouth dry.

"Well, Holban, what's your answer?"

"Yes…," mumbled Ştefănucă, after trying to moisten the roof of his mouth with an almost painful swallow. His lowered eyes could see how Rotaru was shifting his weight from one foot to the other.

"Good! So, in principle, it's agreed. I imagine it goes without saying that maximum discretion is called for. Not only the fate of the movement but our own fates as individuals are at stake. All that remains now is to decide on our next meeting. I propose Thursday afternoon, by the roadside, this time at the entrance to Băneasa forest. At the first junction off the national road, where there's that big advertisement for Dunlop tires."

"Understood!" replied Nicoară for them all.

"On that occasion, I'll give you some grenade training. Holban, make sure you talk to your uncle this very evening!"

"Yes…."

When Rotaru left the church garden, the street lights had not yet come on. In the growing darkness of the evening, it was impossible to make anything out clearly. After looking around to be sure that no one was lying in wait for him, he went on his way with his hands in his pockets. He was soon followed at a few meters distance, however, by some Siguranţă agents who had been waiting in a car parked by the pavement outside one of the houses at the blocked end of the cul-de-sac.

Rotaru walked on calmly. Now that he had a sacrifice squad prepared, the assassination of the prime minister scarcely seemed a problem at all. As it was to be attempted on the occasion of the performance of *A Lost Letter*, the attack was designed to take on a symbolic value too. He had not forgotten Sebastian Răutu's words when they had met in the summer: "Cațavencu, Tipătescu, and Pristanda are endemic among us. What do you expect? We are in the land of the Romanians, on the margins of the Orient."

Rotaru stopped for a moment at the tobacconist's at the corner and bought the latest installment of *The Man with Five Masks*. Then, instead of taking the streetcar, he continued on foot. It was less than a week till Sunday—a short time, but too long for the impatience that had taken hold of him. Taking stock of things again, he now came to see everything through the same ideal prism of the version of events with which he had mystified the boys in the church. Can anyone know the imponderables on which a revolution depends? At the news of the assassination of the prime minister, of the fall of their number one enemy, who could tell whether the groups of comrades across the country might not indeed spontaneously turn to action? By speculating on the psychological impact of the confusion of the moment, especially in the provinces, the state order might indeed be overthrown from one day to the next. The use of violence did not make one popular. All the same, if by its means one happened to win the political game, the vision of public opinion changed overnight. One was glorified by everybody; one became a national figure; one went down in history. Nothing was more arbitrary than so-called public opinion! The theoreticians of democracy imagined that the people might constitute the basis of a political system. However, no war, no revolution, not even the slightest legislative measure had ever resulted from its will. Structurally, the people were amorphous. The elites, who in one form or another, had always led humanity, had since 1789 used the people as the cover for all their actions. The people themselves only played the role of extras. Even the case of the Herald movement, which at one point had given the impression of being a mass phenomenon, did not disprove the rule. What had the masses done apart from giving an unprecedented scale to the street demonstrations in the movement's period of legality? Nothing. As soon as the official persecution had started, they had declined the risks of intransigence and resumed their vegetative existence. The Herald movement remained the work of an elite because only elites or a single individual could be creative factors in history.

Rotaru arrived home and took the key from his pocket. Once inside, he was about to shut the door again when three individuals with revolvers in their hands started pushing their way in after him. Despite the shock of this abrupt return to reality, he did not lose his presence of mind. It was not all going to work out as simply and easily as the Siguranţă agents had surely imagined. The leader of the Heralds could not allow himself to be caught like any ordinary activist.

Rotaru suddenly let go of the door that he had been trying to force shut and leaped back onto the steps of the dark staircase. From there, he began to fire his revolver. In the exchange of fire that immediately broke out, he did not live long enough to know when his body rolled down the stairs.

From the floor above, the crazed voice of his landlady rang out, "Help! Robbery! Help!"

While one of the agents tried hurriedly to wind a bandage improvised from the torn-off sleeve of his shirt around the wounded arm of another, the third bent down over Rotaru's corpse and muttered, "Dead… Damn it! Wouldn't it have been better to have lifted him in the street? You didn't listen to me! What use is it now to know where he lived, if we can't get anything out of him? And Alexandru wounded, on top of that."

"Tough! But that's the way it goes. You'd better hurry upstairs before his landlady slips out at the back."

Chapter II

hortly after Rotaru's departure, Nicoară and Cernat left too. Only Ștefănucă insisted on staying longer in the church to ponder things over in his mind. He had never been able to reconcile himself to the idea of killing someone. For that reason, he had found it impossible to approve of the assassination of the previous prime minister, no matter how many hairs he split to find mitigating circumstances. Rotaru's plot had shaken him. Out of the blue he now found himself ready to become an assassin. As his two classmates had given their consent at once, it had been hard not to declare that he too agreed. But however necessary the assassination might appear, Rotaru should at least have allowed them some time to think. Taking responsibility for an assassination called for a struggle with one's conscience. Even if the planned murder had not actually constituted an order, he could easily see that its imperative character was to be taken for granted. There were no two ways about it: they were being set a test of discipline, the hardest of all.

Ștefănucă approached the altar and went down on his knees. He tried to pray, but the words took shape mechanically and seemed to adhere to nothing. Before his eyes, the shadowy iconostasis began to take on a crushing materiality that made it no different from a wall.

Ștefănucă left the church and made his way slowly home. This time he no longer felt the restfulness of the sloping street. In his mind, it was already Sunday, and he was at the theater, in the box determined by Rotaru. In one seat, a little to the rear, sat Nicoară, who had been silent all evening. How could he look so calm? He himself could barely sit still and kept fingering the pocket where the grenade was. Cernat had gone out again to light a cigarette in the corridor. The auditorium was full. A gala audience. All around, black jackets alternated with evening dresses. In the director's box, the armchairs with their red velvet upholstery were still empty, waiting. The ringing of the bell, announcing the imminent start of the performance, made Ștefănucă more attentive. The movement around the entrance doors intensified. At the second signal, the crush grew to the point that the ushers with their programs could no longer keep control. The bell rang a third time and there was darkness. Illuminated only by the footlights, the heavy folds of the curtain began to tremble slightly. Far from settling down, the bustle in the auditorium continued as before. Just as the gong rang out solemnly, the director's box was filled. Straining his eyes, Ștefănucă recognized Sebastian Răutu talking with his Uncle Matei. Good Lord, how could it not have occurred to him that the director of the theater was destined to fall together with the prime minister? He took his head in his hands, feeling everything turning cloudy in his mind. The opening lines spoken on stage and the laughter of the audience fell meaninglessly on his ears. He started at the touch of Nicoară's hand and the question, "Will you throw or will you let me go first?"

"You can go first…."

Nicoară took a step back, stretching out his arm with the movement of a discus thrower. But what was happening now?

It was all gone. Ştefănucă found himself standing in the street with someone gripping his arm. In his total confusion, he could not even answer the individual who was threatening him with the words, "Don't you try to slip away or cry out, or you'll have hell to pay. Let that be clear!"

In the cramped cell, Ştefănucă felt as though he were buried alive. The darkness was heavy and oppressive in a way he had never known before. The lack of air was stifling. He could only stand upright, with his body forced into a rigidity that gradually led to numbness, while his knees felt ready to give way. Then there were the screams from above, screams that might have come from an animal being stabbed. Long and piercing, they penetrated his ears to the very marrow.

Ştefănucă lifted his hand to the cold sweat on his forehead and then slowly lowered it to his face, feeling the need to recover the identity of his features through touch.

It was all still too much to take in with the logic of thought. He had been at the theater on Sunday evening, just as Rotaru had determined. At the moment of the attack, however, instead of the expected explosion, there had been the strange occurrence at the end of Strada Antim, when an unknown man had seized him and had then handed him over in a place with duty officers and winding corridors, where his shoelaces had been taken off and then this door had been shut in his face, without his being asked anything. What was true in all that he had experienced? His thoughts pursued their gymnastics in the void, trying in vain to grasp the trapeze bar of a certainty.

After a while, Ştefănucă's dizzy head fell onto his chest, and there it remained, unconscious.

In the office, by the clear light of day, the nightmare of the pitch-dark cell at first seemed to dissipate. Ştefănucă's thoughts, now restored to order, gave him a certain presence of mind, a welcome defensive resource. Very soon, however, this brief relaxation of his nerves proved illusory. As the interrogation followed its course, he got a stronger and stronger impression that he was experiencing a new form of torture, perhaps even worse than what he had gone through in the night. The gentlemen who were conducting the investigation never stopped interrogating him, asking questions by turns, pointing a finger at him like a revolver barrel. Their questions, in fact always the same question, but asked in a different form each time, were a continual attempt to catch him in a contradiction. It was all about confessing why he had met Rotaru, Nicoară, and Cernat at the church. How many times had they met like that before? Was he aware of Rotaru's true identity and the role he had played recently in the leadership of the Heralds? What had they discussed together? From the start, Ştefănucă kept to his version, set down also in writing, maintaining that there was no question of any conspiratorial meeting with the unknown bearded individual wearing sunglasses that he had happened to encounter at the church. All he and his classmates had done was to light a candle for their baccalaureate. Later, without giving away any sign that he had lost his patience, one of the investigators began to tell him in a changed tone of voice that they knew the truth from the confessions made by Rotaru, Nicoară, and Cernat, who had, like him, been arrested the previous evening. If he held so strongly to his statement, it was presumably only in the hope that he might provide himself with some mitigating circumstances by helping the Siguranţă to complete the investigation. For the first time, Ştefănucă had the feeling that it was in vain to continue with his lies. If what the investigator had said proved to be true, which might very well be the case, even though the possibility had not occurred to him until now, there could be no escape. Weary as he was, however, some last reserve of his defensive instinct made him take nothing back, even when faced with the threat of a confrontation. Obviously displeased, the investigators gathered by the window, where they conferred in whispers. Ştefănucă felt so weak that he did not even try to eavesdrop on what they were saying. He opened his eyes, startled out of his torpor, only at the moment when he was shaken by one of the investigators, the one who sat all the time with his spectacles lifted up on his forehead. "Listen, boy, if you're not willing to answer when we ask you nicely, we have other methods of constraint! While you were in the cell, maybe you heard the screams from the torture rooms."

Overcome by terror, Ştefănucă began to tremble uncontrollably all over. Even before his thoughts, shaken out of the inertia of apathy, could form their own representation of scenes of torture, the investigator revealed the dreadful reality, "It's not just beating till you're unconscious, although that's enough to make even a deaf mute talk. We have other systems, rather more refined. For example, with the spotlight, with boiling water, with matches under the fingernails, with—"

"No! No!"

Ştefănucă started to tell them everything with the enthusiasm of one hallucinating, omitting not a single detail. He began with the first two meetings with Rotaru. Then he went on to their last discussion at the church, recalling how he and his two classmates had been designated to carry out the assassination. As he spoke, the investigators kept exchanging looks, satisfied beyond all expectations. The boy's tone of voice now was so different from the way he had answered before that it was as though he were a different person.

When he got to the end of his statement, Ştefănucă's reserves of energy suddenly ran out. The investigators turned away to talk between themselves, and then one of them left the room. Only when he heard some movement around him did Ştefănucă lift his eyes from his unlaced shoes. The room was now full. Together with the original two gentlemen, there were another three that he had not seen before, one of them in uniform. Then, beside the door, in an indescribable state, he saw Nicoară and Cernat. Disfigured and with a dull look in their sunken eyes, they were almost unrecognizable. There could be no doubt now that it had been their screams that he had heard during the night. When one of the investigators shoved them forward, he could see that they could no longer even walk properly.

Ştefănucă buried his face in his hands, trying to escape the reality of the nightmare that once again overwhelmed him. When would it all be over?

"Now, Holban, tell us again in front of your classmates exactly what happened. Just as you confessed before. Maybe this time they too will be so good as to admit the truth…."

Chapter III

Although the evening meal was long finished, Raluca Holban was still sitting in the dining room. Olimpia, the family's elderly cook, watched her tensely from the threshold, not daring to initiate conversation with a word of comfort.

Ştefănucă's absence had worried Raluca Holban from the first evening, especially as the boy was always in the habit of letting her know when he was delayed in town. She had waited all night for him, her state of unease growing with each passing hour. Early in the morning, she had received a phone call from Cernat's mother, asking if Ştefănucă knew anything about her son. Far from feeling relieved at the almost certain connection between Ştefănucă's absence and that of Cernat, Raluca Holban had been quick to enquire further, and had telephoned the Eminescu printing house, where Nicoară's father worked. She found out that his son had not returned home the previous evening either. She had barely managed to put down the receiver when the housemaid appeared to inform her that the police were ringing at the stair door. At once, all her vague suspicions were proven true. In spite of her emotional state, Raluca Holban had had the presence of mind to go take a look around Ştefănucă's room again, in case there was something compromising to be found there. In the top drawer of his writing desk she had come upon a pistol. She had lost no time in taking it and its spare magazine and throwing them down the lavatory.

She had turned round to find the Siguranţă at the top of the stairs, presenting a search warrant. With her arms folded over her chest to hide the wild beating of her heart, Raluca Holban had been present to witness them rummaging through everything bit by bit. After two hours, the agents had considered that their mission was completed with the confiscation of a photograph of Toma Vesper, found in a box in Ştefănucă's bookcase, and a folder from Lucian's desk. In spite of all her pleading, Raluca Holban had been unable to find out anything more than the fact that Ştefănucă was under arrest. Without a second thought, she had decided to appeal to Adina Răutu, the prime minister's wife and her former schoolmate. But when she went to look for her, she was not fortunate enough to find her at home. It was only at lunchtime, telephoning for the third time, that she had finally managed to speak to her.

After filling her in on Ştefănucă's arrest, she had begged her to intercede with her husband for the boy's release. Adina Răutu had promised her full support, and had left it that she would get back with an answer as soon as possible. Raluca Holban had waited on tenterhooks all afternoon. Late in the evening, just when she was wondering if she should perhaps make the first move herself, she had received Adina Răutu's telephone call. Obviously embarrassed, the latter had informed her that Ştefănucă had been arrested following a meeting with Rotaru, the third of the assassins of the previous prime minister, an individual who had been sought for the past eight months and who had been tracked down two days previously on the basis of a denunciation. From the boy's declarations, the authorities had found out that he, together with two classmates, members like himself of the Herald movement, was to have carried out an assassination attempt on Sebastian Răutu following Rotaru's orders. As the matter was a rather serious one, and the investigation was still in progress, nothing could be done for the time being. All the same, the prime minister had shown readiness not to give the case any publicity, and on top of that, in honor of his friendship with the family, to insist personally that Ştefănucă be acquitted.

As she listened, Raluca Holban had been overwhelmed by what she heard. Her son implicated in plotting an attempt on someone's life! And a family friend at that…. That her son, who was incapable of crushing a fly, should suddenly have the instincts of an assassin! It seemed inconceivable to her. The excuse for all hypotheses had from the beginning prevented a feeling of revulsion from taking shape. Surely Ştefănucă must have given way under the pressure of some brutal treatment or other and proved willing to admit to any nonsense. And even if he had indeed given his consent to some criminal action, he had done so only as a matter of form, out of a puerile ambition not to be outdone by the other conspirators. No one with any common sense who knew him at all could imagine that the boy was really capable of taking part in the planned assassination. After receiving her friend's assurances, Raluca Holban had waited in vain, as the days passed, for Ştefănucă's return. She was reluctant to telephone again to ask, but equally, she did not have the patience to sit around knowing nothing. Eventually, after much hesitation, she had taken her heart in her teeth. When it happened to be Sebastian Răutu himself who answered the telephone, she had been momentarily thrown into confusion. However, for better or for worse, she had found out the essential details in the end. Ştefănucă, together with his accomplices, was to be tried by a military tribunal. There could be no question of his being released before the trial, and he would have to be sentenced, at least as a matter of form. Only then, on the basis of guarantees, and only on the pretext of his shattered health, would it be possible for him to be released. She had put down the receiver with a trembling hand. A lawyer, a friend of the family, consulted in haste, had confessed that he was not in a position to give any opinion before seeing the case files. In the end, Raluca Holban had resorted to fortune-tellers. As it happened, whether they read in cards or in coffee, all concluded that Ştefănucă would come home "by the road of evening." And so she took care that the boy's place was always set at the table.

At the sound of the outside doorbell, Raluca Holban felt a painful twinge in her heart. In the moments of waiting that followed, she did not have the strength to get up from her chair, fearing lest she delude herself yet again with the illusion that it was Ştefănucă.

When the boy entered the dining room, Raluca Holban could scarcely believe her eyes. Unable to utter a word, all she could do was to stretch out her arms. But what was the matter with Ştefănucă? Instead of coming to her, instead of embracing her or at least saying something, he sat down at the table, at the place set for him, and just sat there stiffly.

"Ştefănucă...Ştefănucă...," His name, mumbled through her tears, was perhaps also a way of assuring herself that she was not daydreaming.

Then, eventually, once she had come back to herself, her motherly instinct managed to find the simple question to restore normality. "Ştefănucă, won't you have something to eat?"

The boy remained silent, as though he had not heard the question. What struck her now about him was not so much his physically weak condition, which was only normal for someone just out of prison, as the way his physiognomy itself had changed: the eyes gazing into space, the mask-like rigidity of his features, the mouth thinned to the point where his lips seemed to have disappeared. Raluca Holban could feel that Ştefănucă did not fully realize that he was home, at the usual dinner table, with her. But what could have happened for him to get into such a state? Could he be ill? After all he had gone through, it was only to be expected that his nerves could not have remained unaffected. And as one thought led to another, Sebastian Răutu's words recalled from their last telephone conversation suddenly took on a harsher sense in Raluca Holban's mind. Had he not made an allusion to the boy's state of health in connection with the pretext under which his release was going to be permitted? So the pretext was turning out to be a reality....

Worried, Raluca Holban leaned over the table. "What's the matter, dear? Don't you feel well?"

Giving her no answer this time either, Ştefănucă stood up. He stopped in front of Raluca Holban and kissed her in passing, or rather momentarily pressed his closed lips to her feverish brow. Then he left the dining room like a robot.

Back in his own room, Ştefănucă sat down on the edge of the bed. Since the confrontation with his comrades in the investigators' office at the Siguranţă, it was as though his feelings had atrophied. A doctor had seen him at one point, but he had not seemed too alarmed and had put it down to a simple case of nervous depression. At the trial, Ştefănucă's attitude had not changed. Under cross-examination, his answers had been completely confused. When Nicoară and Cernat were being questioned and witnesses called from among their former teachers and classmates, he had given the impression that he was not even following the discussion.

It was the same at the prosecutor's requisitory and the speeches of the defense lawyers. When the accused were allowed a final statement, he had nothing to say. The next day, in his cell, when his sentence was communicated to him—two years in prison with a secret clause suspending the punishment—Ştefănucă had remained equally amorphous. Nor, a little later, when he found himself alone with a high official who had come to inform him that he owed his release exclusively to the repeated intervention of the prime minister, nor even when he was obliged by the same official to write a dictated statement of solemn repudiation, had he reacted in any way.

The stress of his night in the cell and of the interrogation culminating in the confrontation with his comrades had been more than his nerves could take. After the first writhings of opposition to a reality that seemed one continuous nightmare, he had felt his power of judgment crushed. Then like a drowned corpse, he had let himself be carried wherever the black water of the nightmare would take him. But dull complaisance in the lack of responsibility of a lost will was perhaps also a way of postponing an examination of his conscience. It was as though it were only now, when he was alone again and back in the surroundings of his own room, that it was beginning to dawn on Ştefănucă. He was assailed by remorse, in a way that he had never experienced before.

He had been a traitor. Scared like a child by empty threats, he had given away the planned assassination attempt. He did not even have the excuse that he had been defeated by physical suffering, as he had told them everything without even getting that far. While Nicoară and Cernat were to serve their sentences in prison, he was allowed home, thanks to the kindness of Sebastian Răutu.

Ştefănucă went over to his desk and opened the top drawer, looking for the pistol. But he did not find it in its usual place, between his stamp album and the various issues of *Sports Gazette*. Hurriedly, with an ice-cold hand, he began to rummage through the other two drawers, imagining for a moment that he might have hidden the pistol somewhere else. But he could find it nowhere. So the nightmare even refused him escape by suicide.

Feeling weak again, Ştefănucă returned to the edge of his bed and took his head in his hands.

PART EIGHT

Chapter I

Vasia forced himself to finish the dessert, just as he had the other two courses. It annoyed him that he should lack his usual appetite, especially as he had been determined to live this day like any other, without the least sign of weakness. And then what could be the meaning of the way he caught his eyes lingering on them all? The Holban family's meals never made any bond among those who took part in them. Each remained in their own solitude, making no attempt to break it other than with strictly conventional exchanges of words. Vasia might be a stranger, but he had long understood at mealtimes that he was no more so than the members of the family appeared to feel in relation to one another. And yet there was a unity of atmosphere about the house, to which, to his shame, he had to admit that he had started to become accustomed.

Rising from the table with the others, Vasia scattered with his palm the little balls of bread that his restless fingers had unconsciously been shaping. Then instead of leaving the dining room, he remained standing in front of the window that opened onto the garden. In the heavy torpor of noon, the sunlight beat down on the shiny surface of the table-tennis table. The chestnut tree had drawn back its shadow, which now barely encompassed the basket chair where the tomcat lay curled up. As he moved to light a cigarette, Vasia felt the touch of Liliana's hand. She had waited behind after the others had gone.

"Wouldn't you like to go outside a bit?"

Vasia hesitated. It was the first time the girl had spoken to him since the night he had rejected her. Without looking at her, he turned from the window and crushed the cigarette, from which he had not taken so much as a puff, on the edge of a plate.

"Yes, let's," he answered quietly, in a voice that seemed foreign even to him.

In the garden, the heat was overpowering, and the close walls of the houses held in the oven-like atmosphere. There was not the slightest sign of a breeze among the motionless leaves of the chestnut.

With a slight jump, Liliana sat on the edge of the table, leaving the basket chair for Vasia after taking care to chase Tan away. On the way, she lifted a table tennis ball from the grass and began to play with it, passing it from one hand to the other and back.

"Vasia, I was an idiot. Let's forget everything! Would you like us to be friends again?"

With his eyes fixed on an ant that had climbed onto the toe of his shoe, Vasia murmured casually, "Yes, of course."

"Vasia, what up with you? You don't seem to be at ease."

Vasia clenched his fists, pressing his fingernails into his palms. So he was giving himself away so obviously that even Liliana, who had no idea about anything that was going on, had been surprised.

"Well, won't you tell me? Why so silent?"

"It's nothing. Perhaps just a little regret that the vacation means parting from you people." Vasia told the first lie that came into his head.

"Hey, we're taking you with us! How could you imagine I hadn't thought of that? You should see how nice it is on the estate!" Liliana exploded in a burst of enthusiasm that made her drop the ball.

Vasia finally lifted his eyes and looked straight at Liliana. He saw her blush. Her bare arms, her little breasts hiding under her thin summer blouse, the slight swinging of her sandaled feet, together completed the impression of a femininity touchingly fresh and naïve.

"A cricket! Can you hear it?" asked Liliana unexpectedly, raising a finger to draw his attention to the chirping that had broken out like a tiny alarm clock.

Vasia got to his feet.

"What? Do you want to go?"

"Yes, I have an exam at four."

"Pity…but we'll talk again this evening."

"Yes, this evening."

"Good luck!"

"In what?"

"In the exam. What else?"

"Ah, yes."

Back in his room, Vasia took out his identity papers, tore them up and scattered the pieces in the wastebasket. Then he gathered together his few changes of clothes, his notebooks of mathematical problems, and his washing things in the basketwork trunk that he had come with in the autumn. Once it looked as though he had everything organized, he sat down at the desk and paused to smoke a cigarette.

From the room next door, emptied for the summer of rugs like all the other rooms in the house, he could hear the constant dull thud of Ştefănucă's footsteps. Since the boy had come home, Vasia's ears had become accustomed to this pacing up and down of his. With its mechanical uniformity, it had come to seem little different to him than the ticking of a clock. In a way, he had foreseen early on that things would end badly. Not for nothing had he kept opposing Rotaru, vigorously maintaining that an assassination should not be attempted using children. The result had fully confirmed that he was right. Nothing had been achieved. Aware that the Herald movement had perhaps missed once and for all the moment for the revolution, Vasia had several days ago made up his mind to take action on his own. In place of the massacres and fires that he had dreamed of so often, reality obliged him to content himself with firing a revolver. He had said nothing to anyone, not even to Gheorghiu, the hump-backed doctor, to whom Rotaru had more than once let it be known that he was designated to be his replacement if anything should happen to him. He knew in advance that the neurologist, who now did not allow the slightest move without his authorization, would not consent, and that he would be quite capable of shooting him if he felt that he was determined to act on his own initiative anyway. Gheorghiu, whom Vasia had always considered paranoid, could think of nothing but blowing up Parliament. The plan was pure fantasy in the harsh conditions imposed by the authorities' surveillance measures. Obviously, only a man who lived day in, day out among the insane at the Berceni hospital could refuse to give up such a plan.

In the goldfish bowl, the little fish slid slowly through the water. Though his eyes had been resting on them from the beginning, it was only at that moment that Vasia became fully aware of their presence.

From the dining room, the sound of the clock striking rang through the house. Three o'clock. Vasia started. There was no time to lose. He threw his quarter-smoked cigarette into the goldfish bowl, only momentarily troubling the fish in their somnolent navigation.

Before leaving the room, Vasia opened the window again, though he was not very sure why he was doing so. Below, in the garden, there was no one apart from Tan, curled up in the basket chair. The shadow of the chestnut had spread to one side. In the grass, close to the table, the table-tennis ball that Liliana had played with showed as a little white spot. No chirping of crickets could be heard any longer in the heated air.

Vasia wrenched himself from the window and strode across the room. He slammed the door behind him as loudly as he could to wake himself up to the only reality worthy of him.

After going part of the way on foot, Vasia took the streetcar for fear of arriving too late. It was past the time when office staff came out of work, so he found a place in an almost empty car. As it moved jerkily on, he began to look out of the window at the succession of buildings on the boulevard. He was thinking of nothing as such. He felt very hot, but that was no sign of weakness. The fat lady sitting in front of him was also sweating as though in a steam bath. As the streetcar began to approach Piaţa Victoriei, Vasia stood up and prepared to get off. In passing, his eye was caught for a moment by a notice on the window, an advertisement for a circus show. It occurred to him that he had never been to the circus and so had missed the chance to see a lion, an elephant, or a monkey in the flesh. Until the streetcar reached the stop, he stood behind the driver, who had taken off his jacket and rolled up his shirtsleeves.

On the ground, the heated asphalt seemed slightly viscous under Vasia's feet. As he walked around the square, it seemed to him for a moment that a girl in front of him looked like Liliana. Irritated, he hurried forward, passing her without looking around. From outside the tobacconist's at the corner, where he could observe the prime minister's residence without attracting any suspicion, he saw the car drawn up by the steps and the sergeant on guard duty talking with Sebastian Răutu's driver and police escort. Beyond them, the street was empty, the asphalt dazzling in the sun.

Vasia entered the narrow space of the shop to ask the time. The tobacconist, who was dozing over the row of newspapers on the counter, made a gesture with his head toward the round clock squeezed between the stacks of cigarette packets on a shelf on the wall. A quarter to four. Sebastian Răutu's response to the opposition's questions was announced in all the papers for the four o'clock session of the Chamber: he might leave home at any moment. When Vasia made to go out, the castrato voice of the tobacconist warned him, "Hey, mind you don't get caught on the flypaper!"

Without any more ado, Vasia slowly walked down the street, his hand gripping the revolver in his right pocket. He could feel nothing special. Perhaps just a slight sensation of thirst. As it happened, he was only about fifteen meters from the prime minister's house when the driver quickly took his place at the wheel, followed by the policeman, while the sergeant hurried to open the door. Chilled to the fingertips, Vasia gave a barely controllable start as he recognized Sebastian Răutu, about to step onto the footboard.

Vasia managed to hold out the revolver with a steady hand. He fired once, twice, three, four, five, six, seven, eight times at the man in front of him, who had fallen in a heap at the first shot. Still he stood there, determined to discharge the revolver completely, not realizing that the policeman, who had leaped from his place next to the driver, and the sergeant, hidden behind the open door of the car, had begun firing too. Suddenly his arm went weak. A web of red filled his vision, and he dropped to the ground, his hand still clutching the revolver.

Chapter II

Seated in the basket chair in the garden, Raluca Holban stroked Tan's fur with restless fingers. Not even the third Piramidon pill, which she had just been into the house for, seemed to have any effect. Her head continued to ache just as badly.

Since the morning, when she had picked up the newspaper and learned of the assassination of the prime minister, Raluca Holban had felt chilled. More than by the black border of mourning around the page and the sensational headlines, she had been hit by the photographs reproduced in all their brutal detail. One of them showed Sebastian Răutu, fallen on the ground right beside the running board of the car, with blood all over his face and clothes. Another showed him again, stripped to the waist, on a table at the morgue. Finally, the third showed the assassin, shot at the scene of the crime and lying in a heap on the pavement. It was when she started reading that Raluca Holban received the second unexpected blow. According to the paper, it appeared that initially, there had been no way to establish the identity of the assassin, as no document had been found on him. Only after more extensive investigation had it been established that he was one Voinov, a third-year student in the Faculty of Mathematics and a member of the Herald movement, his last known address being the student residence at 62 Calea Plevnei. The newspaper fell from Raluca Holban's hand and she could feel a wave of nausea coming over her. The housemaid, who had until then been watching her from the doorway, had leaped to her assistance, massaging her temples after first giving her a glass of water to drink. When the children came down to tea, the drama had grown in intensity. Liliana, who already the previous evening had begun to show signs of unease in connection with Vasia's absence, had glanced at the newspaper on the table and had passed out when she read the first lines. Ştefănucă, with a lost look in his eyes, helped by Lucian, with the blood drained from his cheeks, had carried their sister upstairs, where Raluca Holban had set about bringing her back to consciousness.

Stroked by her fingers, the cat purred contentedly with a dull snoring sound. The midday heat made everything around seem drowsy, even the blades of grass. Although the chair where she was sitting was in the sun, Raluca Holban could not get warm: she still felt chilled at Vasia's crime. It was all she could do to keep from shivering. She was also seized with the fear of finding the police at the gate, knowing very well that she could expect them to turn up at any time. Her heart pounded at the sound of every passing car. After much deliberation, she had decided not to let it be known that she had given Vasia lodgings for fear that if she informed the authorities, they might attempt to prove some sort of complicity. Nevertheless, there was not the slightest doubt in her mind that Ştefănucă and Lucian had not been involved in any way. She had witnessed the boys' reaction to the news and could swear that neither of them had been expecting what had happened.

Raluca Holban pushed Tan to one side, feeling the need for movement. She began to walk to and fro between the table-tennis table and the chestnut tree in the corner, taking no notice of the time struck by the dining-room clock, the hour at which they usually sat down for lunch. Every time she turned away from the chestnut, the sun-drenched wall of the house stood before her. In the children's rooms the blinds were down. Where Vasia had stayed, on the other hand, the window lay wide open, just as he had left it the evening before. Finally Raluca Holban made up her mind. The empty space of that window had to be covered. She went into the house, not to see to lunch, but to give orders that the windows were to be shut and that the curtains were to be drawn in the room where nobody stayed anymore.

Meanwhile, Lucian had arrived in Piața Victoriei, where Vasia's corpse still lay. When he made it through to the front of the crowd that had gathered, the scene before his eyes shocked him, no matter how much he tried to maintain his self-control.

Caked in blood, sprawled, filthy, Vasia was barely recognizable. On a placard set up beside him was written in big letters: "May this be the fate of all assassins who disrupt the state order." A few gendarmes were trying their best to hold back the wave of curious onlookers. Made up especially of women, their ranks included all social categories. From time to time, the odd itchy-tongued gawker from the outskirts would come out with some observation, clearly audible against the heavy silence:

"Looks like he was machine-gunned! See, they got him all over: head, chest, belly...."

"He has the face of an assassin...."

"Disgraceful! A student...."

"Easy to see he was a layabout. Look at the state of his shoes!"

Lucian twisted around. With people muttering at him and elbowing him as they pushed through from the back, it was with difficulty that he made it out of the crush. Finally, he set off slowly down the boulevard.

The summer Sunday had brought the city out into the streets. The crowd filled the pavements like a great river bursting its banks. In everybody, one seemed to detect the same sweet complaisance in the inertia of a strolling pace. Here and there, groups of passers-by formed little eddies in the stream, leaving one to suspect the presence of a cinema, a soft-drink stand, or a seller of seeds, popcorn, or peanuts.

Lucian looked around in confusion, repeatedly raising a hand to his spectacles. Premises for a more categorical conclusion he found it hard to conceive. For whom had he worked for months on end at his book on the Herald ideology? It was no great disaster, then, that the work was now lost to him in some file or other at the Siguranţă. For whom had Vasia disposed of the prime minister at the cost of his own life? For whom?

Overcome by a sensation somewhat resembling seasickness, Lucian left the boulevard.

"Hi! What's up with you? You look like a sleepwalker."

Lucian gave a start. He had not noticed his comrade until suddenly, he was just one step away. In contrast to how he usually felt, this time the meeting was a source of pleasure. At last he had come across someone with whom he could feel a sense of solidarity.

Without saying a word, Lucian took Darie by the arm and continued with him on his way.

"Haven't the police come looking for you yet?"

"No, Why?" asked Lucian, startled. He had been convinced that no one knew that Vasia had stayed in their house.

"Come on, what world are you living in? Don't you know they're making massive arrests as reprisals for the assassination? I, for one, am keeping well clear of home."

Lucian remained silent. The thought that he might be picked up too, together with the other comrades, did not trouble him. Arrest might even be a solution in the present circumstances.

"What terrible significance in Voinov's act!" exclaimed Darie, rubbing his unshaved chin.

"Yes…terrible…," came Lucian's answer like an echo, but in a tone that hinted at a change in the meaning of the word.

"I get the impression that you don't think so."

"What should I think? Unfortunately there's nothing to think. I see everyone is strolling on the boulevard just like any other Sunday."

"Were you expecting everything suddenly to change? You're in too much of a hurry…. Let's be clear! With Voinov, what needed to be seen has been seen, namely that in the ranks of the Heralds there are people capable at any time of dying willingly for the objectives of their cause. This isn't a case of someone made a hero by an accident of fate, such as usually happens in history. From the way he carried out the assassination, it's clear that Voinov didn't for a moment think of himself. Well, that says more than anything. The future has always belonged to those who are ready to die. Listen to me! History…."

Darie went on talking, accompanying his words with demonstrative gestures. Lucian continued to hold his arm and listened, no longer trying to think of counterarguments.

The night was stifling. Although Lică had left the window open, not a breath of fresh air could be felt. The same oven-like atmosphere, in which one could neither sleep, nor read, nor smoke. The only good thing, which made the difference between night and day, was that at least there was an end to the plague of flies and the kitchen smell. And it seemed that only the bridle of sleep was able to stop the mouths of the gossips chattering in the yard of this squalid place. The peace that began to fall from ten o'clock onward was troubled by no more than a policeman's whistle or the screeching of cats

Lică had come back late after spending all day in town, walking up and down Calea Victoriei, going in and out of exhibitions, trying to pick up housemaids in the Cişmigiu Garden, cooling himself with ice creams at street corners, and gaping for the third time at the corpse in Piaţa Victoriei. He had come back tired and sticky, his feet swollen in his too-heavy shoes. He had stayed on in Bucharest after the end of the exams only because the theatrical stroke of the assassination had taken place, and he had been eager to witness the aftermath from the orchestra seat that the capital city offered. Now, with his curiosity satisfied, there was nothing to stop him from leaving. He had bought a ticket on the morning stopping train, so as not to travel when it was very hot. Although he had never been content in Pitești, considering the provinces to be a graveyard for anyone with ambition, he was happy at the thought that he was going to cool himself with walks in the Trivale forest or indeed bathing in the Argeș. He had packed his things in his suitcase, shaved now so as not to waste time in the early morning, and put his striped trousers under the mattress. He intended to slip away without saying anything, leaving his rent unpaid. Mrs. Păpurică was away in the country for a brother's funeral. In her absence, the old man generally got up at the crack of dawn and went off to spend the whole day fishing, so there would be no one in the house to notice that he was leaving town.

As he waited to fall asleep, Lică lay with his thoughts focused on the ceiling, like the dazed flies up there in the darkness. It was so hot that he had gone to bed naked, even throwing the sheet to one side. His mind took stock again, especially as his departure for the vacation marked the end of a year exceptionally rich in experiences. The road to advancement through the Herald movement was closed forever. He was going to start everything from the beginning again. A new strategy had to be worked out. Indeed, one could also launch oneself through women, or through blackmail in the press. The three months of vacation that lay before him would offer time to think. He had been easing up on his activity as a police informer, so his reports were now no more than a matter of form, with information he made up on the spot. In any case, the role protected him from the risk of imminent arrest and was convenient in a time when the last crazy fanatics in the movement were running amok, not caring that by their attitude, they were endangering passive adherents too.

Lică was startled out of his thoughts by the sound of unexpected movement in the yard. First he heard a car stopping outside in the street. Then there was the barking of Bombonica, which suddenly turned to a prolonged whine, surely in response to a kick from the intruders. Ever more insistent knocking on the outside door was followed by the sound of Mr. Păpurică's slippers fumbling their way down the corridor. It all happened so fast that Lică barely had time to pull the sheet over his unclothed body.

By the smoky light of the bulb in the ceiling, which his landlord had struggled to screw in place, two Siguranţă agents were walking around the room with sure, professional movements. Mr. Păpurică, with a nightcap on his head and a nightshirt embroidered with wavy lines on his scraggy body, was trembling all over, as if ready to disappear into the wall.

"Ha, so you were aiming to sneak off!"

Lică looked at the agent who had laid hands on his suitcase, unable to believe his eyes.

"I don't understand. There must be some confusion. Who are you looking for?"

The other agent, an individual with a slender

mustache, who had been rummaging through the piles of books, turned around with a bored look, "Come on, get your clothes on. You're not the only one we've got to pick up!"

Despite the cramps that racked him more and more powerfully, Lică sat up. The astonishment in his tone suddenly turned to wounded dignity, "There must be some confusion. Please understand, in the name of God! I myself am on the payroll of the Siguranţă. I work with Major Halunga in Office number IV. What more do you want?"

"Come on, old man, no more talk! You want us to pull you in stark naked?"

The window of the room where Gheorghiu was hospitalized opened onto the corner of the schizophrenia section and the path that led between fruit trees, with their bark whitewashed as though in the yard of an army barracks, to the administration. The double-glazed window could not be opened as its metal handle had been removed, so the air inside was constantly oppressive. The room had been familiar to the humpbacked doctor ever since his student placement in the paranoia section. However, before he had been locked up here, after being arrested by the Siguranţă to wrest from him a confession of complicity in Vasia's attack, it had been a ward of six beds. It was here, he remembered, that the old Lipovan fisherman from the Danube Delta had stayed, the man who thought he was Jesus Christ and who on one occasion, by uttering the

Gospel words *"Thou dumb and deaf spirit, I charge thee, come out of him,"*[20] had actually healed an epileptic child who had thrown himself at his feet in the hospital garden.

Gheorghiu resumed pacing to and fro with the same flapping of his slippers. Praise the Lord, his head was no longer troubling him! It was the first time he had been free of that meningitis-like pain that had remained with him from his beating at the Siguranţă, where he had regained consciousness only after several hours, drenched by all the buckets of water they had thrown to wake him up. He was now waiting for the doctor's visit with greater impatience than ever. He could not conceive that they would refuse him a sheet of paper and a pencil—or at least the pencil, as if necessary, the sketch of the underground passage that continued to obsess him could be drawn on the cement floor in a corner of the room, or on the portion of the wall that was hidden behind his bed, where it could hardly attract attention. It did not bother him that he was regarded by the authorities as mentally incapacitated. On the contrary, he had no doubt that the members of the movement would get him out of here, out of the hospital, more easily than might have been possible from a prison. The locked door, the agent set to keep watch on the ward, the hospital guards reinforced with a few gendarmes— none of these really constituted a serious impediment. The Heralds at that moment were enjoying the great good fortune of having him as the leader. He who was going to bring them a plan of action with which Toma Vesper or Rotaru could have been sure of going down in history among the victors, not the vanquished. A month

---

[20] Mark 9.25

of non-stop work, in two shifts of three individuals, until the underground passage was bored, just large enough to accommodate a man crawling on his hands and knees some three hundred meters from the starting point to the Parliament... and then, at the right moment, dynamite! The whole lot of them blown up at one stroke. From the king down to the last parliamentarian of the regime. That was why he might be entitled to say, like John in the Book of Revelation, *"And I saw a new heaven and a new earth...."*[21]

The doctor's arrival, accompanied by a nurse, made Gheorghiu turn from the window, where his steps had taken him once again.

"Hello! Well, how do you feel today?"

"A bit better. My head has almost stopped hurting."

"Great! In that case, I'm inclined to think we should take out the analgesic. What do you say?"

Having previously been his colleague, the doctor was visibly uncomfortable and seemed to feel dutybound to get Gheorghiu's approval each time, as though consulting him about another person.

Instead of answering the question, the patient pulled him by the sleeve toward the window, where he begged in a whisper, "Listen, please give me a pencil and a piece of paper!"

"Can't be done! Our instructions are not to...," The doctor tried to refuse.

"At least a pencil...! In God's name! I'm not asking you for a tube of dynamite," Gheorghiu insisted, red in the face.

---

[21] Rev. 21.1 (KJV)

"All right, but what use is it if you don't have paper?"

"I'll show you tomorrow!" Gheorghiu winked meaningfully. "You know, my plan! Just between the two of us! I sensed you were loyal to me...."

The doctor slipped the stump of a pencil that he had found in the pocket of his ward coat into Gheorghiu's hand. Poor chap! After the shock of the blows he had received to his head, his obsession with blowing up the Parliament had reached the stage of delirium and turned him into a full-blown paranoiac. Out of a professional tic, he made as if to pat his patient on the shoulder as a sign of encouragement, but when his hand touched the hump he drew it back with a feeling of embarrassment.

Left on his own, Gheorghiu first listened at the door as the sound of footsteps in the ward became more and more distant. Then he turned around, pushed the bed a little to one side, and began to draw on the lower part of the wall a topographical sketch of the basement where he lived, in a small building at the end of one of the cul-de-sacs below the Patriarchate Hill. The drilling would have to be done from the wood cellar. Unfortunately, the quantities of rubble that would accumulate as the passage advanced deeper and deeper could not simply be carried into the inner yard of the building and thrown down the drain there, as it would immediately become blocked. It would be necessary for some comrades, well-vetted by him, to get work as refuse collectors in the municipal vehicle that served the street, so that day by day for several months, under a covering of eggshells and empty cans, they would leave with a load of rubble for the waste tips at the edge of town.

Footsteps rang out unexpectedly, amplified by the cement floor of the ward. Gheorghiu jumped to his feet and prepared to push the bed back to its place. However, the footsteps passed by his door without stopping, so a moment later he was able to crouch down again and get on with his sketch.

Chapter III

On the hammock, where she lay for the greater part of the day, Liliana closed her eyes. From somewhere in the village, the crowing of a cock rang out. It was strange to hear it in the middle of the afternoon. Then silence spread again, all embracing.

For the last two months, since the vacation had brought her back to the estate, Liliana might be considered to have been in convalescence, if one considered the state she had been in immediately after Vasia's death. As her mother could permit herself to feel less anxious than before, she now left the girl alone, waiting for time to heal the pain of losing Vasia. However, her pace of life had completely changed in comparison with past vacations. Liliana no longer went to the banks of the Prut to bathe. She no longer went fishing. She no longer wandered the district on horseback, with those boyish ways of hers that disconcerted the peasants. She no longer played croquet or table tennis. The park, which had previously resounded with her songs and shouts, was this summer under the sway of an oppressive silence, just as in the months when there was no one there but Grigore Holban.

Liliana opened her eyes. The sky shook its blue haze among the leaves above her. Her gaze was absorbed by the void, until the sound of footsteps suddenly startled her out of her inertia.

It was Ştefănucă. Always silent, with lowered forehead, he seemed alienated from everything around him. One got the impression that he could not find his place anywhere.

"What's with that feather in your hand?" Liliana asked, looking long and hard at her brother, who had sat down on the grass.

"Don't you recognize it? It's the feather I wore on my head when we used to play at Indians. I found it when I was going through some drawers."

"And why did you bring it out with you?"

"I don't know either," answered Ştefănucă, his eyes still fixed on the long thin feather, green in color, that he held in his hand.

Liliana let her head fall back. As if reflected in still water, at once the memories came back to her of the day in the previous vacation when the boys had arrived late, in the autumn. For dinner, they had had crayfish from the pond. As soon as the meal was over, Ştefănucă had come looking for her in the park. She had been in the hammock then too, and he might have been standing on the very same blades of grass. Good Lord! Almost a year…. Back then, Vasia had not even entered her life. At the thought of the boy, her eyes filled with tears. The blue haze of the summer sky spread its web among the leaves above her.

Unaware of Liliana's state, Ştefănucă began to speak, still playing with his Indian feather.

"You know I'm leaving? Mother's just brought the matter up with Father."

As with everything since Ştefănucă's acquittal, Raluca Holban had made the decision and carried it out. The boy lived now only as a pawn in her hand. Paternal consent to his departure for Germany had now finally been obtained. As usual, when he was interrupted in his work, Grigore Holban had given his wife a bored look, continuing to sort through some notes as if to let it be understood that he had no time to waste. Raluca Holban had not withdrawn, but had shared with him at length her plan to send Ştefănucă to study at the Polytechnic University in Charlottenburg, pausing in the end over the details of the journey. Grigore Holban, who had been listening with one ear only, in a hurry to get rid of her, had told her that he would let her do everything as she thought fit, as long as he did not have to go anywhere in connection with the necessary formalities for the boy's departure.

"What did you say?" Liliana woke up after a while and rubbed her eyes.

"I said it's been decided that I'm leaving. Father agrees too…."

"What a pity! I'll feel even more lonely…."

"What can I do? Mother is determined. And if I stay here, in the end I'll go mad."

"Yes, who knows? Perhaps it's better this way…," answered Liliana softly, closing her eyes again to leave all her thoughts in the dark.

As the hours slid toward twilight, the heat began to feel less oppressive. All the same, there was still no breeze. The windmills that Colonel Ioanid had left behind a few moments earlier still stood strangely frozen, their arms motionless. For the first time since noon, his handkerchief lay forgotten in the pocket of his cotton duck jacket, as it was no longer needed to mop a forehead and two cheeks dripping with sweat. His rustic basketwork trap, light and fast on its wheels, was now passing between fields of tall maize. Colonel Ioanid drove the horses at a trot, his gaze lost in the vastness of the fields that rolled in waves to where the forest started in the distance. The panorama consisted of long rectangular strips, their colors varying according to what was planted along a scale ranging from yellow to coffee-colored and green. From time to time, Colonel Ioanid caught himself lifting two fingers to the brim of his straw hat, a reflex response to the gesture of greeting he received from the occasional peasant distracted for a moment from his work in the fields by the passage of the trap. The only sound was the measured trot of the horses' hooves as they raised the dust of the road.

Like someone newly returned from exile, Colonel Ioanid was experiencing with enhanced delight the little pleasures of a landowner's existence. An excursion in the trap was one of these, along with tea prepared in the samovar, long games of chess played on his own, and the pursuit of gardening. The year he had spent in Bucharest, with a hotel room, restaurant meals, and hours of duty at the Censorship, all that disordered life in a troubled and chaotic world, seemed to him a monstrous experience and one that he was determined never to repeat. He had given in his resignation after the death of Sebastian Răutu and had returned to the country with a weight lifted from his heart.

The trap turned away from the scattered houses of the village and took the road toward the Holbans' castle, whose strange walls exceeded the height of the trees in front of him. As he entered the park, Colonel Ioanid slowed the pace of the horses. Along the way, he began to notice to his regret the decay that was apparent all around. The barn with its rotten roof. The cow grazing on the croquet lawn. The paths overgrown with weeds. The parterres with no flowers.

Leaving the trap in the care of a servant, Colonel Ioanid made his way slowly toward the castle. Grown man as he was, and an old army man at that, he felt overwhelmed by an ill-defined sense of desolation every time he crossed the threshold. In the hall the size of a cathedral nave, where the gloomy atmosphere made one feel suddenly transported to another season, there was scarcely a piece of furniture to meet the eye. From the salon at the far end came the sound of some piano chords. This was the first, and as yet the only sign of life, but a sign of life so anachronistic in its resonances that one could well imagine that one was the victim of an auditory hallucination. Colonel Ioanid knocked several times on the massive door of the salon but to no avail. He was unable to attract attention any other way than by entering.

When he suddenly appeared before her eyes, Raluca Holban hurriedly got up from the piano. "What a surprise, Colonel! I wasn't expecting anyone. Forgive me, I sometimes do little exercises from Handel and Bach."

"On the contrary, please forgive me for turning up like this, unannounced. However, I'm looking for a book that I imagine old Grigore must have."

"Then let me take you to him!" Grigore Holban's study was a comprehensive library. Wherever one looked, nothing but books, in a jumble that choked and darkened the atmosphere. There was something about it that was reminiscent of old engravings of Dr. Faustus's study. True, there were no alchemist's retort flasks, but little else was lacking. There was even a terrestrial globe of unusually large dimensions, which served on its own to furnish an entire corner of the room. At the far end, behind a desk, the colonel could make out the figure of Grigore Holban. At the sight of the intruder, a slight grimace showed on his emaciated and excessively long face, a face like that of some Byzantine saint.

"Hello, Grigore old chap! Pardon me for bothering you! I just came to ask you something. Could you lend me Mommsen's *History*?"

"The *Römische Geschichte*?"

"If you have a French edition, that would be better. But at the end of the day…."

To the amazement of Colonel Ioanid, who imagined it would be impossible to find one's way around such a library, Grigore Holban immediately worked out where the requested book was, and from a high shelf he took down the five volumes of Mommsen's *History of Rome*.

"Grigore old chap, to think of all that's happened since we last saw one another!"

"Meaning what exactly?"

"Răutu's assassination and all that…."

Grigore Holban pouted. "Mere trifles. Political assassination is a minor incident, a common occurrence in history. And even if there had been a revolution or if a war had started, what does it matter? For a true historian, things begin to take on significance only after the passage of a thousand years. You'll see that in Mommsen."

Colonel Ioanid was left without an answer—a situation in which he seldom found himself. Involuntarily, his thoughts drifted to the episode at the Censorship with Grigore Holban's son. On a different level, the boy's ideas had left him equally baffled. He remained silent, looking in the direction of the window, where the light was slowly fading.

"If you don't mind, I still have work to do. I'll leave you in the care of my wife, who will treat you to a redcurrant preserve. It's her specialty. You can hold onto Mommsen as long as you like. For me, the Romans are of little interest...."

In the clear of the August night, moonless but with stars laden with light like ballroom candelabra, Raluca Holban continued walking her unease along the walnut alley. Sometimes the clumsy flight of a bat made her start and shield herself. The others, apart from Grigore Holban, who usually worked with little regard for the clock, had of course long been asleep, especially as the following day they were to rise earlier than usual to go to the railway stop a few kilometers from the castle. All the same, only she was going to accompany Ştefănucă to Bucharest to make preparations for his journey to Germany. Now that the plans she had made seemed ready to come to fulfillment, she was beginning to suffer from doubt as to whether her decision was a good one. What if, rather than resulting in the boy's return to normal, living alone among strangers were to bring his state of apathy to its ultimate consequences? At least here, Ştefănucă was under her supervision and could be guided step by step.

From somewhere across the fields, a locomotive whistle pierced the night and Raluca Holban felt a pang. Suddenly she could see herself in Bucharest, on the platform, with her handkerchief in her hand. The train had started moving. From the carriage window, Ştefănucă was looking pallidly at her, not responding with any sign of goodbye. Then there was nothing before her eyes but the empty rails, stretching endlessly away.

With the locomotive whistle still sounding in her ears, Raluca Holban returned to the castle. At the entrance, she lit a candle on a tall candlestick and then walked with it the length of the great hall, where the darkness had an almost material consistency. In her own room, the same since she had been a child, she was greeted by suitcases, scattered around just as she had left them when she began to gather her things before going down to dinner. In the depths of the mirror that extended over a quarter of the wall, everything could be seen over again but looking strangely submerged.

Wearily, Raluca Holban began to undress. Leaving the closing of the suitcases for the next day, she lay down in the monumental bed that looked as though it ought to have a baldachin. Unfortunately, her thoughts were not extinguished with the candle. In all that had happened over the past year, Raluca Holban believed she was justified in seeing signs of the Apocalypse. The age of the false prophets, turning even the minds of children….

In the solemn silence that ruled over the night, the procession advanced, holding lighted torches. All had hoods over their heads and were dressed in a sort of long black capes. Their faces could not be distinguished clearly, but from what could be seen by the light of the torches, one was left with an impression of perfect delicacy: girls, or in any case boys with a feminine sweetness in their still hairless cheeks.

Later, the walls of houses began to rise all around, making the procession divide into lines in single file, each of which took a different street for itself. There, leaving a gap of several paces between them, the strange pilgrims stopped still.

At a signal—but whose?—the torches were used to set fire to their garments. As they blazed, the black capes now had the shine of hot tar. In the mime that followed, they all cast away their burnt-out torches, and then stretched out their arms to form a cross. Raluca Holban hurried up to the first pilgrim. Under the hood, she recognized Ştefănucă—his mask from that evening when he had come home a different person. He looked past her, as though she were not there in front of him, right before his eyes. Maddened by horror, Raluca Holban grabbed the boy's arm. It was rigid, like the wood of a real cross.

"Ştefănucă, what's happening?"

"We are dying, like our Lord Jesus Christ, for the salvation of all...."

Hearing his words, Raluca Holban expected his almost carbonized arms to turn into angel's wings. But this did not happen, just as the silence did not resound with bells, but burst suddenly into the whistle of a locomotive.

Raluca Holban blinked in the darkness, drenched in a cold sweat.

The Story of the Condemned Book
Monica Pillat

The trajectory through time of the manuscript of *In the Shadow of the Apocalypse*[1] begins with Dinu Pillat's letter of 2 October 1948 to George Călinescu, in which he writes about his recently finished book as follows:

Dear Professor,

This letter may constitute an act of intellectual sentimentalism, but at the end of the day, we are only human.

Since the beginning of the summer, for three months, I have been writing day by day in my hermitage of Miorcani, which in its present neglected state has come to resemble the fascinating run-down property that attracted le grand Meaulnes on the path of adventure in Alain-Fournier's novel. Today, after finishing my book, I feel the need to write to you. Not as if giving a disciple's report to the master. Nor in any way out of pride at corresponding with a personality such as yourself. But simply because, in this moment in which I return to the other reality, after the hallucinatory reality of narrative creation, I have a feeling of disconcerting loneliness that seeks its solution in a message. And as, over the last three years, perhaps without knowing, you

---

[1] The first version of the title of the novel, which Dinu Pillat was thinking of as early as 1943, was *Tinerii noului veac* (Youth of the New Age). A second was *Vestitorii* (The Heralds).

have been my closest friend on the high level of thought, for all the disappointments sometimes experienced as a result of certain political adjustments, I can find no one else to whom to address my "annunciation" message.

This is not my first novel. And yet somehow, from the sense of plenitude that I feel, I have the impression that only now am I at the peak of my creative powers. It is a book whose eruptive material I believe you are not at all expecting, especially as you have always judged me otherwise, along the lines of a certain family tradition, than perhaps I really am. I do not know when and how this novel will manage to appear, what it will be destined to signify on the relative level of our literary contemporaneity, still less in relation to the absolute of narrative creation, but I was determined that, before all others, you should be/ the first to know of its completion. [...]

The following day, 3 October, also by way of a letter, Dinu Pillat explained to his wife in Bucharest the reason for this effusion:

My Dear Nelli,
[...] Today I have also finished the novel, with surprises even for me in the final part. At the end of three months of daily writing, I now feel disconcertingly alone. After every book completed, I have the same sensation of desolate sadness as after love-making. The leaves of the manuscript lie stacked beside the table. Another experience brought to consummation! Another struggle won against the hallucination of the world configured from the depths!
When I reached the end, with the penholder still

warm from the grip of my fingers, I at once had such an intense feeling of pride at having achieved a truly significant book that I could not refrain from sending a message of "annunciation" to others far away, who did not yet even know what I was working on.

And I wrote two letters on the spot, simple gestures of lyric exaltation (have no fear with regard to the content, for I haven't give away the subject of the book), one to Teodoreanu and the other to Călinescu. [...]

Why did Dinu Pillat avoid giving away the subject of the book in the letters he sent to his two mentors? In the first place, probably, for fear of censorship, and second, I suspect, so as not to put the recipients of the letters in danger by revealing to them in black and white that he had just completed a novel about the Legionary movement, which was a target of communist persecution.

Eleven years after these first testimonies to the completion of In the Shadow of the Apocalypse, in the night of 25–26 March 1959, the night after the Feast of the Annunciation, Dinu Pillat was arrested. After ten days of beatings and torture, he revealed where he had hidden the manuscript, for fear that otherwise there would be house searches. On 5 April, two Securitate agents entered our yard at 6 Str. Ion Țăranu, and asked my grandmother (my mother's mother, Ecaterina Filipescu) to lead them to the attic. They found the manuscript there in a disused stove and confiscated it.

In the course of the terrible interrogations to which he was subjected from July to December 1959 and on 24 February 1960, Dinu Pillat was forced to make full statements about the incriminated novel, which constituted one of the principal grounds for the prosecution at his trial. In the 1960s, Ion Podașcu, his defence counsel at the appeal, had the presence of mind to copy from the archives of the Noica–Pillat trial significant extracts from Dinu Pillat's interrogations, and after the latter's death in December 1975, he gave the family the notes he had made then. The quotations that follow are taken from the pages copied by Ion Podașcu from File no. 201/1960, at the Military Court of Military Region II, where it is stated that: "All the contents of vol. I from p. 170 to p. 450 concern Pillat Constantin. [...] Pillat's novel [is] in vol VI, pp. 339–507." Ion Podașcu's notes have since been supplemented with the information that I found in the Penal File of the Noica–Pillat Trial, P (Penal Fonds) 118988, P 336, in the CNSAS[2] Archives.

Out of the series of fifty interrogations to which Dinu Pillat was subjected, I shall focus on those that relate specifically to his statements about the manuscript of the novel that at the trial was labelled "mystical-Legionary." At his interrogation on 22 July 1959, recorded in P (Penal Fonds) 118988, P 336, p. 343, Dinu Pillat stated:

"In the Shadow of the Apocalypse is a completion and continuation of the novel *Strange Youth,* written during the second war. From 1944 to 1948, I gathered documentary material, and I wrote it from the spring to the autumn of 1948, while staying on our estate at Miorcani [...] [I was interested in] the clandestine

---

[2] The National Council for Studying the Securitate Archives, founded in 2000, the institution responsible for administering the archives of the secret police of the communist period in Romania. (Tr.)

Legionary movement, which has not been written about.

The Legionary movement is presented under the name of the "Herald" movement. Toma Vesper stands for Corneliu Zelea Codreanu, Sebastian Răutu for Armand Călinescu. The figure of Dr Rotaru was inspired by Dr Noaghia, a Legionary—and district doctor at Miorcani—who told me much about the Legionary movement. The end of Dr Rotaru was inspired by the shooting of Valeriu Cristescu, Legionary commandant in 1937–1938, the details of which I read in [the newspaper] *Universul* in the Library of the Romanian Academy. […] Dr Aurel Vlad, a friend of [Dr Nicolae] Radian's, told me much about Legionary life, and […] I gave him my novel to read.

[As my] source of ideological documentation [for] the founding of the Legionary magazine in the novel, [I had] texts in Cioran's book *The Transfiguration of Romania* and in a collection of articles, *Roza vânturilor* [The Rose of the Winds] by Nae Ionescu, edited by Mircea Eliade. The type of the Legionary philosopher is represented precisely by Emil Cioran, Mircea Eliade, and Constantin Noica. I was told about the reactionary episode at the Faculty of Letters, where the Legionaries forced the Jews out of the lecture room, […] by Mihail Sebastian.

The episode of the shooting of Toma Vesper [Corneliu Zelea Codreanu] I read about at the Academy, in the newspaper *Universul*, and many other Legionary aspects I was told about by Ionel Teodoreanu, who was counsel in many Legionary trials. The character Voinov and the terrorism in the novel were inspired

by the book of the Russian anarchist Boris Savinkov
under the tsarist regime, a book which I read on loan
from Ionel Teodoreanu. For the [character] type of
Toma Vesper, I also made use of the book *Pentru
legionari* [For Legionaries], written by Corneliu Zelea
Codreanu, which I received from Nicolae Morcovescu,
who fled to Paris in 1948.

After I wrote [the novel], I showed it to Ionel
Teodoreanu, then to Dr Aurel Vlad, who told me it was
written superficially and that it was obvious that it was
written by an outsider to the Legionary movement.
Then I gave it to Nicolae Radian, who stayed with me
for a month at Miorcani, and later, after adjustments
had been made, my mother and my wife saw it, and
then I didn't show it to anyone until 1955, when the
widow of Professor Popescu-Voiteşti typed it for me.
After 1955 […] I showed it to George Călinescu,
Tudor Vianu, Vladimir Streinu, Barbu Slătineanu,
Dan Cernovodeanu, Sandu Lăzărescu, Andrei Scrima,
Stelian Diaconescu (Caraion), Mihai Muşceleanu,
Emanoil Vidraşcu, Nina Radian, and Teodor Enescu."

At his interrogation on 23 July 1959, p. 353, Dinu
Pillat mentioned:

"[…] other materials studied for the preparation of
the novel, [namely Ion Antonescu's] book *Pe marginea
prăpastiei* [On the Edge of the Cliff], published in 1943,
in which he talks in great detail about Legionary life
and clandestine activity. […] I revise and declare that I
did not receive the book *Pentru legionari* from Nicolae
Morcovescu but from Gheorghe Florian, a Legionary,

who also read my novel and was the only one who had no objection to make.[3] Among the persons who read [the novel] were:

1) George Călinescu, to whom I took it together with my studies *De la Alexandru Macedonski la Emil Botta* [From Alexandru Macedonski to Emil Botta] and *Liniile de forţă ale romanului românesc contemporan* [Force-lines of the Contemporary Romanian novel]. I told Călinescu that I had brought him my novel *In the Shadow of the Apocalypse*, which might interest him, because up to a point it was similar to his novel *Bietul Ioanide* [Poor Ioanide], published in 1953, though the two were written from different perspectives and in different forms. A month later I visited Călinescu at his home to take back my works. [...] He told me that he had only leafed through the critical studies, he had not been able to read them fully and could not give his opinion about them, but he had read the novel to the end of the second chapter, and he told me that he did not like the beginning of the novel, because I was trying to excuse the Legionaries and to justify their criminal and terrorist actions. He told me that the Legionary movement constituted a rich subject [...] but—in writing [about it]—the realist-caricature style should be used, as he had done in *Bietul Ioanide*.

2) Also in 1955, I showed the manuscript novel to

---

[3] To avoid denouncing his friend Gheorghe Florian, Dinu Pillat had initially declared that he had borrowed Corneliu Zelea Corneanu's book from Nicolae Morcovescu in 1948, before the latter's flight abroad. He would proceed similarly in the case of Cornelia Ştefănescu, his colleague at the Institute of Literary History and Folklore, to whom he had entrusted the second copy of the novel, saying during the first interrogations that he had given it to Father Andrei Scrima before the latter left for India in 1956. Both attempts proved in vain, however, as in the end he divulged their names under torture. Cf the interrogations of 17 July 1959, p. 317, 23 July, p. 353, 12 August, p. 382, and 10 September, p. 410.

Tudor Vianu, the director of the Academy Library, who read it in its entirety at home. [...] Vianu likewise told me that he did not like it, because [...] I saw things from a unilateral psychological angle, without providing a historical-political and sociological explanation of the Legionary phenomenon, regarding which Vianu too said that "it is an interesting subject."

3) In 1955, I gave the novel [...] to Dan Cernovodeanu, who liked it [...] but told me that I might attract trouble on the part of the Legionaries—whom he had known in prison until 1954—as I presented them in the novel in various lights, and not as "heroes" and men "determined" to the end, as he said the Legionaries considered themselves to be.

4) In the same year—1955—the novel was also read by Sandu Lăzărescu, Legionary, editorial secretary at the Casa Scânteii legal publishing house. Sandu Lăzărescu highly appreciated the subject and the style in which I wrote my novel, but was not completely in agreement with my vision of the Legionary phenomenon, in the sense that among the members of the Legionary movement there was a "cohesion," they had a command structure, and acted in an organized way, not individually and each at his own initiative as appears from the novel. Sandu Lăzărescu also said that among the Legionaries there were not only criminals and desperadoes and people with a terrorist mentality, but there were also "luminous elements" [... and] I should also have presented in the novel such "luminous figures" among the Legionaries.

5) Vladimir Streinu did not [like it], but told me that he had enjoyed the recollections about Armand Călinescu, with whom he had been in politics.

6) Emanoil Vidrașcu liked it.

7) At the end of 1955, the novel was also read by the monk Andrei Scrima, who appreciated it very highly, declaring that it was "the first mystical-apocalyptic novel in Romanian literature," and that it would be good to put more accent on the transition of the Legionaries to monasticism, as he had heard that in prison certain Legionaries intended to become monks once they were released [...] I had this discussion with Andrei Scrima in his cell at the Antim Church [...].

8) In 1956, I took my novel to Stelian Diaconescu (Caraion) at his home, and after reading it, he let me know that in general he liked it [...though] objecting to the fact that, in his opinion, the characters described in the novel were demeaned from the moral point of view, as Diaconescu said that [...] he had met in prison Legionaries whom he appreciated as "upright" and "of character."

9) Also in 1956, I gave it to Mihai Musceleanu, a very mystical man, who liked it.

10) Radian, who had read it before it was typed, [liked it.]

11) In 1957, I read three extracts at the cenacle in Barbu Slătineanu's home, where Dr Vasile Voiculescu, Șerban Cioculescu, and Vladimir Streinu were also present, and all made different comments; Barbu Slătineanu kept it to read in its entirety.

12) Dr Vasile Voiculescu liked it, knowing nothing of the Legionary movement.

13) Teodor Enescu was the last who [read it and] liked it."

At his interrogation on 14 August 1959, p. 390, Dinu Pillat said:

"I gave the novel *In the Shadow of the Apocalypse* to [Dr C.] Răileanu.[4] He told me that he didn't like it because I hadn't understood the heroic spirit of the Legionaries."

At his interrogation on 31 August 1959, p. 390, Dinu Pillat stated:

"Another Legionary was Arşavir Acterian, [who] ran the clandestine second-hand bookshop. I gave him my novel and he lent me [Antonescu's] *Pe marginea prăpastiei*. I asked him to obtain for me a French Legionary book, *The Envoy of the Archangel* [*L'envoyé de l'archange*], a reportage on the life of Corneliu Zelea Codreanu, written by the Tharoud brothers. He brought it to me at the hospital, where Radian worked and told me to read it quickly, which I did; the next day I gave it back to him and he gave me back my novel."

In his interrogation on 25 November 1959, p. 422, it is mentioned that:

"Dinu Pillat spoke about [Sandu] Lăzărescu and his influence on the writing of the novel *In the Shadow of the Apocalypse* and then about the analysis he made of the novel. He also spoke about Aurel Vlad, to whom he gave the novel and with whom he discussed the mystic-Legionary issues in it."

At his interrogation on 24 February 1960, p. 450. the following sentence was entered in the record: "The novel is presented to him and he recognizes it."

---

[4] As he suffered from tuberculosis, in the 1950s Dinu Pillat had gone to Dr C. Răileanu for sessions of pneumo-thorax treatment.

Finally, in the record of his interrogation on 24 February 1960, I found among other things the following statements by Dinu Pillat:

"I deny that I was ever part of the former Legionary movement. I wrote for a journal, *Perspective*, in 1948, director Gheorghe Florian and editor Alexandru Lăzărescu, an independent journal [that] was not published under the auspices of the Law Faculty. [...] I began the novel *In the Shadow of the Apocalypse* in 1948 and finished it in 1955. I gave it to Radian, Lăzărescu, Voiculescu, Ranetti, etc. to read. Some didn't like it; others did. I hoped the regime would change and I would be able to publish it. I took my inspiration from the mystical psychosis of the Legionary movement, and did not write it with any subversive intention."

At the trial, Jaures Benea, Dinu Pillat's defence counsel, underlined that the accused "is the product of the old society and has not had the possibility of re-educating himself because, given his origins, he could not fit in." He went on to state that he "suffers from pulmonary tuberculosis and, in conclusion, asks for a just punishment, so that he can realize that he has erred and, after the completion of the punishment, become an element of use to society."

Dinu Pillat was tried for "the crime of treason against the country and for the crime of conspiracy against the social order," and received the most severe sentence possible, namely twenty-five years' hard labor and ten years' civic degradation. After being detained in the prisons of Jilava and Gherla, he returned home after five years, four months, and three days, on 28 July

1964, following the general amnesty applied to the political prisoners in the Noica–Pillat batch.

Several years after his release, Dinu Pillat tried to recover his novel from the State Archives, but he was officially informed that this *corpus delicti* had disappeared from the penal file and was not to be found.

In the 1990s, Silvia Colfescu, the managing director of the Vremea publishing house, searched the Archives, as the first editor of the documents of the Noica–Pillat trial,[5] and on this occasion, at the request of Dinu Pillat's family, she attempted to recover the novel, which she had undertaken to publish. She received a negative response from the officials, who informed her that the manuscript had been destroyed.

Also in the 1990s, the writer and sociologist Stelian Tănase studied the Archives with a view to writing a book about the trial of the intellectuals,[6] and he in his turn tried to track down the lost novel. He was told that the manuscript had been burned. In the same period, the researcher Carmen Brăgaru, preparing her doctoral thesis on the destiny and work of Dinu Pillat,[7] made a meticulous study of the documents of the trial, but was unable to find out anything about the book that had disappeared from the penal file.

It must be emphasized that, thirty-seven years after the sentencing of the intellectuals in the Noica–Pillat batch, "in its public session on 10 March 1997,

---

[5] *Prigoana. Documente ale Procesului C. Noica, C. Pillat, N. Steinhardt, Al.Paleologu, A. Acterian, S. Al-George, Al. O. Teodoreanu, etc.* Bucharest: Vremea, 1996, 2nd ed., 2010.

[6] Stelian Tănase: *Anatomia mistificării*, Bucharest: Humanitas,1997, 2nd ed., 2003.

[7] Carmen Brăgaru: *Dinu Pillat, un destin împlinit*, Bucharest: DU Style, 2000.

the Supreme Court of Justice admitted the annulment appeal initiated by the Prosecutor General against sentence no. 24 of 1 March 1960 of the Military Court of Military Region II and decision nr. 77 of 7 April 1960 of the Supreme Court—Military College [...] All the appellant accused were absent, eleven being deceased."

After an examination of the *corpora delicti*, namely Constantin Noica's studies *Anti-Goethe* and *Povestiri din Hegel* [Tales from Hegel], Dinu Pillat's novel *In the Shadow of the Apocalypse*, Mircea Eliade's novel *The Forbidden forest*, Emil Cioran's book *The Temptation to Exist* and his article "Scrisoare către un prieten din depărtare" [Letter to a far-off friend], Constantin Noica's reply to this article, and Vintilă Horia's introduction to the volume *Antologia poeților români în exil* [The anthology of Romanian poets in exile], the Supreme Court of Justice in 1997 ruled that these writings did not contain:

"Legionary ideas, against the social order then existing in Romania, such as to justify the ruling of the court of first instance and that of appeal that the writings in question and the discussions among the accused concerning them presented a danger to the security of the Romanian state. On the contrary, the subject matter treated and the ideas developed within the afore-mentioned writings eloquently demonstrate their artistic character of value, achieved by the authors with their specific means of creation, some original and others inspired by foreign prose that has enjoyed uncontested appreciation on the part of world literary criticism." (see also pp. 2–168 of vol. VIII.)

Literary critic George Ardelean, the latest seeker of Dinu Pillat's manuscript, reported:

"During 2004 (and continuing also in 2005) I had the occasion to consult at the CNSAS the *File on the Noica–Pillat Trial*, an immense file of 21 volumes (6,356 leaves). At the CNSAS, this file bears two numbers, P 118988 and P 336. The purpose of my research was the writing of a doctoral thesis on N[icolae] Steinhardt,[8] who, as is well known, was one of the accused in this trial. I knew something about the case of the novel *In the Shadow of the Apocalypse* by Dinu Pillat, the principal grounds for his prosecution. I knew that two copies had been confiscated, and I had found out—from the trial documents themselves—that one of the copies had been destroyed and the other kept in order to constitute *corpus delicti* in the trial.

Now, at the beginning of the first volume of the trial there is a nineteen-page inventory listing the documents in the first eight volumes. In this inventory, the following documents are mentioned for volume VI: *Order for attachment to the file of the corpora delicti*, leaves 1–3, *Anti-Goethe* by Constantin Noica, manuscript and typescript, leaves 4–338, and the work *In the Shadow of the Apocalypse* by Dinu Pillat, typescript, leaves 339–507.

I was thrilled, thinking that I had discovered what had been considered lost. Very excited, with my hand on the phone to tell Mrs. Monica Pillat the good news, I requested volume 6. Then total disillusion! Volume

---

[8] George Ardeleanu: *Nicolae Steinhardt și paradoxurile libertății*, Bucharest: Humanitas, 2009.

6 did not correspond at all to the inventory. Instead of 507 leaves there were only 84, and the documents were not those specified in the inventory. It was the only case of this sort: all the other volumes corresponded with the inventory. Moreover, all the volumes (apart from 20 and 21, covering the annulment appeal of 1996–1997) had covers showing wear and tear and inscribed with the style "Republica Populară Romînă" (which made sense, given that the trial took place in 1960). Volume 6, on the other hand, had brand new covers and was inscribed "Republica Socialistă România" (which no longer made sense).[9] This gave rise to a series of new suppositions, disillusions, and the timid expectation of a "revelation" that failed to appear."

The miracle occurred, however, on 1 March 2010, when, in the CNSAS reading room, on the occasion of the launch of the 2nd edition of Silvia Colfescu's book *Prigoana. Documente ale Procesului C. Noica, C. Pillat, N. Steinhardt, Al.Paleologu, A. Acterian, S. Al-George, Al. O. Teodoreanu, etc.* [The persecution: documents of the trial of C. Noica, C. Pillat, N. Steinhardt, Al.Paleologu, A. Acterian, S. Al-George, Al. O. Teodoreanu, etc.], a researcher from the host institution, Raluca Spiridon, announced the discovery of Dinu Pillat's novel in the CNSAS Library Fonds at the Archives Centre in Popești-Leordeni.

---

[9] Republica Populară Romînă (the Romanian People's Republic) was the official name of the Romanian state from 1947 till 1965. It became Republica Socialistă România (the Socialist Republic of Romania) in 1965, and remained so till the fall of communism in 1989. This latter name could thus not have appeared on the original covers of a file from a trial in 1960. (Tr.)

On 10 March 2010, the manuscript that had been kept in detention for fifty-one years was returned to me. I am most grateful to Silvia Colfescu and all those who, over the years, have tried to track down this novel that was so dear to my father, and for which he and his friends suffered indescribable torture. My thanks also to Dragoş Petrescu and Virgil Târău, chair and deputy chair of CNSAS respectively, and to researchers Cristina Anisescu and Raluca Spiridon, who helped me gain possession of the book.

Dinu Pillat's words, uttered during his interrogation on 24 February 1960, "I hoped the regime would change and I would be able to publish it," now have their long-awaited fulfilment.

9 789898 574470 5